Praise for

If Fried Chicken Could Fly

"Take a puzzler of a mystery, season with a dashing ghost, add a pinch of romance, and you have a blue ribbon–winning recipe for a tasty read."

—Jenn McKinlay, *New York Times* bestselling author of the Cupcake Bakery Mysteries

"I guarantee your spirits—pardon the pun—will be lifted . . . Paige Shelton has created a vivid setting, fun, friendly characters." —E. J. Copperman, author of *Ghost of a Chance*

"*If Fried Chicken Could Fly* simply warms your spirit with delicious homespun goodness." —*Blogcritics*

"*If Fried Chicken Could Fly* has terrific characters, including a wonderful ghost, and a perfect setting."

—*Lesa's Book Critiques*

"All good fun and a nice twist on a cozy—a little bit of the supernatural added in." —*Book Reviews and English News*

"A charming cast makes this a delightful read in this wonderful and appealing debut series." —*Dru's Book Musings*

Praise for Paige Shelton's
Farmers' Market Mysteries

"[A] puzzling and satisfying whodunit."

—*Richmond Times-Dispatch*

"[An] absolute delight . . . A feast of a mystery."

—*Fresh Fiction*

"Each page leads to more intrigue and surprise."

—*The Romance Readers Connection*

Berkley Prime Crime titles by Paige Shelton

Farmers' Market Mysteries

FARM FRESH MURDER
FRUIT OF ALL EVIL
CROPS AND ROBBERS
A KILLER MAIZE

Country Cooking School Mysteries

IF FRIED CHICKEN COULD FLY
IF MASHED POTATOES COULD DANCE
IF BREAD COULD RISE TO THE OCCASION

Specials

RED HOT DEADLY PEPPERS

If Bread Could Rise to the Occasion

PAIGE SHELTON

BERKLEY PRIME CRIME, NEW YORK

THE BERKLEY PUBLISHING GROUP
Published by the Penguin Group
Penguin Group (USA) Inc.
375 Hudson Street, New York, New York 10014, USA

USA | Canada | UK | Ireland | Australia | New Zealand | India | South Africa | China

Penguin Books Ltd., Registered Offices: 80 Strand, London WC2R 0RL, England
For more information about the Penguin Group, visit penguin.com.

IF BREAD COULD RISE TO THE OCCASION

A Berkley Prime Crime Book / published by arrangement with the author

For information, address: The Berkley Publishing Group,
a division of Penguin Group (USA) Inc.,
375 Hudson Street, New York, New York 10014.

ISBN: 978-0-425-25223-9

PUBLISHING HISTORY
Berkley Prime Crime mass-market edition / August 2013

PRINTED IN THE UNITED STATES OF AMERICA

10 9 8 7 6 5 4 3 2 1

Cover illustration by Phil Parks.
Interior text design by Laura K. Corless.

For Lisa and Paiger, and an ankle tackle
that has given us hours of laughter.

Acknowledgments

When I first started writing this story, the bakery was a shoe factory. It turned out that a shoe factory didn't work so well with a cooking school mystery, so the bakery was born. However, I kept the building the same as the one that inspired the ghostly location in the book. It's located in Rolla, Missouri. When I was a little girl, my parents and grandparents drove me past it lots of times, always commenting on how many of their friends had worked there. Back then I was pretty certain I saw a ghost or two peering out one of the big windows. The building no longer looks the same as it did when I was a child; time and building codes have modernized it. But I still enjoy driving past it.

A special thanks to everyone who does whatever they can do to see that old buildings are saved and preserved in their finest forms. After all, it is these sorts of places that inspire stories.

Chapter 1

"I wanna talk about me, I wanna talk about I," **Gram sang.**

"Hmm," I said to myself as I stood up from my office chair and hurried next door to the infrequently used classroom. "Gram?"

But whatever she was looking at in the file cabinet drawer was firmly holding her attention.

"Gram!" I said a little louder.

It wasn't until she peered up that I could see the earbud cords trail over her Texas A&M T-shirt and into her jeans' pocket. She pulled the buds out of her ears and smiled. "What's up, Betts?"

"You wanted to talk about you?"

Gram laughed. "It's a Toby Keith song. I was just singing along. That man's got a voice that makes me . . . mmmhmm."

I smiled. "I didn't think any of the students were here

yet. I just wanted to make sure you were okay and weren't already greeting someone."

Gram looked at her watch. "They'll be here in about an hour, huh? How exciting. What a great group we've got this year."

"I'm excited, too," I said.

This was always the most thrilling moment, the time right before the new crop of students arrived for our nine-month course in down-home country cooking. We'd looked at applications, we'd pondered who would fit the best, we'd thought about both the chemistry of the food we'd be using and the chemistry of the students' backgrounds and past experiences, and then chose fifteen we thought would be brilliant and amazing.

We'd had to turn away more applications, more people, this year than any year before. Gram's Country Cooking School was only gaining in popularity. Her simple and delicious ways with food had always been popular and sought after, but her reputation was growing, and more and more people wanted to venture to Broken Rope, Missouri, for our nine-month course.

The few hours before the students arrived for the first time were always filled with the most anticipation. This was the time when we could still envision that everyone would get along, that everyone would be willing and cooperative, that there would be only friendly competition among the group of daytimers—our nickname for the full-time students.

We never spent much time worrying about the nighters—the locals who took our night community education classes. Those classes would begin again in a month or so, and were just small bites, designed more for fun than bona fide Gram-cooking-ability certification.

Of course, reality would set in soon. When the students arrived they'd be cheery and excited and somewhat scared, but once they mellowed into a routine, we'd find that not everyone is, by nature, cooperative, not everyone gets along with everyone else, and despite our deep consideration about each and every person's potential skill level, not everyone could handle themselves in a kitchen.

We'd never had one failure, though. Even if it took extra hours with a student or students, we were bound and determined to make sure that all issues got the attention they needed so that they were no longer issues, but, instead, challenges well met and defeated.

Still, that didn't stop us from wallowing in a few hours of pre-arrival hope that the upcoming school year would be magically perfect.

"Hellooo!" someone called from the kitchen a moment after the front door buzzer sounded.

"Someone's early?" Gram said as she pulled the iPod out of her pocket and set it and the earbuds on the desk.

"Guess so."

Gram led the way out of the classroom and into the long well-furnished kitchen. Someone was, in fact, early or lost, or something. A young man, who couldn't have been much older than twenty, stood at the far end. He'd placed himself halfway through the swinging doorway, but he'd set a large suitcase on the floor in front of him. He had a head full of brown curls, and even though he was at one end of the room and we were at the other, I could clearly discern the bright, mint green of his eyes.

It didn't register at first that we hadn't accepted anyone under the age of thirty this year, not because of their age, but that's just how it seemed to have worked out. Both Gram and I were clued in that something was wrong, though, when the grinning young man said, "Hi, I'm Freddie, am I at the right place?"

I was sure that Gram's mind was working through the same gymnastics as mine. *Freddie? I don't remember a Freddie or Fred or Frederick.*

"Freddie who?" Gram said as we stayed on our end of the row of butcher blocks that ran down the center of the room.

"Freddie O'Bannon," he said as he came all the way through the door, stepped around his suitcase, marched down the side aisle toward us, and extended his hand to Gram. "You must be the legendary Missouri Anna Winston."

Again, my mind worked silently. *Freddie O'Bannon, Freddie O'Bannon. Who is this guy and why does he have a suitcase?*

"I am Miz," Gram said cautiously as she extended her own hand. "Can we help you?"

Freddie laughed. "I hope so. I'm ready for nine months of intense training, Miz. I'm ready to learn how you fry chicken, mash potatoes, and bake amazing cakes. But mostly, I'm here to learn all about your bread—the doughy kind that is. I don't need to know how much money you make." Freddie winked. "Need—K-N-E-A-D—get it?" He laughed again. "My plans are to open the best bakery in all of the state of Maine, and I know you're the one to teach me the ways."

One of those *uh-oh* silent pauses hung in the air for a

moment. Gram and I both memorized the names of our daytime students before they arrived, and there was not one Freddie O'Bannon on the list. There wasn't anyone with an O-apostrophe, either, so I didn't think we'd mixed up a name.

Gram opened her mouth to speak, but I put my hand on her arm.

"Freddie, I'm Betts Winston, could you excuse us for a minute? Please have a seat in the front reception area. We'll be right back."

"Sure. Happy to," he said a beat later, his smile dimming only slightly. He retrieved the suitcase and backed through the door. "So good to finally be here," he muttered, and then the door swung back and forth a couple times.

"Who in tarnation is that?" Gram said to me.

"Come on," I said as I signaled her to follow me.

We traipsed back the way we'd come and I pulled the stack of student files from off the file cabinet in my office.

"I thought we should take a minute and make sure. Double, triple-check that this guy's not supposed to be here. I'd really hate to insult a student if he is one."

"Good point, but . . ." Gram said. "There's nothing about him that fits. Even his age. He's pretty young. I don't think we had many applications from people his age this year."

"I think you're correct, but let's just see. Some people look a lot younger than they really are."

I thumbed through the stack of fifteen. We had students coming from all over the country; one from Portland, Oregon, one from Alabama, one from Arizona, and a bunch from many different Midwestern states. There was only one from the East Coast, and he was from Massachusetts, not

Maine. There were, in fact, no students who were named some version of Frederick. There was someone with the last name of Riley, but that was the closest thing to O'Bannon I could find, and that was a pretty big stretch.

I closed the last file. "Why would he be here? Why would he even think he was supposed to be here?"

"Let me see the other applications, the ones we had to deny," Gram said.

There were many more applications than there were accepted folders, but the applicants' names were right at the top of each page so they were easy to thumb through. We thought we might have solved the mystery when we found a Frederick Stallion, but a closer look at his application showed that he was from Florida and had graduated from MIT in 1977. Freddie O'Bannon wasn't even a glimmer in his father's eyes in 1977 if he was truly as young as we thought he was.

"I don't understand who he is or what he wants, but this is silly. We just need to talk to him." Gram sighed.

I sighed, too. "You're right. I guess the only way to find out is . . . Oh, wait! Gram, you don't suppose he's a ghost?" I asked.

She looked at me with drawn-together eyebrows. "No, of course not. They're different and they all have a scent. He wouldn't be able to carry real luggage, either. We'd . . . I'd know."

"But things are . . . changing a little," I said as gently as I could. Things on the Broken Rope ghost front were changing, transforming. From all indications, those changes were mostly because of me; somehow my onset of ghost communication ability had triggered nuances to the specter visits that we were still trying to understand. Our most recent ghost, Sally Swarthmore, had disappeared back to wherever they disappear back to only a couple weeks earlier. We'd helped her by finding the truth about her past, and she helped us solve a murder and kidnapping. But we'd also been able to release her from a terrible burden—this was something Gram hadn't ever been able to do, but apparently I had a talent for it.

One day, a couple weeks after the crimes were solved, she was just chatting with us and told us she probably should bid us farewell. She was gone in the next instant, leaving behind a quiet we hadn't known since she'd arrived.

"Well, there she goes," Gram had said before she turned her attention back to the knife she was sharpening.

"Yes, there she goes," I had said. I was working on not getting attached to the ghosts, but I wasn't quite there yet. When Sally left I'd swallowed a lump of sadness, and I still missed her a little.

"Things might have changed, Betts, but a ghost is still a ghost. Freddie isn't a ghost. It looks like whatever the mistake is, it's not our mistake. Let's go talk to him and see if we can just send him on his way." She turned and left my office.

When she was gone I patted my front pocket. I still carried the coin that reminded me of the first ghost I'd gotten to know. I didn't pine away for Jerome Cowbender as much as I used to, but I still missed him sometimes. I smiled to myself.

"Quit being so goofy, Isabelle Winston," I said.

Gram was quick enough to have made it to the reception area by the time I got to the kitchen. I picked up speed and hurried to join her.

But the lobby was empty except for Gram standing with her hands on her hips as she bit at her bottom lip.

"He's gone," she said.

"Gone? As in, maybe he really was a ghost?"

Gram looked truly perplexed. This didn't happen often.

Only a moment later, though, Freddie O'Bannon came back through the school's front door, this time his scent was strong and awful. He and it were pushed inside by a small breeze.

"Whoa," Gram said.

"What's the smell?" I said.

"Oh, sorry about that," Freddie said. "It looks like my cologne bottle broke in my suitcase. I heard a snap, a crack when I set it down out here. I got it outside before it could stink the place up inside, but when I took the bottle out of the case, I'm afraid I got it all over my hands. And shirt. And of course on everything that's in the case. Any chance I could wash up?" He stood with his hands up and out. His smile was much less confident now and he looked even younger.

Out of the side of my mouth, I said to Gram, "I guess he's not a ghost."

"I'm beginning to wish he was," Gram mumbled, but then she turned to Freddie and said, "Come on, young man. This way, and then it looks like we're going to need to have a chat."

She led him through the swinging door and to the bathrooms at the back of the building, a sandalwood incense-like fog moving with him.

I followed a second later, but not before glancing briefly out at the cemetery next to the school. It was still too early for the leaves on the trees to have begun changing, so the graves and tombstones were still under a full green canopy. I looked at the two markers I was most familiar with—Jerome Cowbender's and Sally Swarthmore's—and smiled. There were lots of other graves out there, many more chances for ghostly visitors, but at the moment all was quiet and undisturbed.

"Well, it looks like we might have enough excitement *without* a ghost this time," I said to no one, or to whomever might be listening.

All remained quiet and undisturbed, but that rarely lasted very long in Broken Rope, Missouri.

Chapter 2

"No, I have my acceptance letter. It's in my suitcase," Fred-die protested.

He'd cleaned up pretty well. Gram made him take off his cologne-stained shirt so she could run it under water and wash out the stink. She hung it over a shelf in the kitchen and lent him a Broken Rope T-shirt. It was bright pink with blue lettering that said, I GOT HUNG UP BY A BROKEN ROPE IN MISSOURI across the front. Neither she nor I could remember why we had a box of them in the back room, but the shirt had been a better option than an apron.

"The suitcase that's out front and scented with cologne?" Gram said.

"Yes, that one," Freddie said with a small shrug. We were in the kitchen part of the school again and it had taken both Gram and I some effort to pull Freddie's attention away from the shiny appliances and get him to focus on our questions.

"Let's go get it," I said.

"Sure," Freddie said as he turned and led the way. He moved slowly because he was still focused on the heavily outfitted kitchen. I could see only the back of his curly-haired head moving, but I was certain his eyes were dancing over the butcher blocks, the gas stoves, the shelves of pots and pans . . . everything. Basically, he was behaving like most of our students. He probably couldn't wait to get his hands on some of the utensils and cook or bake something in the ovens.

A sense of regret started to build in my gut. Gram and I both knew that Freddie O'Bannon wasn't set to be a student at her cooking school. Either a strange mistake had occurred or we were being scammed. Though I couldn't, offhand, understand what was the expected end result of such a scam. How in the world could it even be a scam? Why would anyone pretend they were a student?

And if someone wanted to be a student so badly, why didn't they just apply? As I followed Freddie's moving head and Gram's short gray-haired one, the thought occurred to me that maybe Freddie was actually someone who had applied. Maybe he'd used a different name and maybe we had rejected him because something on his application seemed off. Gram's a big believer in the fact that people can and do change, and a few of our students have had criminal records, though nothing too scary.

I wasn't frightened of Freddie, but by the time we made it out the front doors and to the suitcase, the regret I'd felt had become lined with a thin layer of suspicion.

Freddie crouched down and reached into a side pocket of the suitcase. He pulled out a single sheet of paper and held it toward Gram. I stepped next to her as she took it.

"I'm afraid it's been damaged, though," Freddie said. "But you can see it's your letterhead and Missouri Anna's signature. Right there at the bottom. Look."

The piece of paper had become a victim of the spilled cologne. But he was right, the letterhead at the top of the page was most definitely a picture of the long white building that used to be a church, then a bingo parlor, and was now the cooking school. Underneath the building, it said: *Gram's Country Cooking School. Broken Rope, Missouri.* It was a simple logo, but there was no doubt that it was our bona fide insignia.

The entire middle section of the sheet of paper was a mess of cologne-scented ink. At the bottom, though, there was a signature, and it did say, *Sincerely, Missouri Anna Winston*, but it was impossible to know if it had been Gram who signed the words. They were legible but warped and blurred by the cologne.

"Do you remember what the letter said?" Gram said.

"Of course," Freddie said. " 'Dear Mr. O'Bannon. It is my pleasure to welcome you to Gram's Country Cooking School for the term beginning this fall. We expect you to arrive ready to learn the delicious ways of simple country cooking by August twenty-seventh. If you need assistance in finding lodging, please contact me or my granddaughter, Isabelle. We look forward to seeing you soon. Sincerely, Missouri Anna Winston.' "

He'd recited the letter perfectly. It wasn't a long correspondence, but still, the fact that he'd memorized it so well must have meant something. That suspicious layer that had appeared made me ponder that perhaps Freddie had found a copy of our acceptance letter and made one to match it, memorizing it as he copied. Or, perhaps he was really someone else, pretending to be Freddie.

But it was probably most likely that Gram and I had made a huge mistake, the origin of which neither of us could pin down. I doubted that both of us could have such a lapse in memory, but anything was possible.

"I hate to be rude, Freddie, but Betts and I need to discuss this again. Would you excuse us for a minute?"

"Certainly," Freddie said, but I heard the hesitation in his voice. I was sure Gram did, too.

Marching back inside the reception area was both uncomfortable and definitely rude, but it couldn't be helped.

"I don't understand, Betts. Do you have any idea what's going on?"

"Not at all. I don't remember his name. It occurred to me that he might be someone we rejected and he's changed his name, but even I admit that's farfetched."

"What should we do? He's got an acceptance letter. I think that's what it is at least."

"We've never had sixteen students, but I guess I don't see how it would be much of a problem. We'll see if he's prepared to make the first tuition payment."

Gram bit at her bottom lip again.

The process, the thought, the sometimes upset stomachs and headaches we went through as we chose a group of students were components of a "whole" that felt almost sacred. It was thrilling to tell someone yes, sometimes heartbreaking to tell someone no. The emotional roller coaster we rode was significant and in a way important, if only to us. Because if we'd gone through the emotions, if we'd ridden that coaster, then we'd done our jobs to the best of our abilities. We'd given all our applicants fair consideration and we'd made the best possible decision for everyone involved.

And now we had Freddie. Per both of our memories, he hadn't figured into the process. Discussing how he might fit in with the other students or whether sixteen was an unlucky number seemed like a total waste of time, though. Either we were going to welcome him and deal with the results or we were going to send him away.

We'd let him keep the T-shirt, though.

Gram sighed. "I don't think we have any choice, Betts. I haven't considered the legal ramifications of our word against his soggy letter but I don't want to call Verna." Verna was our local attorney-at-all-type-of-law. "Bottom line, I think we'd be somehow wrong to turn him away."

"I guess I do, too," I said.

I didn't continue to vocalize my thoughts, but something was strange about Freddie; his behavior wasn't totally right. I couldn't quite pinpoint what exactly was wrong, though. Maybe it was more me than him anyway. I hadn't been much for suspicion before the ghosts came into my life, and though they hadn't caused any real harm, my attitude had changed. Of course, when reality as we know it alters even a little bit, a few attitude changes here and there are to be expected.

"This is what we'll do. We'll ask for references, see if he pays," Gram said. "We'll have to tell him we weren't expecting him, and since the mistake must somehow be ours, we'll let him stay but he has to supply those references. We'll check them, and if we find anything wonky, we'll throw him out on his keister."

I smiled.

"Well, we won't mention the keister part," she added, but she smiled, too, halfway at least.

"I like that plan," I said.

Since we were in the front part of the school with no open windows, we couldn't really feel the gust of wind. But we heard it blow through the cemetery and over the roof. It also rattled the front glass doors, opening one just enough to allow some scented air to enter.

Once we both caught the scent, it was as if we went up on point, just like any good hunting dog, so we could sniff more deeply.

"Wait, is that bread?" I said.

Gram looked at me, her eyes suddenly big and then shiny with tears. She blinked them away quickly and then cleared her throat.

"Gram?"

"Yes, I do believe that's bread."

"And you know who this ghost is?"

"I know exactly."

The last ghostly scent we'd encountered had been lavender. At first, Gram hadn't remembered who brought the lavender scent with them. And, of the two ghosts I'd already gotten to know, neither had made Gram tear up enough to make her want to hide her reaction from me. According to her, they were mostly nuisances.

"Tell me," I said.

"I suppose you'll know soon enough anyway. It's Gent Cylas," Gram said with a sigh.

"Gent Cylas? I don't know that name. What's he famous for?"

Gram thought a good thirty seconds before she answered.

"Breaking my heart, time and time again," she said before she turned and pushed her way out the front doors of the school.

"Oh," I responded a long few beats after she was gone. Gent wasn't my grandfather's name, but I knew that Gram had been "a handsome woman" and "though a spitfire, considered a good catch." I often rolled my eyes at those old-fashioned sexist descriptions, but a part of me always enjoyed hearing about her popularity no matter how it was described.

Visions of dashing movie star men from her time like Clark Gable and Cary Grant played in my mind. What would this man look like? I'd never even heard the name Gent Cylas before, and I suddenly couldn't wait to meet him.

"Oh," I said again, this time with eager curiosity, and then followed her trail out of the school.

Chapter 3

Gram hadn't gone far. She stood at the bottom of the two short steps outside the front doors. She had her hands on her hips and inspected the scene. I stood next to her and did the same.

Freddie O'Bannon, with his beautiful green eyes and bright pink shirt, sat on the ground next to his stinky suitcase. He smiled and waved hopefully. I smiled back, but I wasn't sure whether to deal with him first or with the young man leaning on the school's front sign.

If the person I saw was indeed Gent Cylas, he wasn't dashing as much as he was adorable. His ghostly form, forever frozen in time at his age of death, was probably about seventeen years old. He wore the same sort of getup as Jerome had worn: long tan pants, thin linen shirt. He didn't wear a cowboy hat, though, and he had no shoes. His bare feet were long, narrow, and curiously obvious.

Gent was tall and trim but seemed solid and strong. His shoulders were wide and confident even as he leaned. His brown hair was shaggy in that Beatles way, and his smile could probably break the heart of every teenage girl in the general vicinity if only they could see him. Charisma's one of those difficult things to define, but there was no doubt that his ghost was overflowing with the stuff.

"Missouri Anna Winston, the prettiest thing about Missouri," he said, and then he smiled his killer smile. And then he bowed.

Yep, lots of charisma.

Gram nodded his direction. It would not only be rude to speak to the ghost in front of Freddie, it would be weird and potentially frightening. Of course, maybe Freddie would leave if we scared him. I gave the idea serious thought but only for an instant.

"Listen, Freddie," I said as I stepped away from Gram and toward him, "we think we made a mistake, but we're willing to work with you. You're welcome to stay . . ."

"Oh, good!" he said as he stood.

"But, we need your first tuition payment and some references. We like personal, but we'll take professional, too. If we find anything questionable, we'll have to ask you to leave."

"You won't find anything questionable, but I don't understand. Don't you have my application?"

"No, we don't."

"Then how did I get the acceptance letter?"

"We're asking ourselves the same question," I said.

"I'm confused."

"Us, too," I said. As I looked at the hurt that crossed his face, I realized that my suspicion had caused me to completely disregard his feelings, which was callous and unlike me. If he had truly applied to the school, had been accepted, and Gram and I had each lost a block of memory, we were not treating him like we should. I decided that we should consider him the student he thought he was until we could prove otherwise. Innocent until proven guilty. I hadn't forgotten everything from my brief and incomplete time in law school.

"Welcome to Broken Rope, Freddie. Welcome to Gram's Country Cooking School. We're very glad to have you here," I said.

"Thank you." His emerald eyes lit brightly. "I'm happy to be here."

"Come on inside. I'll set you up with a phone and a computer. You can gather, or regather, your references. The other students should be here shortly." I glanced at my watch. Very shortly. "We'll welcome you again with everyone else."

"Thank you," he repeated, still with utter enthusiasm.

I eyed Gent and then Gram as I escorted Freddie into the school. Gent seemed surprised that I was looking at him. He didn't know yet that he and I would be able to communicate, but I hoped the glance told them both I'd be right back out to get the story, or stories, that went with his life.

I had Freddie set up in record time before I hurried back outside, only to be sadly disappointed. Gram sat on the small stoop in front of the doors.

"Oh, he'll be back," she said as she peered up at me and used her hand to shade the sun from her eyes.

I sat next to her and looked around the cemetery. There wasn't a ghost or tourist to be seen. The August day was almost as perfect as a Southern Missouri day could get. The humidity that was thick and stifling only a week earlier seemed to have disappeared, but that was probably just a tease. It could come back any second and with a late-summer vengeance that always made me wonder if my hair would ever be able to un-frizz. It usually did by the end of September, mostly at least.

The Ozarks, the large body of water that contributed to the thick humidity, weren't far from Broken Rope, but I hadn't had a lake adventure this summer. I'd been busy, with murders, ghosts, student selection, and becoming reacquainted with my high school boyfriend, who, through some sort of bump in the time-space continuum, was now a Broken Rope police officer as well as my *new* boyfriend.

It had been a good summer, productive and adventurous, but in less than half an hour it would be over and we'd be back into the swing of the school year. I wasn't sad about my missing lake adventure, and even though I was excited about the upcoming nine months, a small wave of seasons-changing melancholy surprised me.

"He didn't have any shoes on," I said. "Why?"

Gram shrugged. "We've never been able to figure that one out."

I paused but only briefly. "Want to tell me how he broke your heart, Gram?"

She smiled. "That was a bit dramatic, wasn't it?" She swiped something off her jeans-clad knee. "Well, it's also true, but not in the romantic sense. We were friends, best friends, in fact. We both grew up out in the country."

She nodded the direction her family's cabin in the woods had been located. It was long gone by the time I was born, but from what I'd heard, it had been as ramshackle as any cabin could be. Gram's family had been poor and marred by their own Broken Rope tragic deaths, giving them more than their fair share of struggles.

"We were country hillbillies, Betts, but it sure made for a great childhood. Imagine being able to run wild through the woods, climb every tree in sight just because it was there, find and watch wild animals, run through clear streams that weren't polluted with what they're polluted with today."

"Sounds fun."

"Oh, it was." Gram glanced toward the cabin's location again but then shook off the past and looked at me. "Gent and I were some of those wild children. We played together all the time. We did everything—we even helped each other with chores so we could go back into the woods and climb another tree or—oh, remind me to tell you about the moonshine apparatus we came upon. No time today, but it's a good story. Anyway, when Gent was ten, his family moved into Broken Rope to work at the bakery."

"The Kennington Bakery?" I said.

The old building was still standing in a residential part of Broken Rope, right off the main boardwalk and behind the courthouse. It was a three-story brick behemoth with large windows up and down its sides. The windows had been broken as the result of passersby who couldn't resist throwing a rock or two just to see if they could hit their targets. It wasn't a tourist stop, though, and there was no way to turn it into one. It had become dangerous and was headed for eventual demolition, though it wasn't a high-priority project.

Even Jake, my best friend and the town's self-appointed historical archivist, who hated to see old things demolished, wasn't doing anything to fight for the building.

The bakery had been founded and owned by two gentlemen who had an idea for a cakelike pastry with a cream filling. They thought their idea was sweet, delicious, and destined to become a nationwide favorite. They were right; their Puff Pocket became a snack that grocery stores throughout the country stocked and sold. Customers devoured it.

"One and the same," Gram said. "Gent left and I didn't have a close playmate any longer. I still remember the sense of abandonment I felt, and how lonely I was." Gram smiled again. "I was a kid and didn't understand how that, of course, would pass."

"I'm sorry," I said.

"Well, time went on and then six years later we moved into town, and we got a house right next to Gent's family's house."

"Oh, good."

"Gent and I were sixteen by then, and sixteen is a very different world than ten. Suddenly, the whole boy-girl thing became an issue. A real issue. We were both confused because we still liked each other but couldn't make sense of liking each other just as friends. I'm an old woman and this all seems so silly now, but I still remember the feelings."

"Uncomfortable."

"Yes, but we were figuring it out, Betts, and whatever the two of us might have become together ended up being tragically denied."

"What happened?"

"Gent and his family were all killed in the bakery fire."

"Wait . . ." I said as I switched my brain into gear. I knew about the fire, of course. It was a part of Broken Rope lore but it wasn't mysterious as much as it was just tragic. Its cause had been determined as coming from a faulty oven, something electrical, I believed. The two partners who'd started the bakery two decades earlier when they'd been young men had been killed, but they were the only ones. The fire had also demolished half the building, but it had been rebuilt. Unfortunately, the Puff Pocket could never regain the popularity it once had. The "lore" part of the story contained the superstitious idea that the magic of the Puff Pocket died with the owners. Not long after the rebuild, the bakery was shut down and many Broken Rope residents, many who'd come to Broken Rope for employment at the bakery, were left without a job. If I suddenly remembered correctly, the real reason Jake didn't fight to keep the building standing was because even though he thought the place was beautiful, he thought it was also somehow more bad luck than good. I'd have to ask him for more details.

But, I was certain that the owners had been the only ones who'd died, and even though I couldn't remember their names offhand, neither of them had the last name of Cylas, I was sure.

"Gram, I don't understand. The owners died, but no one else did."

Gram shrugged and kept her eyes away from mine.

"It was horrible, truly horrible," she said. "I didn't meet Gent's ghost until many years later, long after I'd met many other ghosts. I was twenty-seven then and he was still seventeen. He told me that his family had died in the fire. I believe him. Betts, I keep telling you that you can't become attached to these ghosts. They aren't people, but they are parts of people and they can—well, you know, they can become more important than they should. You need to be able to let them go, because they always do go. They don't stick around; I don't even really understand why they're here in the first place except that it's Broken Rope and it's what we do."

There was no doubt that she had really cared for Gent, and still did. I'd never seen Gram struggle much with anything, her emotions included. I'd seen her bury two husbands, and though she'd been sad, she was always so solid and resilient. Her obvious emotions about Gent were unexpected at the least.

"I know. It's not so easy sometimes, though," I said with a mixture of sympathy and curiosity. "But, Gram, I really don't understand. I'll check with Jake, but I'm positive that it was only the owners who died."

She shrugged again and said, "Some of Broken Rope's stories aren't totally true, Betts, you know that."

"But . . ."

"Every time that boy comes back, he gets to me a little more. It's not a romantic feeling, of course; it's just that he represents many things in my own personal past—friendships, youth, unsolved mysteries. It's much easier to let go if you didn't know the ghost when they were alive, but apparently there are no real rules with all this. Anyway, I'll be fine. It's just always such a jolt to see him. I told him you could communicate with him, too. He'll be back and I'm sure he'll want to talk to you."

She was lying. She was keeping the real reason that seeing

Gent bothered her so much hidden, feigning *friendship* and *youth*. She valued these things, but she was also realistic enough to know that sometimes friendships don't make it and youth never sticks around for very long.

"I'm surprised he didn't stay." So far, the other ghosts I'd met had been happy to have someone else to talk to. I was as novel to them as they were to me. "I'd like to know more about his family dying in the fire, too."

"There's something else you need to know about Gent, well the entire Cylas family, that is."

I nodded.

"Though his family can't come here to the school, or really go anywhere, when Gent comes back, his family comes back, too. They are in the bakery building."

I sat up straight and looked toward town. The bakery was around a curve and down a hill of the two-lane highway, and though I couldn't see it from where we sat, I knew I was only a few short minutes away from a family of ghosts. It was difficult not to jump into my old blue reliable Nova and head to town, but the students would be arriving any minute.

"I've never told Gent that the bakery building won't be around forever. Do me a favor, Betts. Don't tell him, either, don't tell his family. They don't know and what they don't know won't hurt them."

I blinked and swallowed the protests that were forming in my throat. Of all that Gram had just told me, of all that she *hadn't* shared, she wanted me to keep from Gent and his family that the bakery building wouldn't last forever? That part hadn't even occurred to me yet. How was that a priority over understanding his family's deaths? What did the building coming down someday mean to them anyway?

I'd call Jake as soon as I could, but I was certain there was no record of the Cylas family's demise. How did Gram get to where she got—asking me to keep a secret that had a bunch of other stuff in front of it that I wanted to understand?

Unfortunately, for the moment and the many foreseeable hours and perhaps days to come, I couldn't take the time to think about the twists, turns, and unanswered questions. Two cars pulled into the parking lot.

"Here we go," Gram said before she stood and went to greet our arriving students.

"Yes, here we go," I agreed.

Chapter 4

It didn't take long to figure out which student I would like the best. Roger Riggins was a character. He was big but not in a heavy way. He had a head full of bright red hair, broad shoulders, and was really tall, so tall that everyone asked him where he played his high school and college basketball. The second day of the term, I heard him say at least five times, "I never played basketball. I was a *big* chess player, though."

No one, including myself, got the joke until I finally overheard a conversation he had with another student.

"So you're good at chess?" Brenda Plumb said.

"No," Roger said.

"I don't get it . . . Oh, wait. You're a big person, so when you play chess, you're big, but you're not big into it."

"Exactly."

Brenda had paused and then added, "That's kind of stupid."

Fortunately, Roger laughed off her insult and then walked away from the conversation. I liked his style.

Though he was barely thirty-four, he also reminded me of my dad, in that math teacher way. He wore wire-rimmed glasses, and for the last two days, at least, he'd shown up in button-up, short-sleeve shirts and ties, which probably meant that's what he always wore. Dad was now the high school principal, but he'd started his career in education by, among other mathematical things, trying to explain the Pythagorean theorem to a bunch of kids who didn't care much to learn it, and his wardrobe was chock-full of the same sorts of things I'd seen Roger in.

Then there was Brenda Plumb. I thought she would prove to be our most challenging student, but by the middle of the second day, Gram wasn't ready to agree with me. And the other students, with the possible exception of Roger—though I witnessed he and Brenda later laughing together about something—seemed to like Brenda, or like her enough to keep it cordial. But, it was early yet.

I caught her shooting snarky looks at the other students when they weren't looking her direction, when they were asking a question or making a comment. I saw her writing things in a small notebook that she never left out in the open for long. She would write something down, close the notebook, and put it in her pocket or in her purse. After each note, a sense of satisfaction pulled at the corners of her mouth.

Brenda had come from Mobile, Alabama, and she looked kind of like me. She had long, wavy-ish, probably prone to frizzy—though I hadn't seen one flyaway yet—auburn-almost-red hair. She could have used a couple extra curves, just like I could have. I estimated that she was probably an inch or so shorter than me, but from behind we probably looked a lot alike. Her eyes were brown, though, and mine were green so that kept the front view different enough.

She'd heard about Gram's habit of wearing T-shirts or sweatshirts in support of any and all colleges and universities, so when she arrived she gave Gram a University of Alabama T-shirt. Gram wasn't swayed by bribery so I didn't think that's why she didn't notice the curious behavior I observed. I even pointed out to her a moment when Brenda jotted down a self-satisfactory note, but Gram waved it off as me being too critical too soon.

Gram and I often discussed how we felt about certain students, but only to each other. And if either of us felt like we were taking something too far, delving into a deep gossipy well, we'd put a stop to the conversation. As teachers, you weren't supposed to have favorites, and if you did, you certainly weren't supposed to announce who they were.

And it never failed; every year there'd be a large group of students you couldn't help but like and root for, and a smaller group you still rooted for but in a different way. You wanted that smaller group to change something: their attitudes, their inability to follow instructions, their egos, something. Sometimes, by the end of the nine-month course and their participation in the contest that kicked off the Broken Rope summer tourist season, the Southern Missouri Showdown, those students, the ones who were somehow the most trying, would change and shine like no one could have predicted. Sometimes not, though.

As I watched Brenda make another note, I looked forward to that possible transformation but I doubted she'd be able to pull it off.

"So, my father had this sourdough starter that he got from his own father. This was, um, about a hundred years ago." Jules Broadshed laughed. "Oookay, so maybe not a hundred years, but a good fifty or so. A long, long time ago."

I smiled at Gram. Fifty years ago didn't seem all that long ago to her, but we both definitely liked Jules. She was the perfect definition of a ditzy blonde, except that she was a brunette who packed an overload of personality into her petite frame. She'd come to Broken Rope from Phoenix, Arizona, and she had the dark tan to prove it. She was thirty-two and had tried college twice but, and this was how she put it, "the whole college thing had rubbed me the wrong way." All she wanted to do was cook or bake. The only jobs she would consider were those around food. She was even happy to work in fast-food restaurants until the time when her real dream of master chef was fulfilled. She claimed that she was the star of the McDonald's when she worked there because she had such a good attitude about everything. She hadn't made a lot of money, but she still got to work with food even if it wasn't in a creative way. She was an unusually chipper and easygoing person.

"Anyway," Jules continued as Brenda put the notebook in her back pocket, "it died. My dad was devastated. He's never been able to reproduce the same flavor of the sourdough food that he loved so much. He made the most amazing pancakes. Yum."

"I've actually heard about that happening with a restaurant. Sort of. Someone sabotaged their starter," Roger said.

"They were famous and could never reproduce what had made them so famous. They had to shut down. It was really sad. No, wait! Someone was actually murdered, too. I'll have to look up the details, but it was tragic."

"That's terrible," Gram said. "Where was this?"

Before he could answer, a loud crash rang through the long kitchen. It was followed by the shuffle of a stool, a few curse words, and then a puffy cloud.

Freddie, his face sheepish and red with embarrassment, looked up from where he'd dropped the bowl full of flour. "So sorry."

"No use crying over spilled flour, Freddie," Gram said. "I'll grab a broom and we'll get it cleaned up and then get back to the bread."

The plan wasn't to make sourdough bread that day, but just some plain old-fashioned white bread. Gram had been giving a general overview about the different types of bread and what made them do what they did—have a hard or soft crust, a softer or chewier center, etc. We'd become sidetracked by the sourdough discussion, but that was normal and welcome. Gram knew how to stay on task and make every sidetrack relevant to the conversation.

"Here, let me help scoop," I said as I crouched down next to Freddie.

"I'm so sorry, Betts," Freddie said. "My elbow just flung out or something."

His words were so sincerely pained that I looked at him. "It's okay, Freddie. Stuff gets spilled here every day. It's part of being in a cooking school. Don't worry about it."

He nodded. Evidently, he was concerned that he still might get kicked out. Neither Gram nor I had taken the time to check his references. In fact, we hadn't left the school since yesterday morning. That happened every year. We think we have a great lesson plan but then we meet the students in person and find we have to switch things up a bit. We usually spend the entire first night reworking the year. Gram often said, "Someday we'll have enough of these 'reworks' that we can just reference something we've done before." I wasn't sure that would happen. I didn't mind, though, even if there was a ghost I was anxious to meet hanging out at the bakery building. With his family, apparently. Unless Gent would hold the record for staying the shortest time possible, he'd be there in the next day or so. Making the year right for the students was the number one priority, and there was something about the group of them that made Gram decide we needed to start the year out with bread instead of the original idea of creams and sauces.

"You're fitting in nicely," I said to Freddie, hoping to help him relax a little.

He nodded again and smiled weakly. A part of me wanted to tell him that we wouldn't kick him out, but I couldn't—not yet. We would definitely have to check his references. That was only fair to everyone else. I hoped we'd find good things. I liked him, Gram liked him, everyone liked him. He was friendly, happy, and knew the right questions to ask. Even in the two short days we'd had with the students, I knew he'd be missed if he had to go.

"Here, let me help, too." Jules hopped off her stool and joined in the scooping.

A few seconds later, Gram, foregoing the broom idea, brought out the DustBuster and took care of the flour in a quick and noisy manner. As she worked, I stood and stepped back. I looked up just in time to see Brenda finishing another note. What in the world had been so interesting that she'd felt compelled to write it down?

Once the DustBuster and Brenda's notebook were put away, Elian Sanchez picked up the sourdough conversation again.

"My mom has a starter that was first created during the Civil War," Elian said. "She calls it her 'Scarlett O'Hara' because it came from a woman whose Georgia plantation was burned to the ground at the beginning of the war. The woman got away with the clothes on her back and her own mother's starter—it was that important to her. They, she and the starter, traveled north, and once her family was all gone, it passed through many families until it somehow reached my mother's in Boston. It's quite a story but I don't remember all the details. It's probably become larger than life over the years, but it always gets everyone's attention." Elian stood out from the crowd only because he mostly didn't. His unusual name called for an accent and an exotic look instead of just simply being cute like Elian truly was. Elian was short with bland brownish hair and bland brownish eyes. He listened intently but didn't ask a lot of questions. He must have been fond of the color orange, because he'd worn an orange shirt both days, but even that bright color hadn't made him stand out. I was interested to see if the trend continued. His contribution to the sourdough stories caught me slightly off guard, and I hoped that his previous quiet contemplation was just his way of getting comfortable before jumping in. Participation was always good.

"You know, you can purchase starters," Gram said. "But, it's good to know how to do them yourself. There are some excellent ones out there, some even that you can get by just sending a self-addressed, stamped envelope to non-profit groups. There are options, but as you are all beginning to see, creating and having a sourdough starter is like beginning a story that might be passed on for years to come. If anything says *country cooking*, it's stories that can be passed along to future generations."

"I'm actually surprised so many people know anything at all about sourdough starters," Shelby Knot said. "I didn't know one thing about them before today—I've had sourdough bread, of course, but I never even thought about the *starter* part of the equation." Shelby was in her early thirties and from Oregon. She owned and operated a vegetarian hotdog truck that had become so popular that Gram had called her before we accepted her application to ask if she really wanted to leave her extremely successful business for nine months. Did she have someone reliable who could cover for her? She really wasn't thinking of closing that business just to go to school, was she?

Shelby had created the recipe for the veggie dogs she cooked and served, and her creation was a huge success. Large food companies had offered her big money for the recipe, but she wasn't interested—Gram really wanted to know why.

Shelby's answers had been reassuring enough for us to accept her into the program and interesting enough to make us look forward to meeting her. Her significant other would handle the business just fine. Her "significant other" was the term she used for her boyfriend. Even though Gram hadn't asked for details, Shelby told her that they didn't believe in marriage but had been together since high school.

Their ultimate goal was to open and operate a number of different restaurants throughout Portland. They understood cooking and baking from a vegetarian standpoint, and while they didn't eat meat themselves, they wanted to understand it and be able to prepare it deliciously. Gram's country cooking methods were skills she wanted to add to her repertoire as well as her resume.

As for the money from the big corporations, her answer had been less anti-establishment than Gram thought it would be. Shelby said that the second she started doing something more for money than for enjoyment, she'd have known she'd have chosen the wrong path. She admitted that the money sounded wonderful and tempting, and she didn't begrudge anyone their financial success, big corporation or not, but when that initial company approached her and gave her a figure, the first thought that came to her mind was what she could do with the money, not what they would do with the product. It wasn't the type of person she wanted to be so she declined.

When Shelby arrived, it wasn't surprising to see her arms covered in colorful tattoos, her hair short and dyed a bright blue, and a number of interesting piercings in her nose and ears. She also had the biggest, brightest, and friendliest smile I'd ever seen. I thought Roger and his clearly conservative ties and button-up shirts would be put off by the much more free-spirited Shelby, but they seemed to hit it off the second they met when Roger asked her for details about the significance of the wolf tattoo on her right upper arm. They'd sat next to each other since class introductions, and I could tell they'd be just fine.

So far, those were the students who stood out the most,

but it was only the second day so who knew how things could continue to unfold. The most intriguing feature of the two days had been how easily Freddie had fit in. I really hoped his references panned out well.

"That's not too unusual," Roger said to Shelby. "If you haven't been exposed to starters, you haven't been exposed. I suspect Miz and Betts like us to be honest about those things."

"You bet," Gram said. "Okay, so here's the thing about making a sourdough starter—first you have to know that your goal is to create a bacteria, or more specifically make a bacteria that's already part of the flour—the wheat—that you use. When it's time, we're going to do our darndest to each create our very own starters."

"Starters are difficult to make, uh, create?" Freddie asked.

"Well, you have to go into it with the right attitude at least."

"A positive outlook?"

"Something like that."

"You all enjoy cooking, and no matter what you're cooking, there's nothing like baking your own bread, right? Kneading the dough, watching it rise, the smell?" I added.

"Of course," Roger answered as everyone else nodded.

"This just adds another element to the tasty and complex artwork you're creating. Starters are leavening agents. Making your own starter adds to the entire satisfaction of your bread-making projects," I added.

"You know what, let's go ahead and jump in and do that now," Gram said because it seemed like the right thing to do and, again, switching gears to fit with the students' needs and desires was comparatively easy at the beginning of the year.

Gram's decision was crowd pleasing; the group rumbled

with anticipation. Those were the types of moments that she and I lived for.

I handed out the supplies: small plastic containers with lids, a few tablespoons of flour each, and a half cup or so of unsweetened pineapple juice per student.

"You can use water, but the citric acid in the pineapple works to ward off another type of bacteria, a type that could kill your starter, so I use this trick," Gram said.

"Does it change the taste?" Shelby asked.

"That's the thing about a starter, you don't really know what it will taste like, or what taste it will give your food, that is. That's one of the fun things about it. It's a mystery, I guess," Gram said.

"It's a simple process to begin," I added. "Flour in container, juice in container, and stir. You need to stir a few times a day. If it's going to work, you'll start to see bubbles after about forty-eight hours, maybe a little longer. No bubbles usually means it didn't work. We'll move on to step two in a couple days, which is just adding more flour and juice."

"That's it?" Roger asked.

"Yeah, it's a pretty easy thing to begin," I said.

"But there are no guarantees it'll work, are there?" Brenda asked, no notebook in sight.

Gram laughed. "There are never any guarantees about anything."

A few minutes later, each student had combined their flour and pineapple juice and had given their mixtures a good stir. They wrote their names on the outsides of their containers and stored them on a shelf.

"We'll go back and stir them again later," Gram said.

The day passed quickly and messily. After the starters

were created, we moved our focus back to the other breads. In the years I'd been teaching with Gram, I'd never seen so many students spill so much flour and break so many eggs. There was usually a "theme" to each year, or a nickname of sorts that encompassed the students, that Gram and I came up with, a word or a phrase that in our minds described the group as a whole. She and I hadn't discussed it yet, but I sensed that *klutzy* would be considered this year.

It was a great day, nonetheless. The students worked hard with lots of enthusiasm and encouraging words for each other. They really got along, even if Brenda was, in my opinion, somewhat standoffish. I didn't catch her making more notes after Freddie's first flour spill, and she had a decent conversation or two with the other students.

And it turned out that Freddie was everyone's biggest cheerleader. I thought he might be putting on an act or trying too hard to please us, but he was genuine and he and Gram really hit it off big that day. They "got" each other's humor and started to bounce jokes off each other.

It was one of the best and most exhausting days I could remember at Gram's Country Cooking School.

After the students left, some heading back to their temporary lodging, some to look for more permanent housing, some over to Bunny's diner for dinner, and others to the grocery store to buy groceries to fix dinner for themselves and perhaps some of the other students, Gram and I sat on the front steps with glasses of very cold iced tea. After we'd told the last student that we'd see them tomorrow and Gram assured me that we didn't need to have another all-nighter, I asked if she'd go with me to the bakery so I could properly meet Gent. She agreed, but only after an iced tea break.

The almost two full days with no ghost in our lives had been good for Gram; whatever burden Gent's appearance had given her had dissipated. Unfortunately, my mention of traveling to the bakery brought it back—it was something that dimmed her eyes and tightened a corner of her mouth.

I hadn't asked her more questions about him. I hadn't had a chance to text Jake a hello, let alone talk to him about the fire. I'd decided that meeting the ghost and his family first was the best way to begin. Maybe there was a simple explanation for the things that Gram had told me, and Gent would be the one to ask; ask first, at least. Or maybe it was just the shortcut that I was most curious about pursuing.

Gram took a large gulp of tea and said, "I'll go with you, Betts, but you need to know that meeting Gent will be unlike anything you could have imagined. It's going to be even weirder than everything else so far."

I gulped a swallow, too. "I don't know. It wasn't long ago that I never imagined I'd be communicating with ghosts at all. I think I'm ready for anything."

Gram looked at me and licked a small drop of tea off her bottom lip. "Well, I suppose there's only one way to know that for sure. Let's go."

It was a good thing she stood up then or she might have seen the shiver of concern that shook me. Despite my brave words, adding something even weirder to the ghostly mix didn't sit well with me at all, but that was the last thing I'd want her to know.

Chapter 5

The building was built in 1931, funded by the riches of a couple of friends from New York City. They moved to Broken Rope with the hopes of living Wild West lives. When they found that sort of living was fraught with more death and danger than they were either used to or prepared for, they chose to go into business instead. And what a business it was. The Kennington Bakery brought an amount of respect to Broken Rope that our deadly reputation never could.

At one time or another, the bakery employed everyone who lived in Broken Rope, or so it seemed. Often, I'd heard people say things like, "Yeah, my great-grandfather (or some other ancestor) worked at Kenny for ten years. Made bread until he got promoted to the Puff Pocket crew." Many people "back in the day" even braved the violent stories of our town and moved here *because* they knew they could find employment at the bakery, a much safer place to work than saloons, brothels, and the like. So, while the bakery offered employment in a safe environment, the Wild West still raged wildly throughout the rest of Broken Rope.

My best friend and the town historian, Jake, had once told me that he gives complete credit to the bakery as the reason that Broken Rope thrived when other Wild West towns died.

If it weren't for the bakery, the one place we don't highlight as a historical tourist attraction, we might not be here and have the chance to show off all our other, stranger parts, he'd say.

Broken Rope was a performance town, the main street still holding pace with time from an earlier era, a hundred years ago, with a dirt main road and wooden walkways that led to the same sorts of shops that had been part of the original Missouri town. We'd added a modern flair with things like air-conditioning and ovens that were fit with knobs instead of burning wood, but we kept those technologies well hidden from the tourists.

The condition of the bakery building and its location contributed to its stark existence even as it sat in a heavily traveled (well, heavily traveled for Broken Rope) residential neighborhood. But I always sensed there was more to why it was mostly forgotten. Jake's wonky feelings about the building's karma somehow made sense to me, and I suspected that those were common, shared feelings among the locals.

There were so many things to do in Broken Rope that no one paid much attention to it anyway. Every now and then, though, I'd see someone standing in the weeds that had overtaken the long skinny front strip. They'd be pointing their camera up to the structure or toward one of the large broken-out windows. It was an eyesore to be sure, but it must have garnered some wayward tourists' interest.

It was dusk by the time Gram parked her Volvo behind the back of the building, and I tried to look at it with different eyes, perhaps with more of an appreciation, but I couldn't make the leap; it was still just an unappealing old structure to me.

"I tried to get in here a couple times when I was in high school," I said. "It was impossible. We talked about getting a ladder so we could climb in one of the windows, but even we could see how foolish that would have been. Too much broken glass, too far a drop on the inside."

Gram shook her head. "There's no way in except for Gent. He'll let us in."

I blinked. "Well, that sounds downright awesome," I said as I smiled her direction. The light from an old streetlamp came through the driver's side windshield and illuminated her face. She'd been the Missouri Anna we all knew and loved when she was teaching the new crop of students, but the arrival of Gent had sent her off-kilter slightly. She glanced up at the building through the windshield, the light making her wrinkles a little deeper and curiously more meaningful.

It took her a second but the corner of her mouth finally twitched at my playful tone. "I know, I know, I've got to shape up."

"It's fine, Gram," I said as I touched her arm. I wanted to remind her about my own ghost angst, that I still thought about Jerome and how much I sometimes missed Sally's happy laugh and desire to always be doing something, but it wasn't necessary to vocalize either of those things; she knew.

"Come on, Isabelle, you're in for quite a treat. This place is amazing when Gent's around. Step carefully. Even with shoes on, there's lots of dangerous glass until we get inside," Gram said as we got out of the car. We stepped forward with caution.

"Oh, bad shoes, Betts," Gram said. "I should have noticed."

I'd put on flip-flops after all the students left for the day. Gram was right, they were horrible for what we would be trekking through, but I hadn't brought my sneakers with me.

"I'll be extra careful," I said.

Gram sighed, thought a minute, and then said, "All right, but be *really* careful," before we continued on.

The back of the building was solid wall except for a long row of windows across the top. There were also three delivery bays, each with an extra-large rolling door that was boarded up tightly. Every once in a while the boards were sprayed with graffiti, but mostly they were left alone. Each bay was at the bottom of its own downhill driveway. The bays made good hiding spots, this I knew, though they were, as Gram had mentioned, littered with glass from the vandalized windows above. She'd parked the Volvo at the top of one of the bays where the glass was still present but not so thickly.

"You're not afraid we'll get caught?" I asked her.

"Nope, you're dating a police officer. We'll be able to talk ourselves out of any trouble with the law. And, no one can go in there unless they can see Gent. If they can see him, we should probably know about it."

"Everyone knows your car," I said as I followed Gram's veer toward another door. I didn't think my dating Cliff would keep him from being curious about Gram's empty car, though she was probably right in that we wouldn't get in too much legal trouble. We wouldn't be arrested for trespassing, but Cliff would be concerned about our safety.

Gram shrugged. "Never been a problem before."

"Okay."

She stopped walking and looked at me. "Betts, don't bring up the fire. Let me do it. It's part of the memory issue. Gent and his family need some time to find the memory themselves. I've tried to push it before, and it only confuses them, and confused ghosts are even more annoying."

I looked at her, in the dark now, the streetlight at her back. She'd already told me not to bring up the fact that the building would probably be demolished someday, and now the fire. What were we supposed to talk about? I would do as she asked, but her reasons for asking weren't what she said they were, I could tell.

"Sure, Gram, no problem," I finally said.

"Good." She turned. "This door," she said as she gave me her hand.

I held it as she took a step onto a small landing up and out of the bay. I continued to hold on as I used her for leverage to get myself up, too.

The door was just a regular solid door, similar to my front door. But this one had a thick piece of plywood nailed across its top and one across its bottom. The knob would have been exposed if there'd been a knob instead of a hole where one used to be.

Gram leaned toward the door. "Gent, we're here."

A long minute passed accompanied by only the sounds of crickets and someone starting a car somewhere in the general vicinity.

Gram chewed her lip, knocked on the door in the space between the two boards, and said, "Gent, we're here," a little louder.

Things began to change.

The boards over the door disappeared and the knob appeared. Except it wasn't a knob, it was an ornate handle.

"Uh, Gram, what's going on?" I said as I blinked at the transforming reality.

"This is going to be weird for you, Betts. It was the first few times for me, too. But you'll get used to it, I promise."

The door was now a smooth dark wood, and a small plaque at the top of it was made of shiny brass. It said: KENNINGTON BAKED GOODS.

I stepped back. It was one thing to see ghosts, another thing to be able to communicate with them, but this was a whole new aspect to add to the already strange experience. Though my encounter with Sally had shown me that whatever was going on during the current time period could be influenced by spirits from the past, I'd never guessed that I could also step into the past, or a setting of the past, or whatever was happening.

I'd sensed that I'd jumped a ride on a slippery slope when I first met Jerome. Communicating with ghosts of the long-dead *might* be harmless, but it also *might* mean that I was exposing myself—that Gram had been exposing herself—to something dangerous, something that live people as a rule weren't supposed to be a part of.

Mostly, though, I'd ignored any sense of danger. It had been there, though, in the back of my mind, a tiny glimmer.

That glimmer suddenly grew larger and brighter, as the light around the door did the same.

"Gram?"

She stepped back and handed me her car keys. "Betts, I'm sorry. I should have prepared you better. Here, go, take the car and go. I'll stay and talk to Gent. I want to. I'll call you when I'm done and you can come get me. I'm sorry, sweetheart. You don't have to do this, Betts, you don't have to do it at all."

No, I didn't *have* to. Given the option to go though made it clear that I truly didn't want to leave. I was just a little scared but not enough to step off the platform. Yet. I swallowed hard as the door opened.

The ethereal sense faded, leaving behind only light, regular old light, and Gent Cylas. But he wasn't as I'd seen him earlier. Instead of his clothes reminding me of Jerome, they reminded me of a high school lunch lady. Gent wore a white shirt and white pants, all covered in a long white apron. Unlike the lunch ladies I knew, though, he wore a cap, something that reminded me of a sailor, and not a hairnet. The cap sat on the side of his head and made him even more adorable. But he was still barefooted.

"Gram, is there a chance we might not be able to . . . go back?" I asked as Gent seemed not to see us; he searched the area where we were standing as though he was looking for someone, but his eyes didn't quite land on us.

"Look down, Betts," she said.

I did and saw that the cement below my feet was distinctly aged: pitted and broken. But that wasn't the case a foot closer to the building and a foot closer to Gent in the open doorway. There it was smooth and even. Gram moved her foot so it straddled both.

"I was once worried about the same thing, but then I noticed that neither of my feet disappears even when they're in both places. It wouldn't be prudent to get into any sort of discussion regarding time, time travel, or even what in the hellfire it is that you and I can see, but I've never had any problem stepping out of that door and coming back to . . . well, to now," she said. "But, Betts, you don't have to do this. I keep telling you not to let this stuff get to you and then I bring you here. I'm sorry."

I shook my head. "No, I want to go in. I just wanted to make sure we can get back out." That was mostly true. Bottom line, I didn't want to miss the . . . opportunity, if that's what it was, no matter how much more slippery the slope just became.

I took a step forward and onto the smooth concrete. Gram moved with me.

"I'll be," Gent said, "you are the spittin' image of Missouri, girly."

Gent's use of *girly* was just what I needed. A sense of silly suddenly washed over me and I smiled at Gram.

"Yes, well, Gent missed out on that whole gender-equality and political-correctness stuff," she said. "His intention isn't to offend. He thinks he's adorable and friendly, and he is, but perhaps more appropriate for an earlier time."

"Missouri Anna Winston, I can surely speak for myself." He took off his cap and swooped his hand in a welcoming gesture. "Pleasure's mine, ladies. Come in, come in."

"He was seventeen when he died?" I mumbled to Gram.

"Yes, but very self-assured," Gram mumbled back.

Though I'd never found a safe way to enter the dilapidated building, I had been hoisted up enough to peer into a window. Then, I'd seen only a large open space strewn with junk, leaves, and mysterious items I thought must have been remnants of old machinery.

But in this state, and even in the dim light, the place was magnificent, and before I could even consider giving Gent my full attention, I had to soak in what I was seeing; something that was so detailed with touches of its own time that it could never have been duplicated accurately in the twenty-first century.

The floor wasn't the concrete I'd seen a moment earlier; it was made of dark wood planks and looked fairly clean. Briefly, I thought about how difficult it must have been to keep it that way, but there was too much to see to dwell on the floor.

Since windows lined the top of the entire building, I figured that the solid wall I saw not far away must have been placed in the middle of the long warehouse-type room. There were ovens lining the entire wall; I didn't count, but there must have been fifteen to twenty of them. Set apart but still in front of the ovens, there was a long rolling conveyer belt that was probably a good four feet wide. Set back farther, toward the windows, were two long rows of shelves.

I didn't understand how the details contributed to the sense of *old-fashioned* until I looked more closely. The oven doors were made of lead, ornate with curlicues and big handles. The shelves weren't metal like the cooking school's shelves, but were wooden and worn perfectly. There was something ragged yet not unappealing about the conveyer belt.

"I couldn't have ever imagined this, Gram," I finally said.

"I know, it's extraordinary."

We'd followed Gent but slowly enough to lag more than follow. He'd noticed my curious stares and waited patiently. Finally, I turned my attention to him. "I'm Betts. It's nice to meet you."

"You, too." Gent winked and then bowed. "Any granddaughter of Miz's is a friend of mine." He stood straight and put his hands on his hips. "Though I gotta tell ya I swear to kingdom come that I never thought I'd meet anyone new ever again. I love coming back to talk to Missouri and visiting my family, of course. Do you suppose I'll get to meet more people?"

"I hope not," Gram answered.

"I suppose you're right about that, Miz." He turned to me. "Did she tell you about how we were best buds when we were growing up in the country, Betts? Oh, Lordy, we has us some fun, we did."

"She mentioned it. She said you had the entire woods to yourselves and that you were wild and out of control."

Gent laughed. "That we were. We were the self-appointed king and queen of the entire state of Missouri. We made thrones of downed trees and we stole towels and sheets—they'd be drying on lines and we'd just steal them to make capes." Gent suddenly looked distracted and he scratched at his head. "I don't think I've ever remembered that before, have I?" he asked Gram.

"Of course you have. It just takes a little time, some memories come back," Gram said.

Gent scratched his head again.

"Come on," Gram said, changing the subject, "let's introduce Betts to your family."

I thought Gent might have preferred to focus on remembering something, perhaps more about their towel thievery, but the intensity with which he was thinking made me wonder if there was something more serious to the story. An instant later, though, his attention snapped back to me and Gram.

"Okay," he said. "Let's start with my momma."

Being inside the time-warped bakery wasn't like floating on a cloud or walking through a foggy scene. It was lit funny, but it was just a normal place, normal for its time period at least, which made it simply weird. Everything from the past was there and in a condition that made it seem real. But, as our focus shifted to the different items, those items became better illuminated. I'd learned that when I was in close vicinity to the ghosts in the dark, they would become more dimensional, more solid, but this trick of light was more about bright and dark than it was dimension. The items in the bakery looked continually solid, just not always properly illuminated.

I'd already seen Gent's mother standing in front of the long conveyer belt under the ovens. Her back had been to us and it was clear that she was doing something with her hands. But as we stepped closer to her and gave her our full attention, she and her space became brighter. She was short and very thin but clearly strong, her shoulders and back straight and firm.

"Mother, some people to see."

Gent's mother turned and smiled.

"Missouri Anna, well, it's always such a pleasure," she said. "And, oh my gracious, I don't understand." She looked from me to Gram a number of times. "It's you, but younger."

"No, Ellen, this is my granddaughter Isabelle Winston, Betts. And this is Mrs. Ellen Cylas."

"I'll be darned. You are the spittin' image of your grandmother."

"So I've heard. It's good to meet you."

"You, too. I didn't know I could ever meet anyone again. It's more than good, it's pretty wonderful. Is it because she's your relation?" she asked Gram.

"Probably, but we don't know," Gram said. "Ellen, you know I've never really understood any of this."

"Well, whatever it is, it's just lovely."

The same intense focus I'd seen on Gent's face a moment earlier suddenly swept across Ellen's face.

"Mother?" Gent said.

"Ellen?" Gram said.

She snapped back to attention a second later.

"Gent, I remembered something, something you and Missouri didn't get to finish, something the two of you didn't take care of. It was like I almost remembered the details but they went away again. I don't know why it happened all of a sudden."

"The same thing happened to me, Ma. Maybe it'll come to us soon."

"I don't know," Ellen said. "It was something bad."

I was thoroughly confused, but it wasn't unusual that these ghosts threw me for a loop. Gram stood next to me and I noticed that even she seemed unsure.

"What's going on?" I asked her quietly.

"I don't really know," she said.

"This isn't normal?"

"No. Shaky memories are normal, but something bigger is going on here. Maybe we're upsetting them. Or upsetting something. I think we should leave."

It was way too rude and inappropriate to point out aloud that Gram had never before been concerned about upsetting the ghosts. It wasn't that she didn't care about them. It was that she'd come to the conclusion that no matter how you felt about them, they weren't coming back to life and they weren't going to become any deader, so concern for them was a waste of time and energy.

"I'd like to stick around and see what happens," I said. "You okay, Ellen?"

She looked at me for a moment as if she'd forgotten I was there, but then she smiled again. I hadn't met his father yet, but Gent looked like his mother, with almond-shaped dark eyes and big V-shaped smile. Ellen wasn't an unattractive woman, but her looks worked much better on her seventeen-year-old son.

"I am fine, so happy to meet you. Wait, I already said that." Ellen laughed. "I should get back to my bread. Excuse me."

She turned and faced the conveyer belt again. Her arms, hands, and shoulders went to work, but whatever they were working on was invisible to me.

I looked at Gram and didn't need to tell her what I *wasn't* seeing. She figured it out.

"If you step closer, you'll see the bread," she said.

I moved next to Ellen and the bread she'd been working on appeared on the belt. She was slipping oblong, perfectly browned loaves into paper packaging. She was quick as she grabbed a paper bag from a spot behind the belt and slipped it over a loaf of bread. This maneuver took her between two and three seconds for each loaf and she didn't miss a beat.

The scents were suddenly there, too. I sniffed deeply.

"You all right?" Ellen said.

"It just smells so good in here."

"Does it? I guess I never noticed." She turned her attention back to the conveyer belt.

I stepped back, and in one blink, the bread and the aromas disappeared.

"You were right, Gram. This is the strangest thing I've ever experienced," I said.

Her forehead crinkled and her lips pursed tightly. "Me, too, Betts. At least, I thought that the first time it happened. This is as strange as it gets, or at least as it has ever gotten. I've never experienced anything odder than this. It's probably good to know that."

"Yes, it is."

"Come meet my sister and my daddy," Gent said, signaling us deeper into the big room.

With each step, the spaces we moved into lit up a bit more. I took a deep breath and realized I was calming down. It would be impossible for this experience to be dangerous, wouldn't it? We were in the middle of something that was bigger than imagination but smaller than reality. Like the Puff Pocket itself, we were in some pocket of time that surely protected us from harm. It had done so for Gram, apparently. I was becoming more certain that we would be fine.

"This is my dad, Homer Cylas," Gent said as we approached a table.

As the space lit, a big, happy man stood from the stool he'd been sitting on and wiped his flour-covered hands over his middle and then put his fists on his hips. He was dressed like Gent and Ellen, all in white, but the ends of his short red hair curled out from underneath his cap. The red was so bright that it was almost cartoonish.

"Missouri Anna, it is always a pleasure. And this young woman must be one of yours, she looks just like you did."

"This is my granddaughter Isabelle. It's great to see you, Homer," Gram said.

"The feeling's mutual, Miz. Lovely to meet you, Isabelle. Boy, if I could remember, I'd tell you stories about Missouri that would curl your hair like the Missouri humidity. If we're here for a while, I bet I'll remember something. These two were always getting into trouble."

Right as he said *trouble*, a noise sounded from an even farther and deeper space in the bakery, from a short wing that jutted out from the center of the building.

It didn't immediately register with me that Gram had made her own noise, a small one, a squeak maybe.

"What was that?" Homer asked as he turned toward the louder sound.

"I . . . I don't know," Gent said, but it sounded like maybe he did know, or maybe thought he knew but didn't want to say.

I looked at Gram. She'd put her hands on her hips, too, and was chewing at her bottom lip again as she looked into the murky space toward where the noise had come from. She studied it. Hard.

I leaned a little closer to her and just happened to catch the glance between her and Gent. They knew something about the noise, but with that glance they told each other not to talk about it.

It was just a random sound. What was the big deal?

"Gent, what was that?" A young girl emerged from the shadows and stood next to the table. A second later, Ellen joined us, too.

"I don't know," he said. "Betts, this is my sister, Jennie."

Jennie might have been ten when she died. She had also been a beautiful child who would have surely grown into a stunning woman if she'd been given the chance. She didn't look like anyone else in her family and had been blessed with a heart-shaped face and long blond curls. Her hair was pulled back in a ponytail that flowed down to the middle of her back. Her white cap was slightly off-kilter like her brother's, and she looked like a child who could have modeled for an old-time soda pop advertisement or a Norman Rockwell portrait.

"Betts. What kind of a name is that?" she asked me.

"Short for Isabelle," I said.

She thought about it a minute and then said, "I like it."

"Thank you." I hadn't looked before, but now I noticed that the rest of Gent's family wore shoes. Jennie's were a clean bright white.

She turned back to her brother. "Gent, what was that noise?"

"Nothing, I s'pose." He reached for her hand.

I swallowed the lump that suddenly grew in my throat.

It was normal to feel at least a little sense of sadness regarding the ghosts and the fact that they were dead. *They* weren't sad, but seeing the young Gent and Jennie together definitely touched that sympathetic nerve.

Gram cleared her throat. I looked at her, but she was looking at Gent. He shook his head slightly and shrugged.

I wished I knew what they were secretly and silently discussing. The rest of Gent's family seemed not to notice or care.

"I think it's time to go, Betts," Gram said.

"You just got here," Homer said.

"We'll come back," Gram said.

But an instinct rocked my gut and told me that we never would. I didn't understand how that knowledge was so clear, but it most definitely was.

"I'll be out to the school to see you, too," Gent said, though I heard doubt in his voice.

Gram squinted, thought a moment, and then nodded. "Looking forward to it."

Gent released Jennie's hand and then hurriedly walked us to the door. As we moved away from the others, they became more emerged in darkness, but not pitch blackness. I could still see *them* as they moved back to their now *invisible* tasks.

Weird.

Gram reached for the door handle as Gent looked directly at me. "You know, you're welcome here anytime. If I don't come to the door, we've gone, but we'll be back someday. We always come back."

"Thank you," I said. Was he inviting me to return to the

bakery, perhaps without Gram? Maybe I was reading more into it than there truly was.

"Come along, Betts," she said as she moved through the open doorway.

I followed but looked back and waved to Gent as he disappeared and the current boarded-over door reappeared. The scene changed with a simple fade—past to present, old-time to just plain old and run-down.

I had to stand still and stare at it a moment. It wasn't easy simply to accept what Gram and I had just done. I'd been scared to my toes when I first realized I was able to talk to ghosts. That moment had been cold and gut churning, but this was different, this was more denial than fear.

"You okay?" Gram asked.

"I'm fine." I smiled at the funny lilt to my words. Okay, so maybe I was a little shaken.

"Come on, let's get home. We can talk about this stuff forever and a day and still not understand it."

"Wait." I grabbed her arm. "What about . . . Well, you didn't get to talk to Gent about the fire."

"Too soon."

"What was the noise, Gram?"

"Gosh, Betts, I don't think anyone knew."

But she did, I was sure. However, I knew Missouri Anna Winston better than I probably knew anyone. It wasn't the time to push her. I'd regroup and approach it all again tomorrow, after we'd both slept at least a little and had some good strong coffee in us.

"Let's go. Time to get home," I acquiesced.

Even in the mostly darkness, I saw relief flash in her eyes

before she gave me her hand. "Help me down and then I'll grab you from down there."

We were off the platform and in the Volvo quickly. As she steered us away from the old building, she turned up the CD player, I suspected to make it more difficult to have a conversation. So, it was while Tim McGraw was singing "Something Like That" that I happened to look back. I was certain I saw a shadow in one of the broken-out bakery windows; something that looked like a man in a cowboy hat and reminded me a lot of Jerome.

I about twisted my head off my neck as I craned it for a better look. There was nothing there but a space where a real window used to be. It was hiding a blackness that in turn hid things that were even more unreal than the cowboy shadow itself.

"What is it, Betts?" Gram asked.

I bit my cheeks. I wanted to tell her. I wanted it to have been Jerome, but telling her what I *thought* I saw suddenly seemed ridiculous.

"Nothing, Gram. Just getting one more look."

She turned her head and briefly looked back at the building. "Gent can visit us at the school. We probably won't go back there."

I was impressed by my earlier intuition, but I still wanted to go back, now probably more than ever. I didn't say a word.

Gram drove us back to the school so I could gather the Nova. I told her a cheery good-bye, hopped in the car, and started it, but pretended to be looking at something on my phone as I waved a farewell. The Volvo pulled out of the parking lot, the normally quiet woods still being serenaded by Tim McGraw. Once her taillights were out of view and

I could no longer hear Tim, I turned my car off and got out of it again.

I hurried toward the cemetery and then stepped over the low rope dividing it from the parking lot. Though there was a large light on the front of the school building, most of the cemetery was buried in spotty blackness. I could make out tombstones here and there but nothing specific, and because I was looking into the darkness and not at my feet, I didn't lift one up as high as I should have. My toe caught painfully on the rope.

"Dammit," I said. I'd avoided all the glass at the bakery, but the rope I was accustomed to had proved the real danger.

I never liked being at the school alone at night, definitely never liked to traipse through the cemetery in the dark. The mere idea had given me the willies even before I knew about the ghosts. I switched on the light on my phone and directed it out toward the plots and tombstones, which ended up making everything only creepier.

"Nice," I said quietly. I cleared my throat and said, "Jerome, are you there?"

My behavior was a little nutty, and I hoped that no one but me and possibly him was paying attention.

I ignored the burning pain in my toe and walked to Jerome's tombstone, my shoes flipping and flopping much more loudly than normal. I'd visited his grave a few times since he'd left, but mostly I'd stayed away from it. I aimed the light at the epitaph. It said: HE COULD CHARM THE LADIES, BUT HE COULDN'T SHOOT DIDDLY.

I smiled.

"No, you couldn't shoot straight, could you? Good thing you didn't have to," I said.

No answer.

With the possible exception of the crickets' chirps, some frenetic moths around the light on the building, and a dozen or so lightning bugs, there was no one else in the cemetery, unless, of course, we were counting the dead and buried. No spirits lurked above the ground. The crickets, the moths, the invisible ghosts, no one cared about or noticed my silliness.

I was, however, surprised to see a coin on top of the tombstone. The one I carried with me for luck was real gold, but this was clearly a fake, perhaps the same one that Jake and I had found before I'd met Jerome. Someone had put this one there or had returned the original token, but I wasn't sure why. Neither Jim, the police chief, nor Cliff, my recycled boyfriend and a police officer himself, knew about the ghosts, so they wouldn't think to put it there as some sort of honor. Jake, who knew all about the ghosts, must have been the one sentimental enough to place the coin there. I'd ask him.

I stood still for a few minutes and then looked around one more time. Finally, I took a big sniff searching for Jerome's wood smoke scent. The night smelled of musty leftover humidity, green from all the trees, and spiced with a far-off tinge of lake water from the Ozarks.

Finally, I turned away from the tombstone and tromped back to the Nova. By then, I was certain I'd only imagined the figure in the window.

My skills of observation weren't as sharp as they should have been, though. Gram and I pulling in, my explorations of the cemetery, and then me leaving it—everything had been observed. Someone had been lying in wait. The good news was that they weren't waiting for Gram or me.

But the bad news was that they were waiting for one of our students, who, unfortunately, ended up being at the wrong place at the exact wrong time.

Chapter 6

Oh no, had I slept in? What day was it? Was school in session? Was I home?

These were the thoughts that sped through my mind as I was awakened by my cell phone's buzz and vibrating dance on the nightstand.

I sat up, still half asleep but half alert from adrenaline, and grabbed the phone. It was Gram calling.

"Hello," I said with a morning croak. I cleared my throat. "Hello, Gram? I'm sorry. Am I late?"

"Betts, you need to get down to the school right away. Don't spend time getting ready, just get down here."

"Okay."

She clicked off the call before I could say anything else. I blinked a few times to make sure I was seeing the time correctly. According to the phone, it was only 6:00 A.M., which was an hour before I was planning to get up, and an hour and a half before I usually got up.

I didn't have a clock on the nightstand any longer, so I hurried to the kitchen to check the clock on the stove. It matched the cell phone.

The phone buzzed again as I held it.

"Cliff, hey, what's up?" I answered. We hadn't moved in together, but we'd been spending most nights together. The last week or so I'd put all my focus on the beginning of the school year, though, so he'd been at his house and I'd been at mine. Normally, I'd be excited to hear from him after even an afternoon of no contact but I sensed he wasn't calling to wish me a good day.

"Are you coming down to the school?"

"Yes. Gram just called. Are you there?"

"I am. You need to get here, okay?"

"Sure, but what's up?"

He paused. "Get here, Betts. We're trying to get ahold of the other students too."

"Cliff, what's wrong?"

"Just get here," he said before he ended the call.

I wasn't sure whether to be concerned or angry. I chose a little of both as I threw on some jeans, a T-shirt, and the same flip-flops I'd worn the night before. I pulled my hair back into a ponytail as I hurried down the short flight of stairs off my front porch and cranked the Nova up with one turn of the key.

Broken Rope was a sparsely populated town, but it was spread out into a number of different sections. The residential area I lived in was considered to be on the other side of town from the school, but it still took less than ten minutes for me to reach it. In the middle of the heavy tourist season and with a big influx of traffic, it could sometimes take about twelve minutes, but I didn't think it had ever been more than that.

The heaviest part of tourist season was over but there were still a few visitors here and there. Even though the trip took only about seven minutes this morning, it seemed like an eternity passed from the moment I pulled away from the curb and then into the school's parking lot.

It was obvious that something was terribly wrong. The parking lot was full, and it was rarely full. The vehicles that took up the space were worrisome by themselves.

I assumed that one of the two police cars in the lot had been driven there by Cliff; Jim probably drove the other one. Broken Rope had a well-equipped fire station as well as its own fire marshal. A fire truck and two ambulances took up a large amount of space, and a couple other cars flanked the far side of the lot. I assumed they were students' cars that I would come to recognize as the year went on, but it was still too soon to have paid much attention to who drove what. Gram's Volvo was parked next to the cemetery, close to the school's sign. The driver's side door was open. Nothing was in truly designated parking spaces, including Gram's Volvo.

I parked behind the other cars and got out with the intention of rushing toward the school and finding Gram. But I was interrupted.

"Betts," someone said.

I turned to see three students exiting the small blue compact that I'd pulled behind. Freddie, Elian, and Jules walked toward me. I conducted a silent self-pep talk about remaining calm around the students.

"Betts," Freddie said as the three of them approached. "What's wrong?"

"I'm not sure, yet," I said as soothingly as possible, "but I'll find out. It'd be best if you all stay back here until we know more."

"I think I saw a body," Jules said, "but there were so many people and vehicles in the way . . ." She sounded more put out by the fact she hadn't been able to see what was going on than the fact that someone might have been hurt. Or worse. Of course, I realized this was probably just her way of coping. Her Arizona tanned skin was currently more green than tan.

I didn't have one word of reassurance. "I'll find out. Just stay back; perhaps sitting in the car is the best idea."

Jules didn't appear to have heard me. Instead, she was silent as she peered toward the epicenter of the activity. Freddie put his hand on her arm and led her back to the small blue car.

"This is messed up," Elian said to me when the other two were out of earshot.

"Well, let's find out what's going on before we get too worried."

"I saw the body, too," he said. "And I'm not happy about it at all." He turned quickly and went to join the others.

"Me, either," I said quietly as I turned the other direction and hurried toward the school. Though I hadn't noticed her, yet, Gram must have seen me arrive.

"Hang on, Betts," she said as she appeared from around a vehicle and met me halfway. She put her hands on my arms and held me back with her typical Missouri Anna strength.

"What's going on, Gram? You're okay, right? Is someone hurt?"

"I'm fine. But, yes, someone was hurt. It's bad, okay?"

"Tell me!"

"One of our students, Roger, he was . . . Oh, good Lord, this is hard. He's dead, Betts."

"What!" A picture of Roger in his short-sleeved shirts and skinny ties flashed through my mind. "That's not possible."

"I'm sorry, sweetheart. It is. I found him here this morning."

"How? I don't understand."

"I found his body in front of the school. He was dead when I got here."

The dead bodies found at the school count had risen to two? In just a few short months? Gram and I had found Everett Morningside's body in our supply room back in May. And now . . . a student?

"How?"

"I don't know. There was no blood that I could see. I saw something, maybe his mouth was foaming, but I can't be too sure at this point. He was draped over the dividing rope. I hurried to see if he was okay, but it was clear he wasn't. I called Jim right away."

It wasn't rare that Gram was at the school early, particularly at the beginning of the school year. But it was somewhat rare that a student was here this early. As the cooking competition neared, some students were at the school twenty-four/seven but it was too soon for that sort of enthusiasm.

The scent of fresh-baked bread suddenly filled the air. It

was such a contradiction to the acidy panic I tasted in the back of my throat that I was thrown off for a second. The thought to ask Gram who was baking crossed my mind, but then I realized that I'd smelled the arrival of Gent.

He stood back from the crowd, toward the end of the parking lot and the beginning of the road, his hands in his pockets. He wore the pants and loose shirt I'd first seen him in. Without the white uniform and hat and with his somewhat unruly hair, he looked much younger and even less modern than he did in the bakery. I suddenly had a thought that must have sprung up from my subconscious, because at that moment, I couldn't have cared less about the details—but, Gent Cylas wasn't buried in this cemetery. I hadn't memorized all our dead residents' names, but I was certain that there was not one member of the Cylas family buried close by. I shook the random thought away.

"Oh, not now," Gram said quietly as we both looked his direction. Just as she was going to somehow signal him that we couldn't talk, Cliff rounded the ambulance, blocked our view of Gent, and strode toward us. We must have been looking intently at the ghost because Cliff turned to see what had captured our attention. All he saw was the end of the parking lot and a big white truck passing by.

"Miz, you okay?" Cliff said as he joined us.

"I'm okay, not the best I've ever been, but okay."

Cliff nodded. "Betts. Miz told you what's going on?"

I nodded.

"I'm sorry, but I need to talk to Betts a second, Miz. Can you excuse us? Jim would like to talk to you some more. He's by the front door."

"Of course."

"I wanted her to sit down," Cliff explained as Gram rounded the same ambulance that he just had. "Jim will take care of her."

"What happened, Cliff?"

"That's what we're trying to figure out. I can't officially question you, but I was hoping we could talk a minute about the deceased and the other new students."

"Why . . . Oh, you can't question me because we're in a relationship?"

"Yes."

Cliff Sebastian and I had had one of those perfect high school romances; so naturally, it was bound to end imperfectly. We'd parted ways for college; he was going to become an architect and I was going to become an attorney. I'd planned on our paths crossing after we finished our educations and that we'd fall madly in love again and resume all that perfectness. And, that's close to what we'd done. Cliff's detour had been a failed marriage, and my detour had caused me to quit law school and come back to Broken Rope to help Gram at the cooking school. Of course, the biggest surprise of my life (other than a ghost or two) had been Cliff not only leaving his marriage but his architectural career to become a Broken Rope police officer.

We'd most definitely found at least some of that perfectness again, though ten additional years and a few bad life choices caused us to see everything differently, mostly in good ways, but it would be impossible for us both not to have become a little jaded and cautious with our emotions.

I took a deep breath. "Sure, but can we maybe sit down, too. I don't feel so great."

Cliff led me away from the front porch and toward the back of the ambulance. Jim hadn't sent them away yet, so the EMTs stood outside their vehicle and waited. It would be wonderful to say that Broken Rope's crime rate wasn't one that caused our EMTs to be busy, but that wouldn't be true. Not only did Broken Rope have a history of strange and unusual deaths, we also had a number of tourists who overdid their activities, and sometimes the Missouri heat didn't agree with them. Since Roger was dead though, it looked like their services wouldn't be needed.

I didn't hear the exact words Cliff said to them, but a few seconds later they were somewhere else and I was sitting on the bed of the open ambulance with a small paper cup of water in my hands.

"Better?" Cliff asked.

I nodded, but now I couldn't take my eyes off Gent who was only about twenty feet away. I still hadn't seen Roger Riggins's body. Gram's Volvo was thankfully in the way. Gent continued to anxiously wave me toward him. I opened my eyes wide for a moment, hoping he'd get what I was trying to say: *Not now.*

"Good. Betts, do you have any details that could help lead us to Mr. Riggins's killer, if in fact he was killed? Hopefully, Morris can tell us what happened quickly. We suspect maybe a seizure was somehow involved, but we just won't know until Morris tells us. Roger was a student. Neither Jim nor I have had a chance to get to know any of them. I know you've only had a couple days, but we need to get as much information together as we can. Anything you can tell me would be helpful." He paused. "Jim and I did meet Freddie O'Bannon when he stopped by the station to ask us how to get to the school, but we don't know him any better than the others."

"Freddie stopped by the jail?" I said.

"Yes, he was lost."

Suddenly, I forgot all about Gent. "Cliff, that's strange."

"Why?"

"Because, we include specific directions and a map to the school in each welcome packet we send. And Freddie's arrival was a surprise anyway."

"I don't understand."

I explained Freddie's unusual arrival and why Gram and I let him stay. I told him about the references we still hadn't checked. He asked for a copy so he could check them, too. I nodded to the blue compact car and told Cliff that Freddie was the one with the green eyes. I agreed that we hadn't had time to get to know anyone yet, either. It was too early to gauge if our instincts about the students were correct, but I did the best I could to offer whatever impressions I'd already gotten. I even included Brenda's strange note-taking habit.

"Did you check references on all the other students?" Cliff asked.

"We always do."

"Anything suspicious? I know Miz believes in rehabilitation. Any previously incarcerated individuals this year?"

I felt a smile pull at the corner of my mouth. This was all far too serious to have a reason to smile, but it was difficult not to find Cliff's use of cop words odd, cute, and endearing.

"What?" he asked.

"I'm sorry. I'm just getting used to you as an officer of the law." I smiled, though it turned out to be a sad smile.

"I know. Me, too, but don't tell Jim."

It had been only ten years since high school, but I'd noticed some significant physical changes in several of our fellow classmates. Cliff had changed only a little and his changes were for the better. He was still tall, with long muscular legs and wide shoulders, but everything had filled out over time, in a pleasing way. His short brown hair was still impossibly straight—I'd never seen such stubbornly straight hair on anyone else. But he wore it so short now that I didn't notice its inability to bend as much. He also still had a dimple on his right cheek, which had probably been the first reason I'd fallen so head-over-heels for him when we were younger. The dimple was still on the list of reasons why I was falling for him again, but just not quite as high as it used to be.

"I won't tell him. No, to our knowledge, none of our students have ever been incarcerated. We'll take a closer look at Freddie, though."

"We will, too."

Cliff plopped his hands on his hips and looked toward the road. I watched him and a zing of hope tightened my chest. Did he see Gent? My best friend since high school, Jake, knew about the ghosts but couldn't see them. I'd felt somewhat disloyal to Cliff that Jake and I discussed our spectral visitors, but I hadn't been able to find a way to tell Cliff about them yet.

Gent noticed Cliff looking his direction, too. He stood a little straighter and waved hesitantly. Cliff looked back at me.

"You know, we found some blood. Just a small amount, but enough for us to notice that it wasn't old. We think it must have come from either the victim or the killer—if there was a killer—and the victim didn't show signs of an injury that would bleed. At least that's something else for Morris to process."

Morris Dunsany was the county coroner. Considering the big influx of tourists during the summer and Broken Rope's reputation, county officials thought it would be best to place Morris's office in Broken Rope. His white SUV hadn't made it to the scene yet.

"Where was the blood?" I asked.

"On the rope between the parking lot and the cemetery. It was just a small amount, but it hadn't dried all the way to a flakey brown, which means it's somewhat fresh."

"Uh . . ." I began. I looked down at my flip-flop-clad feet as well as at the Band-Aid covering the tip of my right big toe. "Cliff." I pointed.

He looked down, too. "That's your blood on the rope?"

"Maybe. I guess I'd have to see the spot. Gram and I were . . . We didn't leave until late last night. I caught my toe on the rope. I didn't notice that I'd scraped it enough to have bled until I got home, but I bet it's mine."

"Roger's body is still there. Do you want to wait until Morris comes for it before we go take a look?"

I shook my head. "No, let's look now. It might save some time for everyone."

Cliff stepped forward and signaled a couple different directions. My attention was on Gent again, who even more urgently than before signaled me to go to him. I shot him another wide-eyed look and held up the give me a second finger. That didn't satisfy him, so along with a number of other people, he moved around the fire truck and Gram's Volvo and toward Roger's body.

I tried to keep my eyes away from Roger, but I got a good enough glimpse to feel a well of fear and sadness build in my chest. I didn't know and I couldn't remember if he had a family, but this was a terrible way to go.

I thought back to the night before. At first, I'd only pretended to leave but I walked toward the cemetery from my Nova, so I couldn't really estimate where I'd stepped over the rope based upon the spot Gram had dropped me off. The rope was close to the ground and had about ten sections, or ten lengths, in between short wooden posts stuck into the ground.

Once the group—me, Cliff, Jim, Gram, another officer I knew only as "one of the Rasson family boys," and Gent—was gathered, Cliff said, "Betts thinks the blood we found on the rope might be hers."

"How's that, Betts?" Jim asked. I'd known Jim Morrison for years. He'd been the police chief since I was little and he and my parents were friends. I'd been to weddings and barbeques that he'd attended, but I'd also gotten to know the police officer side of him much better lately. I liked both Jims, but I preferred the one at social events over the official one.

"Gram and I left the school late last night." I didn't need to look at her to see if she'd go along with the story. She would. Explaining that we'd gone to the old bakery first would cause more questions than offer answers, so I left that part out for now. "Gram left first. As I was leaving, I thought I saw something in the cemetery. I got out of the Nova to take a closer look. As I stepped over the rope, it caught my toe. I didn't know it had bled until I got home. I'm pretty sure it was right in the middle of that section." I pointed to the portion of rope next to the one that was taken up by Roger's body."

"You were alone, saw something in the cemetery late at night, when it's really dark, and you got out to look at it?" Jim asked.

"Yes," I said.

"That sound like a smart thing to do, Betts?"

I shrugged. "It was one of those horror movie moments maybe. I couldn't stop myself."

"Did you call anyone, maybe Cliff first?"

"No. But, Jim, I'm used to this cemetery. It doesn't freak me out," I said. That wasn't altogether true, but I thought it sounded good.

I heard Gram make some sort of noise, but I couldn't be sure if it was surprise or irritation.

"You see her do this, Miz?" Jim asked.

"No, I left," she said. "But she's right. We're not all that scared by this place. We've been here long enough. If there are ghosts or spooky things, we'd've seen them by now, surely." She looked at Gent, who smiled satisfactorily.

"I suppose," Jim said. "You did the right thing by telling us, Betts. That is, in fact, the area with the blood. I need to get a full and official statement from you. Cliff can't do that. Let's move away from here."

"Sure. I'll be there in a second," I said. "May I have a moment alone with Roger?"

I was sure that Gram, Cliff, and Jim all wondered why I'd requested such a thing. I hadn't known Roger all that long—what could I possibly hope to achieve?

"Okay, but step back from the body. I'll give you some

space, but I'll be watching. I don't want you to touch him at all," Jim said.

I was sure that he would have denied the request completely if he didn't know me so well.

"Thank you."

Everyone but Gent moved away. I didn't look at her, but I sensed that Gram shot him some sort of irritated glance. I kept my back to everyone, put my hands on my hips, and then pretended to look down at Roger, though I kept my eyes on only his dress-shoe-clad feet.

"What do you need, Gent?" I said without moving my lips much.

"I really need to talk to you. I have a lot to tell you."

"Should Gram and I come back to the bakery tonight?"

"No! Not Miz, just you."

"I don't understand."

"I have to talk to you alone."

"Why?"

Gent looked around me and said, "Miz is on her way over. Just come talk to me. I think I have a clue that will lead to the killer."

He disappeared and I tried to look unbothered by his surprising statement.

"Damn ghosts," I muttered.

"See, they can be challenging," Gram said as she joined me. "What did he want?"

"Nothing really. He just wondered what was going on."

"Really?" Gram said.

Morris's SUV pulled into the lot, giving me the perfect excuse to end the conversation.

"Oh, good, Morris is here," I said before I turned and walked away from both Gram and Roger.

Gram knew something was up, though. I'd have to find a way to get to the bakery without her. I knew her well. It wouldn't be easy.

Chapter 7

"That's horrible!" Jake said. I'd been sharing details about Roger.

"He seemed like such a great guy. It's terrible news for everyone," I said.

We were sitting on stools in Jake's archive room, which was the space behind his main office, the town's fake sheriff's office. Jake was a self-made millionaire who loved acting the part of Broken Rope's poetry-reciting fake sheriff. Four times a day, every day during the summer, he'd recite a cowboy poem that he'd written. He'd become one of the town's main attractions, and he was proud of his reputation.

He and I had been best friends since high school. Actually, Cliff, Jake, and I had been close during those younger years, but Jake's loyalty had remained with me during the years that Cliff had led another type of life outside of Broken Rope. They got along just fine again, and Jake was happy we were all back together. But lending me his ear to bend and his shoulder to lean on had gotten me through more than a few tough moments.

"What do they think happened?"

I shrugged. "I don't think they have any idea. He was found dead, foaming at the mouth, but no other apparent injuries. Morris will have to do an autopsy, until then 'no one is to leave town.' "

"That's a common phrase around this place. Well, I'm so sorry. It's sad for everyone."

"It is. Oh, they did find blood, but it was mine."

"Uh-oh, how'd that go?"

"Fine. I explained that I had been there late the night before and stubbed my toe as I was going into the cemetery."

Jake blinked and sat up straighter. "Why were you going into the cemetery late at night? Do we have another visitor?"

"We do, but that's not why I was exploring. Actually, I thought I'd seen Jerome earlier, but now I don't think so."

"The plot thickens. Details, please."

I told Jake the story of Gent Cylas and his connection to Gram. I told him about the strange experience at the bakery as well as meeting the rest of Gent's family. I shared what Gram had told me about the Cylas family dying in the fire even though I knew that wasn't the way history had recorded the event. I mentioned how weird Gram was about me talking to Gent about it. Jake wasn't doubtful about anything I said until I mentioned the cowboy shadow.

"That part's just wishful thinking," he said. "You would have smelled him if he was back. You said his scent was like wood smoke, right?" I nodded. "You smell that?"

"Nope."

"There you have it; wishful thinking."

"I suppose."

"Later, we'll go into this a little deeper. There are some good reasons you need to quit hoping for and now imagining Jerome Cowbender, Betts. Right now, we need to figure out more about Gent. May I come with you tonight?"

"I don't know. I doubt you'll see things the same way I do. It might be more dangerous for you, in fact. If you can even *get* into the bakery building, it'll probably be in the shape it's really in, and that's pretty scary. Now, I mean. Yikes, this is enormously weird."

"I'll wait in the car?"

"Sure, if you really want to."

"I would love to."

Jake scooted off the stool. He was wearing his fake sheriff's costume even though his shows were over for the season. We still had a few visitors passing through, and Jake had become popular enough that many people stopped by just to meet him and his palomino stick pony, Patches. He didn't like to disappoint.

"Now, you say that this young man, Gent Cylas, and his family died in the bakery fire?"

"Well, according to Gram, yes, but even I know the history better."

"I think I do, too, but, Betts, I have learned that Broken Rope's history is frequently manipulated for the benefit of . . . well, something economic, I suppose, though saying that leaves a bad taste in my mouth. Let's see if we can find anything suspicious. I have a few things on the fire. It was a terrible tragedy, that much I'm sure of."

The archive room was purely Jake's creation. It was high-ceilinged, with plastic-folder-filled shelves that covered the back and one of the side walls. There were two windows at the top of the back wall, but they were sealed shut for fear of a weather or dust-related tragedy. I didn't understand what he'd done to keep the room under air and temperature control, but it was scientifically beyond simple heating and air-conditioning and created a low hypnotic hum that seemed to come from everywhere. An old chandelier that had originally hung in the town saloon was now wired for modern easy-on-the-eyes light and hung from the middle of the archive room ceiling; it was the exclamation mark on the entire space's atmosphere. Even those who knew about the room's existence didn't know all the technology that Jake had put into it. We Broken Ropers were good at hiding modern amenities.

Jake pulled a stepladder to the side wall, hoisted himself to the top rung, and then pulled a small plastic folder from the highest shelf. He rejoined me at the custom-made enormous table that took up the middle of the space.

"That's not a very big folder," I said.

"There wasn't much news about the fire. After it happened, the building was rebuilt, but then it closed shortly thereafter. I do think there were *haunted* and *jinxed* sorts of rumors but I'm not sure if they were ever written about. Business just died off. The Puff Pocket, the sugary, creamy concoction that had taken the world's taste buds by storm suddenly became less yummy. It was a truly baffling mystery.

I think of all the strange Broken Rope stories, the bakery fire was one of the least bizarre—it was just a boring old fire. But the aftermath, the real death of the bakery, is still beyond comprehension."

Jake pulled the small stack of papers from the folder and placed it on the table.

"I made copies of the articles from the time. Oh, and I have this, and it's authentic. It's the original business license; actually it was called a certificate back then."

"How did you get that?"

"I have no idea. Someone sent it to me or I found it in a stack of stuff in someone's attic—no, no, I would have marked it if that was where I got it. Someone must have sent it to me."

I reached for the articles that had come from the *Noose* and read, " 'Kennington Bakery Fire Kills Two.' " I read it again, silently, and then looked at Jake. "Well, right there, there's something wrong with someone's story. There are four Cylas family members."

Jake nodded thoughtfully. "Keep reading. Let's see if we can learn more." He moved behind me to peer over my shoulder.

I continued:

The two founders and owners of the Kennington Bakery Co., William Kennington and Howard Knapp, were both killed in a fire at their bakery's building Saturday night. The fire, still under investigation, was said to have most likely started because of something faulty with one or more of the massive ovens. The bakery was not operating at the time, but both Kennington and Knapp were said to have spent many of their free hours in their place of business. Per wishes expressed in their wills, a new management team will be formed to continue operations as soon as the building is repaired.

That was the end of the short article.

I looked at Jake. "There has to be more. Perhaps they found the Cylas bodies later as they investigated."

"I really don't think so. Let me see if I have anything else." Jake moved back to the articles. He mumbled as he thumbed through the few remaining pieces of paper. Then he went through them again. Finally, he handed them to me. "No other bodies are mentioned, but services for Kennington and Knapp are noted. They are both buried in your cemetery—well, the one next to the school."

"That's interesting. I don't really know how, but maybe that's something important. Now that I think about it, I *have* seen those names on tombstones, but I don't know what else they say. I'll look again."

"I don't think that the Cylas family was killed in the fire."

"I wonder why Gram told me that, or rather why she believed Gent when he told her as much."

Jake shrugged. "If Miz was holding you back from talking about it, you can ask Gent for details tonight."

"Can you look up obituary information regarding the Cylas family?"

"Sure, I've gotten pretty far on that database." He sat in a low chair and rolled it to the desk with his computer. He moved busy fingers over the keyboard.

"This is odd," he finally said after much longer than I expected.

"What?"

"I know my obits are updated through 1960. The fire was 1951. I should have their information."

"Nothing on the Cylas family?"

"No Cylases at all."

"This is really strange, right?"

"Possibly. I will concede that I might have missed a death or two, but it's unlikely. Let me check cemetery records." His fingers worked the keyboard again. Only a few seconds later he said, "Betts, there's not one Cylas buried in any nearby cemeteries. So, yes, this is getting stranger. Maybe they moved. Let me do some more research and I'll get back to you later."

"Thank you. May I make copies of the articles?"

"Help yourself."

School was, of course, canceled for the day as Roger's death was investigated, so I left Jake's office with no real destination in mind. As I stood on the front boardwalk, I thought about visiting Cliff at the jail across the street, but I knew he'd be busy for the time being. I thought about heading down to Bunny's for some coffee and pie, but I wasn't even close to hungry, and oddly enough, I didn't want or need coffee. Finally, I spotted someone who might give me further diversion.

Evan Mason was Broken Rope's fire marshal. He'd come to town via St. Louis. He'd lost his family—I'd heard a wife and a daughter, but I wasn't sure—to a tragic car accident and he'd been looking for a new start when the marshal position opened up. I hadn't seen him at the school this morning and, considering one of his fire trucks and at least two of his firemen were there, I was suddenly curious. I also had some fire-related questions that he might be able to answer.

"Evan!" I called from across the street.

He smiled and waved my direction and then seemed surprised when I signaled for him to wait a second. I hurried across the street and to the boardwalk on the other side.

"Hi, I'm not sure if you remember but I'm Betts Winston," I said as I offered my hand.

"Of course. I remember you," he said with a tentative smile. He exuded sadness but who wouldn't after such a tragedy. I'd heard he was extraordinarily good at his job and had already intervened on some construction projects to make them much safer. He'd created a respectful following around the entire county. He was tall, trim but not thin, in shape but not muscular, with gray green eyes and a head full of blond unruly curls. More than once I'd wondered why he wore his hair the way he did since I thought there might be some short-hair regulation for firefighters, but I didn't know him well enough to ask.

"Good to see you again, Evan," I said.

"Good to see you. I heard about the trouble at your school this morning. I'm awfully sorry."

"Thanks," I said. "I saw a fire truck there."

"Yeah, we always send a crew in an emergency situation. I didn't know about the body or I would have been there, too. We're still working on some communication issues between the fire and police department."

"Jenny?"

"Yes, Jenny." Evan smiled.

I'd never met the woman and didn't even know who she was, which was hard to pull off in Broken Rope. Mostly, everyone knew who everyone was even if we didn't know them personally. Except for Jenny. She was the mysterious emergency phone operator who didn't quite get everything right all the time. I'd had my own problems with her, but I didn't think Evan needed to hear the details.

"Believe it or not, Evan, I have some fire-related questions. Can I buy you a cookie or an ice cream?" I gestured toward the end of the street where the cookie shop, Broken Crumbs, and the ice cream parlor, jokingly known as the "saloon" were located.

"I'd love a cookie, but only if I can have some milk, too." Evan smiled. "Can't imagine a cookie without milk."

"Deal."

The walk to the shop was quick and without any tourist impediment. Once inside, we both greeted the owner, Mabel Randall, and ordered a tall glass of milk and two cookies each. Evan wouldn't let me pay, which was awkward, but only momentarily.

"What are your questions?" Evan asked when we were both seated and had each enjoyed one milk dunk and one bite of a peanut butter and white chocolate cookie.

"Do you know anything about the bakery fire from way back in 1951?"

"Absolutely," he said around a mouthful of the cookie Mabel had named the Double Noose. "It was the first thing I studied when I got here. I was interested, I guess. We've got the records from the investigation in the firehouse files."

"Really? I bet Jake would love to have a copy for his archives if you ever think about it and if they're in any condition to copy."

"For that secret room in the back of his building, the one

he has more up to fire code than any other building in town?"

I nodded. "That would be Jake."

"I'd be happy for him to have a copy. I can make one for him easily."

"Can you tell me what you saw in the papers? I mean, was the investigation thorough? I'm curious about it."

"Sure, in fact I've been thinking of talking to the police—I think your boyfriend's one of them?" I nodded, and though I hoped I wasn't one to flatter myself, I thought I might have seen a little disappointment cross his face. Surely, I'd misinterpreted. "Well, I don't think the fire was investigated well at all. They claimed it was an electrical fire, but I see evidence right in the notes and in a couple old pictures that were taken that points toward an accelerant, like gasoline or something, being used."

"The fire was started on purpose?"

"I don't know for sure, but I would like to look into it a little closer, have the photographs examined by some experts. I don't think it would hurt, and I think there's a town budget for these sorts of things."

I nodded and then took another bite of milk-soaked cookie. When I finished the bite, I said, "Evan . . . what about, well, could there have been more than the two people who died in the fire?"

I thought he might laugh at my question, or think I was somewhat off my rocker, but he didn't. Instead, he put down his cookie and his eyebrows came together as he looked off to the side.

"I don't know, Betts, why do you ask?"

I shrugged and sighed. "Broken Rope is an unusual place."

Evan laughed. "Yes, it is."

I liked how his face lit with his laugh.

"Anyway, stories sometimes become gossip and then gossip causes some stories to become real. I've heard things over the years, some recently, that make me wonder if there were more deaths. Can your pictures tell you that?"

"Maybe. I sense there's more to this than you're sharing, but it's okay. I'll try to look at the pictures more closely, and see if I can get another expert opinion."

"Thank you."

"You're welcome." He chewed and thought some more as if he were debating whether or not to say something. I was glad when he continued. "You know, Betts, I woke up in the middle of the night last night and I couldn't stop thinking about that fire. And then you ask me about it today. What's up, was there a recent article or something?"

I shrugged. "Sometimes things like that just happen, I guess."

"Especially in Broken Rope."

"Probably," I said.

"Well, *my* questions all stem from the soot patterns on the floor of the bakery. Whoever took the pictures did a very thorough job even if they are poor quality and, of course, they're only black-and-white. They're from a long time ago and I think it's a miracle we have them as it is."

"Jim might be able to approve something. I'll get Jake involved, too. As much of a tragedy as it was, if it was an even bigger one than everyone thought, I expect it'll garner some more morbid Broken Rope curiosity."

"I'll talk to Jim," Evan said.

I realized that I'd never sat in the cookie shop and had cookies and milk before. I'd purchased plenty of cookies from Mabel and I'd eaten them on the run or taken them elsewhere. But the simple pleasure of sitting at one of the small tables and enjoying the moment was something I'd never done. I decided I'd do it more often.

"This place has quite the history, and people sure love to visit and hear the old stories," Evan said.

I laughed. "It takes a little getting used to, doesn't it?"

He smiled. "A little." His eyes were curious as they stayed locked on mine a beat longer. "You were supposed to be . . . I mean, you were going to school to be an attorney when you decided to come back to town and work with your grandmother?"

"I dropped out of law school. It wasn't for me." It hadn't been for me, but no matter how certain I was of that decision, it still left me with a sense of failure. Dropping out is dropping out, or quitting or leaving. None of the verbs that went with what I did made it sound honorable or even just *okay*.

"You are so suited to what you do that I can't even imagine you as an attorney," Evan said so sincerely that I blushed.

"Thank you."

He nodded and quickly changed the subject. "Tell me about the man who died at the school. The one that was found this morning, not the one from a few months ago."

"He was a student. Roger Riggins. I only knew him for two days but he seemed like a smart, likeable guy." I regretted not knowing him better.

"Do the police suspect murder?"

"I think they think he had a seizure, but there's something about the way they were acting. I don't know, maybe the police always act suspicious."

"Dying from a seizure is pretty rare. There must be some underlying condition that needs to be considered."

"Morris is doing an autopsy. We should know more this afternoon."

"I'm sorry for you and Miz and your other students. That has to be tough."

I nodded and my cell phone buzzed in my pocket. It was Gram.

"Excuse me," I said to Evan. "Gram?"

"Betts, have I caught you in the middle . . . Oh, dadnabit, I'm fit to be tied. I don't care if I did get you in the middle of something. Can you hightail it back to the school?"

I looked at Evan. "Sure, but what's up?"

"I'll show you when you get here. We don't have another body, at least that's the good news."

"I'll be there shortly."

My departure was probably rude and awkward, but Evan understood that Gram and the cooking school were my first priorities. We exchanged phone numbers and he said he'd call soon with any more fire details. I hurried back to the Nova with the thought that Cliff, Jake, and I should all get to know our fire marshal better.

Chapter 8

Though there wasn't another body at the school, Gram was inching closer to adding one to the count.

"You try," she said as she handed me the piece of paper.

I glanced at the list. It was Freddie's references. They were scribbled unevenly down the page, something he'd put together quickly as he sat in the school's classroom two days earlier and were supposedly based upon the official list we'd never received.

"I don't understand," I said.

"There are six references. Four of them go to disconnected numbers and the other two are just voice mails. And the voices on those two sound the same. You try the numbers, too. Tell me what you get."

Just as Gram reached for the phone to nudge it toward me, it rang. Or, rather, it jingled.

We looked at each other and then she picked up the handset and gave it to me.

"You take it," she whispered.

"Country Cooking School," I said.

"Hello? Hello? Yes, this is Miriam McCalaster. Someone named . . . well, I believe they said their name was Missouri just called. Do I have the correct number?" The voice was so thick with a strange accent that it took me a second to interpret the words. I couldn't place the accent but it was something nasally and slow, and forced, I thought.

"Yes, I'm Betts Winston, Missouri's granddaughter. We run the cooking school." I looked at the list. Miriam McCalaster was the second reference listed. Following her name were the words *restaurant owner.* "We were calling to check references for one of our students."

"Go ahead."

"Freddie O'Bannon has listed you as a former employer. Do you remember Freddie?"

"Of course I remember Freddie. He was by far one of the best workers I've ever employed," Miriam said.

"Where's your restaurant?"

"I'm in Connecticut."

"What kind of restaurant is it?"

"Doesn't matter because Freddie was a server not a cook, but if you must know, we're a diner."

"I love diners," I said.

"Uh-huh."

"What years did Freddie work for you?"

"Oh. Oh, well, it was a number of years ago. I believe he was just out of high school."

Over the past couple days, Freddie had mentioned that

he was twenty-six and had attended a junior college in New York state, so the diner experience would have occurred about eight years ago.

"So about four years ago?" I said.

"Yes, that's about right."

I wasn't very good at calculating passing time, but the difference between four years and eight years earlier would have been something I think I would have been able to recognize.

"How long did he work for you?"

"I'm not really sure . . . Oh, I must go. Duty calls. Know that Freddie's the best, but I'm happy to talk to you again if you need more information. Call me in a couple days." The unusual accent had changed by the time Miriam clicked off the call; it had transformed into no real accent at all.

"Hello?" I said to the distinct and hollow quiet that switched to a dial tone a second later. I handed Gram the handset and said, "Miriam's accent was gone by the end of the call. I have no idea what she was attempting to sound like at the beginning, but she was one of the worst actresses I've ever seen . . . I mean, heard."

"These aren't real references, are they?" Gram said.

"That's just the one, but I don't think it's valid. We could be wrong, though," I said.

"We gave these to the police, didn't we?"

"Yep, I made a copy and gave it to Cliff."

"They might not be checking them right away. I think they need to. We need to call Jim," Gram said.

"I agree, but I'll do some research, too. Check the Internet for more information on Freddie. Let's see what Jim says. I . . . Well, the reference thing is an issue, of course, but if Roger hadn't died, I don't know that we'd be all that upset or suspicious about it. We'd want them clarified, of course. I do think Freddie's here under some sort of false pretenses, but even though we might be tying it to killing Roger, we could just be jumping to a conclusion based on circumstance and fear. Besides . . ." If I'd made it all the way to a full-fledged attorney, I'd have to chastise myself over what I wanted to say next.

"What?"

"Well, we like him, Gram."

Gram harrumphed as she thought about what I'd said. The lines around her mouth softened and her shoulders relaxed.

The phone rang again, causing me to jump slightly.

"You were goosed," Gram said as she picked it up this time. "Cooking School."

Her face fell quickly. "I see. Thank you for letting us know, Morris. Uh-huh, yes, I'll let her know, too." She hung up the phone without saying good-bye.

"What?"

"We won't need to call Jim. Morris said he will be here shortly to talk to us both. Morris has determined that Roger was poisoned, and he and the police suspect murder. They'll want to search the school and the grounds from top to bottom."

"Oh no." My breath shallowed immediately. I knew murder was a possibility, but hearing it become more real shook me. "What kind of poison?"

"Something he ingested, something he ate. Morris says he knows what it is, but he couldn't tell me."

"Something at the school or from somewhere else? An allergy?"

"He was clear about it not being an allergy but a poison. I don't know what specifically it was or when he ingested it, but I'm sure we'll all be under close scrutiny even if he wasn't poisoned by something in the school. He was here when he died—unless the body was moved here . . . Oh, I don't like any of this." Gram's voice quieted as though she'd forgotten I was in the room.

I stood up. "Gram, let's look around, you and me. We might be able to find something before they get here. I'm too curious not to." I was, but I also thought it would be good to keep her busy.

"You think that's okay?"

I shrugged. "I'd like to check. We won't disrupt anything. We don't even have to touch anything."

"Your time in law school might be paying off a little today?" Gram asked.

"Nope, got all this from *Law and Order.* Television show," I said, trying to alleviate at least a little of her stress, but it didn't work.

"Got it," she said seriously before she led the way into the kitchen.

The long and continually transforming space was difficult to examine closely. Utensils, small dust layers (though we cleaned obsessively, flour was still flour), chair locations, pots and pans; things moved and changed all the time. There was an organization to the space but a loose one that allowed for some flexibility when it came to storing.

There seemed to be nothing strange or out of place in the kitchen. The only real recent addition to the room was the shelf full of sourdough starters, and they wouldn't get the timely attention they needed to thrive so we assumed they'd all fail. We left the containers where they were, though. We'd throw them away after the school was thoroughly searched. The food inside the refrigerators and freezers also seemed undisturbed.

"But, let's not touch any of it, either," I said. "If someone messed with the food, we might not be able to see it. Jim might want to test things."

"I don't think Roger ate anything from in here. There was no sign of a break-in, so the poison must have been ingested outside the building. They can look around all they want, but I don't think they'll find anything suspicious in here."

"Probably not," I said. I hoped not.

Our inspection of the rest of the building left us with nothing more. We were hesitant to open the door to the supply room since we'd found Everett Morningside's body in there only a few months earlier, but we were met with no surprises there, either. In fact, the supply room seemed more organized than it had ever been.

"Neither hide nor hair of something wrong," Gram said as she plopped her hands on her hips, a small tone of distress still in her voice.

My dad, her son, had recently called Gram "tough as a Mack truck." The description had made me smile. Though she'd been detained during Everett's murder, it hadn't even occurred to me that she—or I, for that matter—would ever again be accused or suspected of a crime. But the idea was there, floating in the air with the stronger concern: who poisoned Roger? If it wasn't one of us, and it wasn't something he did to himself, accidentally or not, it was likely another student. Of course, we'd been focused on Freddie's seemingly fraudulent references so he was at the top of both of our minds. But there were fourteen other potential suspects, and we didn't know any of them well enough to make an educated guess as to who might be homicidal.

"It'll be okay. They'll solve it quickly," I said.

She straightened her back and twisted her mouth funny. "I hope so."

I nodded as the buzzer announced that someone had come into the front of the school.

"Bet it's Jim," Gram said before we hurried to greet our visitor.

She was close; it wasn't Jim but Cliff who pushed through the front swinging doors and into the kitchen as we swung through the back ones.

"Betts, Miz, the two of you need to head on out of here for the day," Cliff said. "I assume you've heard from Morris?"

"Yes. Roger was poisoned, maybe on purpose. Murder," Gram said.

"Yes, on purpose for sure. At this point, we have no doubt it was murder." Cliff's words didn't leave the same room for uncertainty that Morris's apparently had. "Jim's got a crime scene unit coming over right away."

Gram looked at Cliff, then at me and back at Cliff. "You won't destroy the place?"

"Of course not. I'll make sure of it," Cliff said. He turned his glance to me. "Betts, can I talk to you out front a minute?"

"Sure."

"Miz, grab your stuff," Cliff said. "We'll meet you outside."

A heavy beat of hesitation filled the air. Cliff was here,

telling us to leave the scene of a crime and telling Gram to get her stuff without an escort. I knew Cliff was better than that at his new job. Did he already have a strong suspect in mind?

Gram went one direction and I went the other with Cliff.

"Hey," he said with a gentle smile once we were outside.

"Hey. So, what's up? Is there something else going on here?"

Cliff rubbed his finger under his nose, looked out to the road, and then back at me. "Look, you might not believe this, but I'm here because Jim told me to come get you two out of the school. Well, at least that's what I think he told me. He hinted emphatically."

"Do you have a suspect in mind? You didn't want us to further contaminate the scene?"

"Nope, no suspect, but we are both one hundred percent sure that Roger Riggins wasn't poisoned by either you or Miz. If we're wrong about that, we are really terrible cops, but I . . . we don't think we're wrong."

"I see." I smiled. It was good not to be considered a killer. An unreasonable wave of confidence swam through me, but I ignored it.

Cliff continued, "I . . . we just don't want either of you to have to put up with the inconvenience of being questioned again right now. Get out of here, but don't take a quick trip to St. Louis or anything. I'll call you if we need you."

I cleared my throat. "Thank you. That couldn't have been easy on either of you."

"That's the problem. I think it might have been too easy.

Your blood being on the rope is interesting enough, but we're not focusing on that yet."

"Oh, good," I said with exaggerated relief.

We were silent a moment as we looked at each other. Our second go-around at romance was either so much better than the amazing first blush had been or we weren't remembering everything correctly. This time, we'd transitioned from *it's weird to see you again* to *quick friends* to *dating* to *dating seriously* in what felt like hyper-drive speed. I attributed the speed of the cycle to the fact that we'd known each other before and we had so many shared memories and shared experiences. Leapfrogging over some of the getting-acquainted phase was to be expected. I liked where we'd gone and I liked where we were headed.

Cliff might have come out to the school and got us out of there on his own, but I was glad he'd been prompted to by Jim.

"I have something that might help," I said.

I told Cliff about Freddie's references. Though he found our inability to track down what we thought was a good reference somewhat intriguing, he was not as bothered as Gram had been. It was important not to jump to any conclusions based solely on unanswered calls and someone who couldn't hold an accent.

Gram joined us a few minutes later. She'd grabbed her big shopping bag–type purse and had put her sunglasses on the top of her head. She held her arms to her body a little tighter than normal. She was still shaken but was trying not to show it.

"You tell Cliff about the references?" she asked me as she walked toward the Volvo.

"Yes."

"Good. Cliff, let me know when I can come back. I have some work to do and I'd like to get to it as soon as possible." She paused with one hand on the car door, perhaps thinking she was sounding unsympathetic. I knew she was just coping in her own way. Cliff did, too. "I'm not sure when we should resume classes."

"I'll let you know," Cliff said, but he glanced quickly at me as he spoke.

Gram cocked her head and then said, "You two belong together." Then she looked directly at me and added, "And both of you are alive and well. Call me later, as soon as anyone knows anything."

As she shut the door to the Volvo and backed out of her spot, Cliff said, "That's an odd way to phrase *healthy*."

"Well, Gram's odd." I shrugged.

When the Volvo was out of sight and no one could see, Cliff pulled me close and kissed me slowly.

"I realize this is even more unprofessional than telling you and Miz to get out of here for a while. I've got to go back to being professional in a minute, so I took advantage of the moment with no audience."

"Mmm," I said. "I'm so glad you moved back to this crazy little town."

"Me, too."

"How about more bad-cop activity later?" I said.

He laughed. "Sounds good to me."

Disengaging was difficult. Okay, so our teenage hormones weren't completely under control. Duty called, though, and Cliff had to listen.

As I drove the Nova out of the lot, I glanced in my

rearview mirror. Cliff, his hands on his hips, was watching me leave. Just as I was going to lift my hand to wave, something else rolled across my field of vision.

I braked hard, skidding and then rocking the Nova. I thought I'd seen the whiff, perhaps only the memory or maybe just something from my imagination, of a cowboy hat roll across the ground at Cliff's feet.

I got out of the car as Cliff moved quickly toward me.

"What is it?" he asked.

I looked around the lot, the cemetery, and the surrounding Missouri woods. There was no one there other than Cliff and me. There were no cowboy hats, either ghostly or in full form. There was no wood smoke smell. We were alone.

"Nothing. I just thought I saw something," I said. "But I didn't."

Cliff scanned the same places I just had and then looked at me again. "You okay, Betts?"

I smiled. "I'm fine. Sorry, maybe I'm still shaken up."

"Understandable."

We repeated our good-byes, though with much less romance, and reiterated plans of hopefully seeing each other later. I got back into the Nova and pulled out of the lot.

"Calm down," I told myself.

When I'd met Jerome, the first ghost in my life, I had a moment of doubt—was I losing my mind? But that fear had disappeared quickly, until today. Now, I really wondered.

So, I went to find the one live person I could talk to about what might be happening, about the hallucinations I was having, and why in the world I was having them.

Though we'd just left each other, and though she didn't have much patience for my pining away for Jerome, I was still her granddaughter and she was required to love me no matter what.

I knew Gram would go directly home, and I needed some answers. There just wasn't anyone else I could ask.

Chapter 9

"Betts, everything okay?" Gram said when she opened her front door. She looked behind me.

"I don't know, Gram. I'm just not sure," I said.

She squinted and then gave me one of her knowing looks.

"Having a hard time about Roger? Or the stuff that happened at the bakery, it bothered you, didn't it?" Gram said.

"No, actually . . . well, I'm sad and scared about Roger, but that's not it."

"Come on in, sweetie. We'll figure it out. There's not a thing we Winston women can't handle."

A few moments later we were both sitting on Gram's couch, sipping some of her fresh-brewed iced tea and snacking on some sugar cookies she'd baked recently.

Just sitting on the couch next to her, drinking iced tea and eating sugar cookies, had the same effect it always had.

I felt better, perhaps even a little silly about my true concern, but I still had some questions.

"I know it's possible for more than one ghost at a time to come back. I saw that when Sally was here," I said. Gram nodded. "But . . . well, I have a sense that a ghost—Jerome, in fact—is partially here."

"Partially here?" Gram said, though her voice was surprisingly uncritical.

"Yes. Last night, I thought I saw the silhouette of a cowboy in one of the bakery windows as we were driving away. Today, just now as I left Cliff, I thought I saw the . . . well, the ghost, I guess, of a cowboy hat, roll across the ground. Could he be sort of back, or trying to come back, or . . ."

Gram looked at me as she thought. I braced myself for another get-over-Jerome lecture, but she surprised me again.

"Really, I can't answer. You know how I've come to think of them all as a little flakey, not terrible to have around but not always welcome?" I nodded and she continued, "Their spotty memories and appearances and disappearances are sometimes inconvenient enough. When I was younger, of course I had questions for them, wanted to understand them. Who wouldn't? But they don't have answers, either. It was probably when I was about your age that I started getting all wound up about them not having those answers. They drove me crazy. I actually told them that they either had to stop visiting me when they were here, or they had to never come back."

"Really? What happened?"

Gram laughed. "Nothing. They couldn't remember that I'd told them that I didn't want to see them, and even though they're dead, I didn't want to continue to hurt their feelings, so I decided I had to change me; either my attitude or the ways I thought about them. I also had to come to the conclusion that they have absolutely no control over where they are, except . . ."

"Except?"

"Just a sec. Let me grab something." Gram left the couch and ventured toward the back of the small house, probably to one of the bedrooms. She returned soon with an overstuffed photo album. "Your brother wants to computerize all these things. He says I need to find a better way to save and store my photos. I told him he should have seen the shoe boxes I pulled them from so I could put them in the photo book."

I'd seen the album many times before. Its blue burlap-wrapped cover had become more worn over the years and its insides had become even more overstuffed, the covers now resembling a wide-open mouth.

"Do you remember when you were little and people asked you what your favorite book was, and you said 'Gram's picture book'?" Gram said as she sat the behemoth on the coffee table in front of us.

"I do. I spent hours looking at these pictures." I leaned forward.

The book held the only known photos of Gram's parents, stern and stiff in their seated poses and uncomfortable clothes. Gram looked more like her father than her mother, though the black-and-white—or I guess they were now called sepia-toned—pictures didn't show off his dark red hair. There were pictures of relatives whose names I either didn't know or didn't remember, pictures of Gram as she grew up, some of my dad when he was little, and some of his and Mom's wedding. I was less interested in the pictures that followed the wedding. Those of me and my brother, Teddy, no matter how cute we were, didn't interest me. When I was little I'd thumb through the book and try to see the differences and similarities between everyone. I'd concluded that there was a good dose of red hair and crooked smile genetics preserved on the pages.

"I imagine there are some things you didn't notice." Gram swung the cover back and turned to about ten pages in. "Here, here I am with my sweet and patient mother. I think I was only about three."

I looked at the picture. "You were cute."

"Yes, I was." Gram smiled. "But that's not what I want you to see. Look closely right here." She pointed to the space next to her, a space that seemed to be filled with only a window behind them.

"Okay," I said, but I had no idea what she wanted me to see.

"Jerome was my first ghost, too. You know that he saved me and my mother from a fire?"

"Sure."

"Well, and you have to remember that this is all purely my own speculation. I've had lots of years to speculate. No one has given me any answers, but I think that Jerome is actually the reason all the other ghosts can get here, too. I think he opened the . . ."

"Door? Portal?" I said.

Gram laughed. "That sounds so science fiction-y, but I guess that's what I mean."

She pulled the plastic cover up from the page and lifted the photo from the sticky surface. "Look right here." She pointed again. "You might need to turn it a little."

I took the picture and turned it a little more toward the light. There might—might—have been something there.

"I'm not sure but there could be a shadow here that forms something similar to . . . well, similar to a cowboy hat. But it's just a shadow, Gram. I get what you're saying, but it's not defined at all. It could be anything."

"I agree, and I'm not saying that you are definitely seeing a cowboy hat. Besides, and think about this, Betts, Jerome's a ghost. Shouldn't he be unphotographable? Like vampires, or some such thing. I'm just saying that I want you to look closely here and then I want you to look at some of the other pictures in the album. Pictures of me. I'll get us more tea." She stood and took the two moisture-beaded glasses from the coffee table and made her way to the kitchen.

Doubtfully, I watched her go. Nevertheless, I stood from the couch, hoisted the heavy book over to the chair beside the window, and sat it on my lap. I opened the curtain so that a stream of light from the late-afternoon sun hit the pages perfectly.

There were many pictures of Gram. Her family didn't have a lot of money, but they did spend some on a small Brownie camera that Gram's mom seemed to enjoy.

Though I was told how much I resembled Missouri Anna Winston when she was my current age, I didn't see the same sort of resemblance when we were little girls. As a child, Gram was skinny, scrawny, with short hair that stuck up in all directions. My mom called it her ostrich hair phase. When I was that age, I was skinny, but not scrawny and though my hair was unruly and difficult to handle, I wore it long and at least started each day with a ponytail.

First, I flipped through some of the front pages quickly,

watching Gram grow from about the age of five up to thirteen or maybe fourteen. As I looked at the pages again, more slowly this time, I focused on each individual picture. In one, I thought I saw a swirl of something that could be interpreted as a brim of a hat, but it could have just been a trick of light, or some sort of exposure problem with the camera.

But then I saw similar images in the other pictures. All of them. Each and every picture of Gram contained an anomaly of sorts.

I hadn't noticed that she'd come back with the refilled iced teas when I muttered, "No, that could be so many things."

"That's what I thought at first, too, Betts, but look at the pictures without me."

I switched my focus to those pictures. I turned the album every which way, I pulled pictures out and held them up to the window, I double-checked, I triple-checked, but there were no strange images or swirls in any of the other pictures. Not even in one.

"Gram," I said. "I don't understand at all. In fact, if I was confused before, I'm even more confused now."

Gram made a pshaw sound as she sat back on the couch. "That's only because you think you should be confused or—what is it you young people say—freaked out. Look, Betts, you've heard all the sayings about life never being what you expect it to be?" I nodded. "Of course you have, and you've lived it firsthand—no one could have predicted how you and Cliff would have ended up back here the way you have." I lifted my eyebrows and nodded again. "This is just another instance of that. That's how you have to look at it. It is what it is. It could probably drive anyone bonkers if they spent too much time dwelling on it. Instead, just accept that it's part of your life. It's easy to distinguish the differences between real stuff and ghost stuff. Roll with it, go with it and just see what happens. I'm certain they can't hurt us. If they could, it would be a different story."

Her words and attitude sent a thread of comfort through my system. She was right—but she still hadn't answered my real question.

"So, I need to accept that a part of Jerome will probably always be around?" I said.

"Again, I'm just not sure, but don't let it bother you either way. Don't let it stop you from living your life. He got to live one, so should you. Fair's fair."

"I just don't know . . ."

It wasn't that I had a simple crush on the ghost. It was that I thought I had real honest-to-goodness deep feelings for him, something more than a crush, and something that wouldn't go away easily if he was around all the time. And something I couldn't easily ignore so I could put my focus where it belonged, on Cliff.

And how stupid was that?

Gram took a sip of her tea and then set the glass on a coaster on the coffee table.

"You need to figure it out for yourself. Do you want to be with Cliff or wait around for the ghost of someone to appear every now and then, with no schedule except that his hat might be hanging around here and there? Talk about a long-distance relationship."

It was all so absurd, but bottom line, I didn't like that I didn't have a firm answer to that question.

"Think hard, Betts. You already ruined what you had with Cliff once. Do you want to do it again?"

So, she'd saved the harsher words for last. But she was correct. Dammit, she was right on target. I had been the one to "ruin" our relationship, no matter how much I hadn't intended to.

I closed the photo album and we both moved back to the couch. I felt better, truly less confused. I knew I had things I needed to think about, but I was suddenly not interested in spending any more time focusing on me and my strange dilemma.

"Thanks, Gram," I said. "Let's talk about how we'll transition back into the classes. I'm sorry about Roger, but we have to remember what we're here for."

Gram smiled. "That's my girl."

Chapter 10

The conversation between Gram and me turned light and even sillier than the other silly stuff. I think we must have needed it, to laugh a little, poke a little fun at ourselves, find our grooves again.

Even with her kind hospitality and willing ear, I didn't tell her I was going to go to the bakery that evening, but I hugged her tightly before I left and sensed that she knew something was up. I hadn't broached the subject of Gent and his family with her during this visit. I believed there just might be such a thing as ghost overload for Gram, and our conversation about Jerome was more than enough for one day.

As I got into the Nova, my phone rang.

"Hi, Evan?" I said.

"Yep. Hey, Betts, what are you doing?"

I thought a moment. "No real plans for a couple hours. What's up?"

"I'm at Morris Dunsany's office. He's let me use some of his equipment to take a closer look at those photographs. He's also been trained in crime scene analysis, did you know that?"

"I did, but he likes to usually stick with the ME part of his job."

"Right. Well, if you can come over to his office, I'd like to show you a few things."

Between Evan's finds and Morris's results regarding Roger Riggins's cause of death, I couldn't think of any other place I'd rather be.

Morris Dunsany's office was one of the bigger Broken Rope secrets. Like Jake's hidden back room, Morris's office and autopsy facility was hidden behind a smaller room set up for the tourists. Back in the day, dentists and doctors performed procedures with over-sized, wickedly heavy and horrifying instruments. The small room in front of the place where the really gory stuff went on had a big dose of gory itself. Antique dental and medical instruments were secured to the walls, on shelves, and on worktables set up next to a dentist's chair. The setup must have been the original design for torture victims, and an old operating table that would look cold and uncomfortable no matter where it was displayed completed the effect.

The front room was free of tourists when I knocked on the hidden door separating the two spaces. I wasn't sure if there had ever been a town meeting regarding protocol for entering our "secret" rooms, or if we all just naturally knew to be stealthy.

"Hi, Betts," Evan said from a tall stool that had been scooted up to a tall table along one side wall.

"Hi, thanks for the call."

"No problem."

"So, right after our discussion earlier, I hurried back to the station and pulled out the old pictures from the fire and brought them here. Come look and I'll try to explain what I'm seeing, and Morris said to call him up after you're done."

I moved next to Evan as he adjusted the microscope enough that I could peer into it as I stood.

Putting my eyes to the double lenses reminded me of high school. I hadn't enjoyed much about science, but I really disliked dissecting frogs, and for some reason the microscope made me think of those poor splayed and pinned creatures. I maneuvered my eyes and nose appropriately and turned the focus dial ever so slightly; I saw black smudges.

"I'm not sure what this is supposed to tell me," I said.

"The smudge you're looking at right now is where the burned remains of a body were found."

"Okay."

"Now, let me change the picture." He stood and pulled the picture out, and then put another one in. He turned the microscope and then manipulated the dial. "Look again."

I did as he instructed and saw the same sort of smudge. Almost.

"See how this one fans out, like someone might have given it a sweep or two with a broom?" Evan said.

"Maybe."

"I tried to piece together the pictures, and they are thorough, but not all as thorough as I would like. Anyway, there are three more of these—I don't know, *disturbed* might be the word—smudges and only one undisturbed."

"Okay," I said again.

"I think the disturbed marks illustrate that bodies or burned remains were moved from those spots."

"So, three bodies—remains—might have been removed from the scene?"

"I think it's a distinct possibility. I thought so when I looked at the pictures when I first came to Broken Rope. Now, under the microscope, I'm about ninety-five percent certain that that's what I'm seeing."

"Wait, I don't understand. That means that after the fire had been put out, someone was able to remove the bodies and do what with them? In front of firemen and police who did nothing to stop them?"

"Ah, I thought about that, too. The fire wasn't doused here. It was already out. This spot, in these pictures, was in the wing that jutted out from the main building. The building is in a residential area now, but the fire might not have been noticed right away back then. And even if it was, sometimes the only thing to be done was to let it burn. It happened lots back then. This fire burned and died out and then another fire started in the main part of the building."

"Evan, that's all really suspicious. Why weren't circumstances better investigated?"

Evan shrugged. "I don't know, Betts. I asked Morris and he chalked it up to the time in history, the lack of investigative equipment, and potentially something that Broken Rope authorities might have wanted to hide."

"Hide?"

"It's all just a guess."

"So they found two bodies and you think there's evidence that three others were there?"

Evan nodded.

"This is a strange question, Evan, but just bear with me. Is there a chance there could have been a fourth body?"

"Uh, well, I don't know. I don't see anything in the pictures that indicates as much. Why do you ask? What do you know, Betts?"

I sighed and pulled another stool out from under the ledge. I sat and said, "I don't know anything that I can share. Really. I know that my gram is old, and over the years she's told me things about growing up in Broken Rope that are . . . interesting, intriguing, mysterious. One of her stories has something to do with some friends who used to work at the bakery. I don't have many details and Gram doesn't want to talk about it anymore—it's too painful for her, apparently—so it's all just a bunch of hunches based on old stories that have probably changed over time."

Evan had listened intently to me. There was something about his concentration that caught me off guard. He was truly intrigued by what I said.

"I'm not interested in getting anyone in trouble, including your gram, Betts, but is there any chance you could at least share the name of the four people you and she think died in the fire and whose bodies were removed before any official record could be taken?"

I smiled. It didn't surprise me that he was a smart man. Anyone who could become a fire marshal must be smart, but again, there was that deep interest I saw in the glimmer in his eyes.

"You need to get to know Jake better," I said. "Something tells me you would love his archives."

"I think I would." Evan smiled, too.

"The family's last name was Cylas. There were four of them. There's no record of them dying in or around Broken Rope. There's no record of them being buried in any of our cemeteries."

"Maybe they just moved."

"Or, maybe they died in that fire and their bodies were taken and hidden. Maybe no one could figure out what happened to them, and missing people back then were much less investigated than they are now."

"So, you think it was all on purpose?"

I shrugged. "I suppose anything is possible. I don't know anything more than what I've told you."

Evan grinned again. "It just might be enough."

"Really?"

"We'll see. I'm going to ask your friend Jake if he and I could combine efforts. It sounds like a great challenge."

"Thanks," I said.

The door that led to the nitty-gritty, the even more hidden back-back room with the autopsy facility, of what Morris did swung open.

"Well, well, there you are, Miss Isabelle Winston," Morris said as he joined us in the smaller mid-room.

Morris was about an inch shorter than me, and he was round in a pleasant way. Even though he took up a good amount of space in every room he entered, that space only expanded with his vibrant personality. His gray hair was always just a little too long. Even when I'd seen him exit the barbershop, I thought he must have been in there only for a friendly visit because his hair was still too wild as it rode the top of his collar.

Morris's friendly round face was punctuated by his wide nose and his continually happy eyes; eyes that had seen some of the worst tragedies Broken Rope had experienced over the last twenty years.

"Hi, Morris," I said.

"Missouri doing okay? She sounded worried on the phone today."

"I think she'll be all right."

"Good, I hope we'll get Mr. Riggins's murder solved quickly." He waved away his thoughts. "Did Evan show you the pictures?"

"He did. Do you think bodies were moved, too?"

"I think it's possible, and I think that possibility might stir up a hornets' nest, Izzy."

Morris was the only person who had ever called me Izzy. It was a nickname that I hadn't encouraged, but it didn't bother me.

"I guess," I said, "but a historical hornets' nest."

"True, but we're a little protective of our scandals. Altering them might not go over well."

"Does that bother you?" I asked.

Morris ran his hand over his chin and thought a moment before he said, "I don't know. How important is all this"—he waved toward the pictures—"to you?"

It was my turn to think a moment. "Isn't the truth always important?"

Morris didn't wear glasses but he frequently bent his neck down and peered up at people from under his bushy eyebrows.

"The truth tends to cause a lot of ruckus before it sets anyone free, Izzy. You prepared to battle that ruckus?"

"Yes." I didn't need to think about that one.

"Okeydokey. Evan, did you show her the one that got my interest the most percolated?"

"Not yet." He switched out the pictures again. "Take a look."

It was another black smudge, but this one was even blacker, as though it had some depth.

"What am I seeing?"

"I think this is the spot where the fire, or at least the fire that was in this part of the building, started. I think some sort of accelerant was used. Probably something as remedial as good old-fashioned gasoline, or turpentine, or whiskey. Those were the typical fire starters of the day; of any day, really."

I looked again. "You sure?"

"We're both as sure"—Morris nodded at Evan—"as we can be. Experts would be helpful, but they might also balk. These are old, old pictures, and 'experts' don't like to risk being wrong. Evan, here, and I are okay with making a guess or two if it's just for you and nothing official."

"I appreciate it." I scooted back onto the stool.

Morris and Evan looked at each other. I was sure they were wondering why I was getting comfortable again.

"Morris," I said. "Is there any chance you could tell me what poisoned Roger Riggins?"

"Ah." Morris patted his round belly and looked at Evan. "Well, I can't tell you specifically. Jim asked me not to tell anyone. But I can tell you that it was something organic, something found in nature."

"A poisonous plant?" I said.

"Something like that."

The only poisonous plants I could think of were poison ivy and poison oak, but they caused itchy rashes, not death as far as I knew.

"The poison was ingested?" I said.

"Yes. That's what we've determined. It was actually pretty easy to figure it out. Everything was right there in the stomach."

"Was it ingested poison ivy or poison oak?"

Morris laughed. "No, but that could make someone mighty sick."

"What poisonous plants are around here, or around the school?" I asked.

Morris just smiled, though it was a sad smile. He wasn't telling.

The school and the cemetery were surrounded by woods that I'd never been one to roam through. I'd grown up in a residential area with a park and a neighborhood swimming pool. But I knew someone who had spent lots of their childhood communing with nature. Gram. I kept that sudden spark of knowledge to myself. I didn't think her time in the woods made her suspicious, but why risk mentioning it.

Somewhere back in the depths of Morris's hidden gory room a phone rang.

"Oh. Gotta get that. Jim wants me to be available twenty-four/seven. If I don't answer, his tighty-whities get all in a bunch." Morris laughed.

I often thought Morris's constant good humor was his way of coping. His smiles and laughter weren't ever maniacal, but sometimes they could be considered inappropriate. But he was too well liked for anyone to call him on it.

After he disappeared again, I took one more look at the picture on the microscope. I saw what Morris and Evan had explained, but I wasn't sure if I saw it because it was truly there or if they'd planted the idea in my mind. I might see some differences in the dark smudges, but I couldn't really be sure. And, I didn't have any sort of education to back up their ideas.

"It'd be great to find another spot where a body could have been," I finally said.

"I'll look into it," Evan said.

I thanked him and stood to go, but as I reached for the latch on the front secret door, Evan cleared his throat as if he had more to say.

I turned and smiled expectantly.

"You know," he began. "And, I'm not saying this because it's something I know for a fact, but it's a conclusion I came to on my own."

I nodded.

"The poisonous plant might not have been from around here. Think about it, you have students here from all over the country. Maybe someone brought it with them."

"That's . . . well, that's kind of brilliant. Good point," I said.

"Thank you." Evan smiled.

"See you later, Evan."

"Later, Betts."

I exited the hidden room without being seen by anyone and went to pick up Jake.

Chapter 11

I pulled up in front of Jake's and honked the Nova's wimpy horn once. The old blue darling might still be a reliable machine, but its horn had seen better days.

A second later, Jake emerged from his cottage. His home was modest, too modest for a millionaire, but he didn't care about the size or the simplicity of his house. It was the property, the land, that he was most interested in, though I never understood why. Jake had about ten acres, adorned with a barn that belonged in Amish country; it was big, red, in perfect condition, and mostly empty. He liked to garden, but he wasn't a farmer, so most of the property was grassland. He enjoyed riding his tractor mower and would sometimes spend hours just mowing and thinking, or so he said. He always said that he someday wanted a farm with cows and chickens and goats, so, in the meantime, he was just getting things ready.

This evening, Jake was dressed all in black as though we were going to rob the bakery. He also had a big bag slung over his shoulder.

"What'd you bring?" I asked after he threw the bag in the back and then sat in the front passenger seat.

"Full-spectrum camera and some other stuff that will help me do ghost readings."

I paused but only briefly. "Got a Proton Pack in there?"

"No, don't be silly, that was just movie fodder. These are real ghosts."

"That's true. So . . ."

"Oh, go ahead and say it. I know you want to."

"Who ya gonna call?"

"Feel better?"

"Much," I said. "Are you going to try to come inside with me?"

"I don't think so. I think it's best if I just stay outside and see what I can pick up from there. Unless you want me to come with you."

"Nope, I'm good." I was happy to hear his answer; I didn't want to have to worry about his safety, but if I said that out loud, he'd take it as a challenge not a warning.

"I bet I can't get in anyway." Jake sighed disappointingly. "You'll have to share all the details."

"I will. I promise."

I pulled the Nova to the same spot Gram had parked her Volvo. It was darker and even quieter tonight than it had been the night before. The sky was milky black with a thick layer of clouds, and I didn't see any activity in the area; no cars, no pedestrians, no curious onlookers. No wonder Gram was never worried about being caught when she used to visit the bakery. The building sat amid a small population but it was still off the beaten track, and the population mostly stayed inside.

I handed Jake the keys. "I don't think you'll be bothered, but if you need to leave I'll just walk over to the benches in front of the old courthouse. You can pick me up there."

"That works." He peered down the dark abandoned street that I would have to traverse to get to the benches. "Sort of. You sure you want to go that way?"

I looked up and out through the windshield at the building. "If I need to get out of there, I'm not going to want to hang around here and wait for you to come back. I'll want to get away. That's a good spot to meet, well lit even if it's dark on the way."

"Betts, are you sure we shouldn't call Miz? This seems like an unnecessary risk. Maybe. I don't know, but that building looks terrifying. Surely, you could fall through a floor or get bitten by a snake at any turn."

"A snake?"

"It's just what came to mind."

"No, when I go in there, I go back to when it was really a bakery. It's sturdy and solid with no rodents or snakes."

"Hmm." Jake glanced at the building, too. He'd often stated his jealousy about how I was able to see the ghosts, and he couldn't, even with his all-encompassing interest in Broken Rope's history. Jake wasn't afraid of much, but I wondered if this time he might be okay being left out of the paranormal experience. "I still don't think it would be awful to call Miz."

"I'm not calling her. I'll be fine." I got out of the car. I didn't tell him that Gent asked me not to bring Gram on this trip. That fact itself might cause him to call her.

Jake joined me a second later with his bag of tricks.

"If something happens, you'll need to get out of here quickly, too. Can you grab that stuff and just go?" I asked as he put the bag on the hood of the car and unzipped it.

"Not necessary, I'm pretty sure," he said. "If I'm trespassing, they'll just ask me to leave. And 'they' will be someone I know. I can tell them I'm doing something for the archives and they won't even blink twice. In fact they'll probably just leave me be. Everyone knows I like my history. I'm sure I'll be here when you come out." Jake smiled and tried to hide a hard swallow.

"Good point," I conceded.

"Go, go talk to your ghosts. I will see if I can find some on my own." Jake smiled and then sobered quickly. "But be careful."

"I will."

I'd put on thick-soled hiking boots this time, but I still made my way carefully thorough the debris along the path. Once to the spot underneath the landing in front of the door, I turned back to wave to Jake. He'd been watching me and waved first.

I hoisted myself up and then looked at the ground as I moved my foot over the invisible magic border between the two times. The change occurred as it had before, and I was suddenly struck by the fact that it was no big deal. I didn't feel anything different, I didn't hear anything different, like trumpets announcing that things were happening that should never be happening. It was so casual, maybe too casual.

I stepped all the way over the invisible line and knocked on the beautiful new/old door with the brass handle.

"Gent, it's me, Betts Winston." I looked back toward where Jake would be in my time, but I couldn't see him. I saw only a distant sort of blackness. I decided that it was better to just look at the door.

A second or two later, it opened.

"Betts, you're here! I wasn't sure you'd come," he said as he opened it wide. "And you didn't bring Miz?"

"No."

"That's great, come in, come in."

Once again, I stepped over a threshold.

The bakery had transformed to its original state just as it had the night before, and Gent was dressed in white as he had been. I saw his parents and his sister in the gloomy background. They were busy at their tasks, and I was pretty sure they didn't know I was there.

I'd experienced this all before so I shouldn't have been concerned that I wouldn't be able to get back to where I belonged, but without Gram by my side, a sense of doubt swept through me and made me nervous. It was as if whatever tether took me back was now weaker without Gram here. I didn't like it.

"Gent, I'm here without Gram because you asked me to come without her, but I don't know why. I don't like lying to her. You said you were going to tell me who killed Roger, and I wish I understood why you don't want her to know who it was, too."

Gent, with his youthful but intelligent eyes, looked at me thoughtfully and then cocked his head slightly.

"I don't know who Roger is," he finally said.

I sighed. *Stupid ghosts and their Swiss cheese memories.*

"You said you might know who the killer was, that you wanted to tell me. Roger was the dead man at the school today," I said.

"Yes, of course. I'm sorry. I was talking about my killer. I might be able to help figure out who our killer was. I know I've never had this memory before because if I had . . . well, if I had been able to tell Miz the detail I'm remembering, I'm sure I wouldn't have caused her so many years of pain."

"I don't understand, Gent."

"We were killed and then taken from here never to be found again. Miz was here when it happened, but she was spared. I believe she saw the killer, too, but she's never been able to remember much and it distresses her so to talk about it. After years of trying to figure it out, she finally told me I wasn't allowed to speak about it ever again—and, I remember her anger and pain when she made it clear that the topic was off-limits, I always remember. I think it's the only memory I carry with me at all times, because causing Miz pain only makes mine so much worse."

"That's why you asked me to come alone?"

"Yes. I'm sorry. It's selfish, I'm sure, but I couldn't help myself. You see"—he looked at his family members—"they can't rest until our bodies are found. They weren't supposed to be able to come back and their . . . travels tire them."

Gent, defying his serious and grown-up words, sniffed and then scratched at a spot behind his ear.

"Your killer set the fire, killed the four of you, then somehow removed your bodies before starting a fire in the other part of the building?" I said, putting together pieces of this conversation and my earlier one with Evan and Morris.

"No, well, yes, someone did set the fire and I don't know exactly what happened after that, but my family and I were killed first. We knew something, you see, we were called to the bakery that night under false pretenses, I think." Gent shifted his weight from one bare foot to the other and then looked toward the dark corner where the strange sound had come from the night before. "I can't remember why. Miz came with us because we were supposed to be . . . golly, I still don't know. But she was with us. She'll never tell you but she thinks she was hit over the head and taken outside. Then the rest of us were killed and our bodies, what was left of them, were put somewhere after they were burned."

I was stunned speechless for a second. My mind had slowed to ponder speed when Gent had said that Gram was hit over the head, and it took it a moment to catch up again. Gram came horribly close to being killed herself.

"I . . . I don't know how I can help," I said. "It's been a long time."

"Come over here with me. I'll tell you the memory and you can think on it."

I followed him to the far and still-dark corner of the jutted wing. It became illuminated slightly as we approached it, but not brightly.

"My family was here, you see." Gent pointed to a spot that was suddenly filled with a long seat, something like a couch with a thin cushion, but less comfortable, more utilitarian, closer to a bench. "This was a room where we could go to have lunch. I wasn't with them. I think I was with Miz."

"Is this the break room?" I asked.

"I don't know what a break room is, but we could bring a lunch and eat here."

I'd have to look it up to be sure, but there might not have been laws mandating such things as breaks in Gent's time; thus, no "break" rooms yet. There weren't many child labor laws, either; that I knew without needing to research.

"Okay," I said.

"Anyways, for some reason I think I was shot first, but then I think the rest of my family was shot when they sat on that bench"—he pointed at the bench—"My ma has told me she thinks that's what she remembers. We were all shot dead."

"Shot?"

"Yes, ma'am, shot. I don't always remember this so quickly, but this time I did. Miz told me later about the two men they found dead and burned, but they never found our bodies. No one ever knew we were killed. Eventually, I think people realized we were missing but we weren't much of anything to anyone but ourselves. No one cared. Except Miz, of course, and I know she spent some time trying to figure it out. It's been hard on her, painful, but she knew us, knew me when we were alive. You didn't. Maybe you can look at it more . . ."

"Objectively?" I said.

Gent shook his head. "I don't know what that means."

"With a little detachment, nothing personal invested into it."

"Detachment." Gent smiled. "Yes, detachment, without being so upset about it all."

I wanted to tell him that I was, indeed, somewhat upset—it was an upsetting story. But he was correct, I hadn't known him when he and his family were alive so I didn't have that attachment. I looked closely at him. Were he and Gram about to turn into an "item" when he was killed, or were they already one? I thought about asking but that felt uncomfortable, like I might be prying where I didn't have a right to pry. But would I have existed if Gent had remained alive and she hadn't married my grandfather? There're good reasons why the past can't be changed. But that's not what Gent was asking me to attempt to do. He just needed the truth. What had Morris just said—*the truth tends to cause a lot of ruckus before it sets anyone free.*

"Gent, I don't know where to begin to look into this. What can you tell me—the name of the killer, a description, why you and your family were called here that night, anything?"

Gent smiled. "Something, a thing I'd never ever remembered before, came to me last night when we heard the noise in the corner. Oh, I wanted to tell Miz, but I didn't want her to get angry and tell you to ignore me. I don't know where you live so I had to come talk to you at the school. Sorry about that."

"It's okay. Tell me."

"I remembered a name. Mary. We were called here because of something to do with someone named Mary."

"Mary?" I said. Mary was a very common name back in Gent's time.

"Yes. Will that help?"

"I, uh, well, I don't know. I can try." I didn't sound encouraging.

Gent's shoulders dropped, but he smiled and said, "Thank you, Betts. Thank you."

"What else?"

Gent's eyes opened wide. "I don't have anything else."

Mary. That was the big clue. That was why I didn't tell Gram I was coming to the bakery. Just a common first name was supposed to solve a decades-old mystery. Perhaps if Gent had been older, I would have rolled my eyes and laughed. But he was just a seventeen-year-old kid who wanted his family to be able to rest in peace. I didn't have the heart to hurt him further.

"Really, Gent, I will try. I'll do my very best," I said. I would, I just didn't think it would lead anywhere.

His smile brightened and his shoulders rose again. "Thank you."

"Let's try to think about it a little more. Do you remember any trouble? Do you remember you or your family getting caught doing something you shouldn't have been doing?"

Gent laughed uncomfortably. "No, I don't remember, Betts. I don't remember anything else."

I thought a moment longer about what I could say that would prompt more memories to come to him, but I knew it didn't really work that way. It seemed our conversation had come to an end. I thought about asking him about what would happen to him and his family when the building was demolished, but I suspected I knew; they'd somehow be . . . lost. There was no need for small talk, and since the rest of the Cylas family hadn't noticed I was there and that imaginary tether to Gram had continued to fade, I figured it was time to go. Before I left, I said, "I'll be at the school some of the time, but let me give you my home address."

Instead of an address, though, I just gave him directions, using the elementary school and the railroad tracks as markers. He'd be able to find the small white house, three down from the old tracks at the spot where the train station was once located much easier than he'd be able to track down the address.

From all indications Gent Cylas was a nice kid. I liked the idea that he and Gram were young together, but it was difficult for me to make the connection to that time, to those people, even though Gram had been one of them. Objectivity, however, might be the best thing this time around after all. I liked the ghosts, but it would be wonderful not to become overly attached to this one.

Gent walked me to the magic door and bid me a polite farewell. We didn't make specific plans to talk again, but I knew where to find him. I suspected that now that he knew where I lived I'd see him there soon, too. The ghosts' short visits gave them an impatience they couldn't control.

As I stepped easily back into my own time period, my eyes went immediately to where I thought Jake should be.

And he was there, peering up at me but over the shoulder of someone else, someone who had their back to me. It was too dark to see Jake's face clearly, but I thought he was probably trying to eye me a message.

The surprise visitor sensed that something was going on behind him so he turned to look.

"Betts?" Freddie said as he hesitantly waved.

"Hey, Freddie," I said from my perch above. "Hang on a second."

I made my way off the platform, stepped through the debris, and joined the two men watching me.

This was going to be another interesting conversation.

Chapter 12

"I told Freddie we were ghost hunting," Jake said as I joined them.

"Really?" I said.

"Did you find anything up there?" Freddie asked as he sent a dubious glance toward the run-down building. "How did you get in?"

I looked at the boarded-over door. "I didn't. I was just looking through windows."

Freddie's eyebrows came together. He must have wondered how in the world I had done even that much or why he hadn't seen me earlier. I interrupted his thoughts.

"What are you doing here and how do you know Jake?" I asked.

He turned his glance my direction. "I was just out walking around and this is where I ended up. Your car is so recognizable that I stopped to talk to your friend about just how many old blue Novas there were in Broken Rope. He introduced himself."

It would have been at least a little more covert to bring Jake's VW Bug. We would have to do better next time.

"Where are you staying?" I asked.

Freddie shrugged. "I'm at the Tied and Branded for now. I'm looking to rent a room or a house or something. I wasn't as prepared as I should have been before I got here."

"About that," I said. "When you got into town you stopped by the jail to ask the police directions to the school?"

"Yeah."

"Where was your welcome packet?"

"Sitting on my counter in my kitchen back home. I left it there accidentally. I was late for the plane and I had to hurry."

It could be true. He didn't sound like he was lying.

"Where's home?" Jake asked.

"Maine."

"Oh?" Jake said.

"Yes, sir."

"What part?"

"Bangor," Freddie said.

"I love Maine," Jake said.

I had no idea that Jake had ever been to Maine, but I filed that discussion away for later.

"Any ghosts?" Freddie asked.

"No," I said.

"I'll have to check what I recorded, but maybe," Jake said.

I rose my eyebrows his direction. He remained serious.

"Wow, that'd be something, wouldn't it?" Freddie said.

"I'd love to see a real ghost, and this couldn't be a better town for ghosts. I'll be around for a while. If you find anything, would you tell me about it?"

The time wasn't right, but there was something about Freddie's enthusiastic interest in the "ghosts" of Broken Rope and his assumption that he wasn't going anywhere any time soon that got under my skin.

"Freddie, my Gram and I were going to talk to you tomorrow. We're having some difficulties with your references," I said.

"Oh? What kind of difficulties?"

"Some go to disconnected numbers, no one's returning our calls, and when they do, they're fishy."

"I don't understand. Maybe you, Missouri, and I could sit down and try them together tomorrow. I was in such a hurry to get them written down, I could have made some number mistakes or something."

He didn't skip a beat. There was no hesitation to his response. I had no sense that he was making anything up.

"I think that's a good idea."

"Thanks." He casually turned his attention back to the building. "So, are you into ghosts and stuff?"

"Jake and I enjoy ghost hunting," I said.

"Interesting," Freddie said. "Sounds like a fun hobby."

"It is," Jake said.

"I'd sure like to see a ghost," Freddie repeated. But this time, there wasn't enthusiasm. Instead, I thought I sensed sadness.

"Hey, can we give you a ride back to the Tied and Branded?" I asked.

"Oh, no, that's okay. The fresh air is doing me some

good. Such horrible news about Roger, that he was killed and all. I'm having a hard time not letting it bother me. Walking helps. Do you think one of the students is a murderer?"

"I don't know," I said. "Do you have any sense that someone in our group could do such a terrible thing?" I didn't point out that he was a student, too.

"I don't. I'm sorry, I wish I knew something that could help."

I'd been so zoned in on the reference discrepancies that I hadn't considered how Roger's death might be affecting our youngest student if he wasn't, in fact, the killer. I needed to stop making such quick assumptions.

I took a deep breath. "I'm certain the police will find the killer. In the meantime, we should all be careful. Really, we'd be happy to give you a ride."

"I'm fine. I'm not scared," he said, his voice surprisingly even. "I'm just sad."

"I'm sorry, Freddie."

"Me, too."

I thought Jake might intervene and insist that Freddie come with us, but he remained unusually silent.

"Well, have a nice evening. Nice to meet you, Jake. See you tomorrow, Betts," Freddie said before he turned and walked away from us and from the town's semi-well-lit Main Street.

"Interesting guy," Jake said when Freddie was out of earshot.

"Yeah? How?"

"He's not from Maine. In fact, I bet he's never been there before."

"What makes you say that?"

"His accent is clearly West Coast. Maine people have a distinct accent, and West Coasters have one, too, though that one's almost a non-accent. And when I asked him where he was from, he said Bangor. Everyone knows Bangor; that's the first Maine city that comes to everyone's mind. If he was going to lie, the least he could have done was to find a better town or city to come from, one more obscure."

"I didn't even think about a Maine accent. You've been there?"

"I have, but even if I hadn't, I would know that people from Maine don't sound like he does."

Perhaps Freddie had only recently moved to Bangor, but according to the references, he'd worked in Connecticut, which was close to Maine in New England terms, I supposed. And the woman I spoke to had at first had an accent that struck me as odd and forced. We hadn't made Freddie fill out another application, just give us a list of references. Perhaps we should have asked him for the full application. I wondered why we hadn't.

"That is interesting," I said, distracted. My suspicions were continuing to build, but giving those suspicions leverage because of unexpected or unusual accents was a waste of time. "But he really is friendly," I thought aloud.

"Apparently serial killers are some of the friendliest people you'll ever meet. You might want to keep that in mind."

A chill raised goose bumps over my arms. "I hope he's not a killer."

"Someone is."

I peered into the gloom but there was no longer any sign

of Freddie. I looked at the building, and there were no apparent signs that ghosts and a chunk of the past resided right inside, but I knew that they did.

"Sometimes it feels like everything's an illusion," I said.

"Ah. I say it's all about perception, not illusion," Jake said.

I sighed. "So, how about we get out of here and you can tell me what your ghost-o-meter found and I'll tell you about my adventure. Did your camera really . . . what, record something?"

"Maybe."

Once inside the Nova and when the doors were locked, Jake said, "Don't leave yet, just in case . . . well, look at this." He pulled out the flip screen on the camera. "I was so busy watching you go into the building that I didn't even think about recording it."

"Did you see me disappear?"

"Yep. One minute there, the next gone. Wiiiiyald."

"I bet."

"Anyway, I started recording after that and look at what I got."

"Is this scary?" I asked.

"Not really. It's just interesting. No faces or forms, just lines. Here, look."

Jake hit the play button and the screen was suddenly filled with gray static except for a red horizontal line cut through the middle of it.

"Is that what this is supposed to look like?" I asked.

"No. It's a camcorder, but it catches . . . it's just supposed to show you a picture of what I aimed it at just like any other recorder. I thought I was recording the building and the surrounding debris. But when I went to play it back, I saw only this. Just watch the red line."

In another few seconds, the red line moved. It started to jump up and down. It reminded me of lines on a lie detector machine or perhaps a heart monitor found in hospital rooms.

"How long does this go on?" I asked.

Jake shrugged. "I stopped recording about five minutes after you went into the building. Nothing was happening out here and I wondered if I would see anything unusual on what I recorded, milky shadows, hot spots, something. This is what it got, so it's either broken or it does something I didn't know it did. I'll need to research. I should have just let it roll because I never started it up again after Freddie stopped and introduced himself. So, I neither know how long it *might* have gone on nor do I know exactly how you reappeared, or if it would have recorded your reappearance. You want to do it again and I'll try to record it?"

It didn't take any thought for me to say, "No, I'm good." Not totally needing the tether Gram's presence provided was comforting but I didn't want to push it. "So, it must have been seeing something, measuring some sort of energy."

"I didn't think that's what it really was supposed to do, but that's the conclusion I've come to, too. I truly don't know. I'm afraid I purchased this when you first told me about Jerome, but I hadn't done anything with it until tonight. I didn't read the instructions well, didn't expect much, but now I wish I would have read everything closely. I'm pretty darn interested in what this is showing. No matter. I'll figure it out. Tell me what happened in there for you."

I started the Nova and drove us back the short distance into town. I told Jake all about my visit with Gent, what he'd said, and why I didn't want Gram with me. I told him about my conversations with Evan and Morris. I gave him as many details as I had and then I asked him if he would do some "Mary" research. He didn't balk or laugh about how ambiguous the clue was, and he agreed to check into it.

"Here's another thought, Betts. It seems pretty obvious to me that the Cylas family must be buried somewhere on the bakery property. Their bodies were, quote unquote, moved. They were never found. The dark smudges. The entire family is there—well, sometimes they are there. Doesn't that make sense?"

"Maybe. I still don't understand how all this ghost stuff works, but it could just be the last place they were alive. Jerome and Sally couldn't get *into* places. This is my first go-around with ghosts who couldn't leave some place."

I'd stopped at an intersection that was on the edge of the downtown boardwalk while I told him what had happened in the bakery. It was a quiet night and we weren't in anyone's way. I was about to turn right to take him home, but just as I put my foot on the accelerator, he stopped me.

"Hey, isn't that Freddie?" he said.

At the other end of the street, the far end of the boardwalk, a man seemed to hurry toward the Jasper Theater.

"It sure looks like him," I said. "He was going the other direction. How did he get back to town so quickly? And where's he going?"

"Looks like he's heading down and across the street. He could be going into the back alley."

Broken Rope performers stored their props and costumes in sheds behind the Main Street buildings. In between the sheds and the buildings was an alleyway that was a popular spot for breaks or grabbing some fresh air or spending some downtime.

I pulled out my cell phone and called Cliff, who answered on the first ring.

"Hey, meet you in about an hour?" he asked.

"Sure, but I need to tell you something I'm witnessing first."

"Go."

I told Cliff about running into Freddie, using Jake's historical interests to briefly explain why we were at the bakery in the first place. Cliff knew about the questions we had regarding Freddie, but he didn't indicate if he and Jim had looked at him any closer. After I told him about Freddie's disappearance into the back alley, he assured me he'd check it out right away.

"Cliff will check it out. I'm not interested in chasing anyone down a dark alley," I said to Jake as the call ended.

"Me, either."

After dropping Jake off at his house, I took a detour on the way back to my own. The Tied and Branded was a busy hotel, and I thought that there must be other students staying there, at least temporarily. I was pretty sure Jake and I had seen Freddie, but not one hundred percent. I parked in the side parking lot and went inside to the front desk.

"Hi, hey, I was wondering if you could connect me to Freddie O'Bannon's room," I said as I put my hand on the house phone at the front desk. The desk was decorated with two large wagon wheels and someone had glued a spur onto the phone's handset. The woman behind the counter looked flustered but she forced a friendly smile as she moved a computer mouse.

"It appears that we don't have anyone by that name staying here," she said.

"You sure?"

"Uh, yep, I'm sure," she said after another long look at the screen. "No, no Freddie O'Bannon. Sorry." As the phone rang, she looked at me with raised eyebrows.

"Thank you. Go ahead and get that."

I wanted to call Cliff again, but if he was chasing or talking to Freddie, I didn't want to interrupt.

I'd see him soon enough, or at least I hoped I would. I hoped Freddie hadn't been up to something that might result in another tragedy. I hoped I'd called Cliff soon enough.

I hurried home and waited.

Chapter 15

I couldn't sleep. I was exhausted but I couldn't get my mind to shut down, to stop thinking about . . . everything.

I turned and looked at Cliff and smiled. He was a quiet sleeper who always placed his head on his clasped-together hands, just like those old-time pictures of children whose faces were always chubby and peaceful as they slept. I thought it was an endearing trait though Cliff claimed he was not a "cute" sleeper and I was making it all up.

Before we'd gone to bed, he had told me what had transpired between him and Freddie.

Cliff had found him in the alley behind the Jasper Theater. When asked what he was doing, Freddie said he was just looking around, just curious about the town. He hadn't been able to sleep so he'd been roaming.

Cliff informed him that it was a little late to be "roaming," particularly in the back alley. Then he offered—enthusiastically—to drive him back to the Tied and Branded. Freddie accepted the ride and Cliff observed Freddie going into his room. I'd asked Cliff a number of times if he was positive that Freddie had, in fact, entered a room. Cliff wasn't doubtful, and his patience level lowered a little with each time I asked.

His last answer was something like, "One of the important police rules I learned had something to do with observation, being aware, and paying attention to details. I remembered that rule tonight, Betts, I promise."

And when I asked if investigators found anything at the school, I'd managed to whittle away his patience so much that I got no words with his answer, just raised eyebrows.

But along with whatever might have been found at the school and Freddie and what was going on with the Tied and Branded's faulty computer system, my mind couldn't let go of Gent and his story, and someone named Mary. I knew I would have to talk to Gram, probably tell her about my subversive mission to speak with Gent alone. She wouldn't be happy, but I'd deal with it.

I took a deep breath and closed my eyes. *Relax, relax, and let your mind go blank.*

Suddenly, the scent of wood smoke filled my bedroom.

My eyes opened wide and I sat up with a jolt, rocking the bed and causing Cliff to stir slightly.

"Hello, Isabelle," Jerome said. He was leaning against the door frame, and he tipped his hat as he smiled.

I was dumbstruck, frozen silent and in place for a good half a minute as I looked at the fully formed, fully dimensional cowboy ghost. He was as close to real as any ghost could be, his form filled out in the darkness. Rugged, that's what he was. Good, old-fashioned rugged. Strong, put together just right, and topped off with the deepest, most beautiful and most pained blue eyes I'd ever seen. Even when he smiled, even when he was playful and kind of silly, his eyes were sorrowful. I suspected I knew what that sorrow was, the tragedy from his life, but at that particular moment, that half a minute when I was trying so hard to find my breath and find my voice, I wasn't so sure.

Oh, God, there was something else, too. Just looking at him made my stupid heart flutter. I put my fist on that spot and hoped it would calm down.

And then I realized I wore only a skimpy tank top and some undies.

So the first words I said—quietly so as not to wake my living boyfriend—to the ghost I'd been pining away for were, "Uh, can you turn around a second?"

"Oh. Yes, ma'am." Jerome turned and leaned his other shoulder against the door frame, but he dipped his head slightly, his ratty cowboy hat angling downward. "Sorry to surprise you like this, Isabelle."

"It's okay," I whispered again. I looked at Cliff, who was soundly asleep, and then gently scooted out of bed. It was warm outside, but I reached to the bottom drawer in my antique dresser and pulled out a long-sleeved sweatshirt and matching sweatpants. I was overcompensating for almost flashing Jerome, but I felt the need to be covered. "I'm good now."

He led with the cowboy hat as he turned around again. He seemed momentarily surprised by my attire but he quickly smiled. "Hello again, Isabelle."

I smiled, too. "Hello, Jerome. You remember my name?"

He nodded. "I do. I remember everything." He glanced at Cliff. "He can't hear me, but even with all your whispering, he might hear you. Should we go into the kitchen?"

"I have a better idea. Come on." I stepped awkwardly past him though the doorway and led him out of the front door and then to the small side yard next to my house.

"The woman who lives next door can't hear a thing. We won't disturb her. We won't disturb anyone here."

"Good plan."

For another long moment, Jerome and I just stared at each other. I had so many questions; perhaps he did, too, but I wasn't sure where to begin.

Finally, I said, "May I hug you?"

His eyebrows rose, but then he said, "Yes."

I moved forward as I saw uncertainty flash in his eyes.

I put my arms around his waist and my cheek into his solid chest. At first, he seemed hesitant but then his arms closed gently around my shoulders. It was unlike any hug I'd ever experienced. I felt him and I was sure he felt me. We were in complete darkness after all. But the sense of touch had been only that—touch. There was no body heat coming from him and I wasn't sure how much of my heat, the blood rushing way too quickly under my skin, he could feel. I stayed there just long enough to begin to feel guilty.

I disengaged and stepped back about a half a step too far. I laughed uncomfortably. "It's good to see you."

"Good to see you, too," he said with a strained smile and a squint.

"Jerome." I shook my head.

"What, Isabelle? Did I scare you? I thought maybe you'd be used to the ghosts by now. I'm sorry."

"I'm not scared."

Jerome laughed. "Bothered, then? Again, I'm sorry."

"No, just . . . surprised maybe. Your timing is interesting."

"You're sweating up a storm and you're as twitchy as a horse's tail in a summer swarm of flies."

It was my turn to laugh. I was sweating, he was right. The outfit I'd chosen and the warm evening made a bad combination. I wasn't willing to take off the sweats though, so I'd have to deal with it. I was sure I was also twitchy from the overwhelming nervousness I felt, but there wasn't anything I could do about that, either.

"Jerome! I've thought about you. I've wondered . . . I've wanted you to come back. I've . . . well, I think I developed a very unhealthy crush on you. It's a little sick, I know, having feelings for someone who's dead, but I can't help it. I've tried to stop thinking about you. I've tried," I gushed, but it felt good to get it out there.

Jerome rubbed at his jaw as I vented. The smile had left his eyes but the squint came back with a vengeance.

"I'm sorry, Isabelle. I'm truly sorry."

"Wait—no, don't be sorry anymore. No, I'm just explaining why I'm behaving this way. I'm not looking for you to have the same sorts of feelings." His eyes flashed but then normalized quickly so I continued, "I know it's impossible. It's stupid. I just want you to know, to understand. There's something that's safe about it all, too. You're dead, I'm not. I . . . aw, hell, I just needed to say it. To you."

"Isabelle, I need to tell you something. It's why I'm here. It's why I came back, I'm sure."

"Okay," I said, feeling suddenly dragged to an emotional halt.

"Darlin', you're in danger. I'm here to warn you that you need to watch yourself. Be careful."

"In danger? You mean from the person who killed one of our students? Roger Riggins?"

"Oh, I'm sorry about that. I didn't know one of your students had been killed. That's horrible, and, yes, of course, you should be careful. No, I'm talking about the Cylas family murderer. You need to stay away from the Cylas family and that old building."

I shook my head. "I don't understand. Maybe you've forgotten how much time has passed. The Cylas family's killer is surely dead by now."

"No, Isabelle, I know exactly what time period it is and was. I know. And the Cylas family killer might very well be dead, but some things are just meant to be left alone, and this is one of them. I knew you were in danger. I'm back to tell you to be careful."

I blinked. "Wait. You knew? Hang on. You remember? You said you remember everything from your last time here?"

"Everything."

It was a good thing it was dark. The intensity with which he stared at me made me blush deeply. And it had just been one silly kiss.

Jerome took off his hat and ran his hand through his messy hair. I wondered if he knew that his hair never changed shape even after he ran his hand through it.

"Isabelle, I don't completely understand why everything is different, but I do remember. Thank you for . . . your help."

"You're welcome."

Jerome half smiled as he put the hat back on his head, this time it was tilted back a little, reminding me how young he could look.

"So they were killed, and their bodies were removed. It's true, then?" I said.

"I think so."

"Who killed them?" I asked.

"I don't know. I wish I did. I've been trying to figure it out. If I do, I'll let you know."

"How do you know I'm in danger? How could I possibly be?"

"The same way I knew to save Missouri and her own mother from that fire all those years ago. That's the best way I can explain it. I just knew."

"Have you . . . well, have you always been able to come back, or have you always just been here? Gram showed me some pictures, and there seems to be a shadow in some . . . I don't know, it's odd, sure, but we thought we might have seen a cowboy hat."

"No, darlin', I don't think so. I don't know. I've always been somewhat aware of Miz, but now I'm very aware of you, your emotions, the danger you're in."

Another thought occurred to me, and I crossed my arms in front of myself and looked toward my house. Had Jerome seen me and Cliff together? Ever?

"Oh, don't worry, Isabelle, I, uh, don't 'see' you really. I'm just able to feel your emotions." He smiled. "You love that fella in there, don't you?"

I was so off-kilter that I could only mumble something incoherent, but I recovered and said, "Gram's going to be surprised."

"It'll be good to see Miz again. It's always good to see her, but . . ."

"What?"

"This visit is about you, Isabelle, all about you."

"I don't think Gram will mind. You know how she is about you ghosts."

"I do."

After another long pause, I said, "Can you tell me more about why I need to be careful? About what could happen?"

"Just stay away from the bakery, darlin'. You'll be fine if you stay away."

I nodded. "Okay, but Jake and I are going to look into things, look into the fire at the bakery, the missing bodies. We'll do that at the library and in his archive room, though. Will that be all right?"

Relief relaxed his shoulders. "Yes, I think so."

"Good."

"Good." Jerome stared again, with the same intensity that made me blush.

"Anything else?" I said.

"Yes."

"Go on."

"About that, what did you call it, that crush . . ."

"Don't worry . . ."

"Give me a second to say want I need to say, please."

"Sure," I said, but his tone sped up my heart rate even more, and I became very aware of a drop of sweat as it trickled down my back.

He took off his hat again and held it with both his hands.

"You've got a good man in there." He nodded toward the house. "Never mind the logistics of having a 'crush' on a dead person, he's alive, well, and head over heels for the prettiest girl in Broken Rope."

"Jerome."

"Let me finish. Please," he said. I nodded. "Now, I know I'm irresistible in my own way." The corner of his mouth quirked. "But we won't dwell on that. When we . . . When you kissed me, my skin felt something it hadn't felt in years: the touch, the lips of a woman. But I'm dead, Isabelle. My heart quit beating a long time ago."

I couldn't help but be taken slightly aback. "You don't have feelings?"

"I'm dead, Isabelle."

Of course he was dead. I'd known that, hadn't I? Jerome Cowbender died a long time ago, shot in the back by the Broken Rope sheriff. I was so stupid. So very stupid.

"Jerome. I'm a fool."

"Don't be silly. You're . . . you're a good friend. Even though I can't feel the same way as you do, I want you and Miz to be safe. Always."

I looked at him. I sensed some holes in his no-feelings statement, but I didn't want to be a bigger fool by pointing them out. I'd been told by a ghost that he just wanted to be friends. It was a new relationship low and I didn't need to test how deep the waters truly went.

"Thank you," I said, because I wasn't sure what else to say.

"Of course," he said as he put his hat back on his head. He suddenly seemed more nervous than I was. "Good to see you, Isabelle. I'll let you get back to . . ."

"Yes, of course."

Walking around the ghost in my side yard and making my way back into my house was the most awkward moment of my life. Jerome claimed to have no feelings. I suddenly felt every feeling possible. I hurried in and back to my bedroom. I hadn't been unfaithful to Cliff in any way except a random wayward thought about how I'd felt about Jerome, but crawling into bed again left me with a sense of disloyalty.

I wouldn't sleep at all that night. And I wouldn't take off the sweats.

And, I would never know what had happened after I left Jerome. I wasn't there nor did I look out the window to witness what he did when I was out of his sight. If I had, I would have observed something that might have confirmed I was right about him not being totally forthcoming regarding his feelings.

Once I was inside, Jerome removed his hat again. He leaned against the side of my house, punched the ragged hat, and said, "You stupid old dead cowboy. You should have stayed away. You should have just let things happen as they might have. You're a fool to . . . Well, you're just a damn fool."

No, I'd never know anything about that moment. It was probably better that way.

Chapter 14

"So, what do we know?" Elian asked. He'd worn another bright orange shirt. "We know he was murdered, we know he was poisoned, but what else?"

Other than Roger, we were all at the school; Gram, me, and the remaining fifteen students. We were gathered in the kitchen, though there wouldn't be much cooking going on today. Instead, the police wanted to talk to everyone, both as a group and then separately. The police—Jim and Cliff—weren't there yet, but the rest of us were, and it was a good opportunity to vent, discuss, talk, whatever anyone felt like they needed to do.

"I believe the medical examiner does know the type of poison but he hasn't shared that with me. Neither have the police." Gram looked at me, which caused the students to do the same. Today Gram wore a black T-shirt with a single word, MINES, ironed across the top. I didn't know which college or university the shirt represented, but I suspected she'd chosen it more for the color than the school.

I didn't think anyone knew I'd met with Morris and Evan the day before, but everyone knew by now that I was dating a police officer. I shook my head to indicate that the police hadn't shared the type of poison with me, either. I'd been so focused on Freddie's activities last night that that's the one thing I hadn't even thought to ask Cliff about. He probably wouldn't have told me. The students turned their attention back to Gram.

"Look, I'm a big believer of innocent until proven guilty, but I hope that if any of you have seen anything that sat funny with you or made you wonder if something was screwy, you won't hesitate to tell the police. We have a good force. Jim and all his men, including the one that Betts is dating, are good, fair fellas," Gram said.

"That begs a question, Missouri," Brenda said, her pen and notebook nowhere in sight. "If your granddaughter is dating an officer, how do we know the two of you will be questioned appropriately?"

"You won't. You'll have to decide if that's something you can or can't live with." Gram hadn't missed a beat. If I'd answered the question, I wouldn't have been able to hide the fact that I was offended by it, but if Gram was annoyed, she hid her reaction perfectly.

In fact, Cliff's shooing us out of the school the day before might have been good cause for the students to be suspicious. But both Gram and I knew that if there was any chance at all that Jim or Cliff suspected either of us, it would have been handled differently. Gram hadn't been wishy-washy with Brenda, and I had to give her credit for that.

"I can tell you all this: once you're cleared by the police, you are free to go, leave if you'd rather not stick around for the year. We've had a horrible tragedy and I'm as sorry as I can be about it, but we will continue on. Classes will resume full speed ahead either tomorrow or the next day. I will refund anyone's initial tuition payment, no questions asked. I've thrown the no-refund policy out the window."

The students each seemed to silently consider the offer for a moment, but a rumble of conversation soon followed. No one wanted to leave. I watched the dynamics and realized that though not everyone truly trusted everyone else, and though there was some fear amid the group, they all *wanted* everything to be okay. Even if they had to force themselves to believe it would be. It would have made an interesting psychological case study regarding the strength of the human spirit and will. Or maybe just denial; time would tell.

Since my powers of observation were surely dull from lack of sleep and somewhat fried from ghost and coffee overload, I knew that what I was seeing must be obvious to Gram. I watched her observing them and then saw acceptance pinch her eyes. She meant what she said, she would refund any early paid tuition to anyone who didn't want to stay, even if that meant the whole class. No one would leave, though, it was clear.

Of course, that also meant we might have a killer amongst us. I hoped that wasn't the case. I hoped none of the students were capable of such evil, and I put a little extra hope into Freddie not being involved in the murder. He was there because we hadn't kicked him out. Yet if he was a killer, Roger's death was partially our responsibility.

I hadn't had much time to talk to Gram before the students had started arriving. The only thing we'd managed to discuss was Freddie, his wayward visit to the alley, and my call to report him to Cliff. I hadn't told her about my visit to the bakery or Jerome's reappearance. Hopefully, we'd have time later.

A few minutes after Gram's refund offer, Jim and Cliff arrived. Jim spoke to the group about the need to be careful, the importance of being honest and sharing any detail with them that might be pertinent. He sounded a lot like Gram had. He answered a few questions and he and Cliff both moved back to the offices where they could each talk to the students individually. The method worked well. Two students at a time were gone from the kitchen as the remaining thirteen remained with Gram and me.

In only a few minutes, an efficient routine was established, but it didn't last long.

"Uh, Ms. . . . Betts, Miz, look here. Look over here." Freddie stood next to the set of shelves that held the containers of the neglected sourdough starters.

Everyone hurried over to Freddie.

"Look, see, my starter's gone," Freddie said.

Gram pushed her way to the front of the crowd.

"Back, everyone. Betts, get up here."

As I joined her, I saw what the problem was—there were only fifteen containers of starter, and none of them were labeled with Freddie's name. There should have been sixteen.

"You mixed one, right?" I asked Freddie.

"Yes," Brenda said. "I watched him myself."

I was surprised at her observation but I didn't say anything.

"Stand back, stand back," Gram instructed.

Everyone moved back as Gram inspected the area; the other shelves, the floor.

"Go grab Jim or Cliff, one of the officers," she said.

Jules hurried to the back offices.

"Do you think it's important?" I asked Gram, though not quietly.

"I'm not sure, but no one noticed it was missing until right now. Hellfire, Betts, I don't know, but the police should be aware. I guess."

"Can a starter be poisonous?" Brenda asked.

"No, not really. It could go bad and make someone sick, but it's not deadly," Gram said.

She sounded sure of herself. I had no idea if she was correct or not. I hoped someone couldn't die by sourdough starter. I'd never heard of such a thing before.

"Miz, what's going on?" Jim asked as he came through the back swinging door.

"Freddie's sourdough starter is missing." Gram shrugged. "Thought you should know."

"I made one, I know I did," Freddie said.

Jim's eyebrows came together under his bald head as he stood still, probably wondering exactly what a sourdough starter was.

"Everyone have a seat, back on the stools. Gram and Betts, let's talk."

Eventually, the individual interviews resumed, but not until Jim and Cliff became educated on sourdough starters and made a call to Morris to share the information just in case it was important. They dusted for prints around the area, but neither of them seemed confident it would do much good. Still, at least it was *something*.

The rest of the starters were taken away to be tested at a lab. The entire discovery and process might yield a clue or it might not.

Once the interviews were over, Gram and I had the students write down their Broken Rope addresses and phone numbers, and then everyone but Freddie was dismissed. Freddie listed the Tied and Branded as his temporary location, and willingly gave his cell phone number, though it began with a Missouri area code. I thought that maybe the hotel clerk had been purposefully cagey with me, which might have been the result of a policy or privacy law I wasn't aware of.

One more thought occurred to me, though. What if Freddie wasn't his name? I made a mental note to go back to the hotel and ask more questions, but I would base doing that on how his references finally panned out.

"Oh, I see what I did," Freddie said as he pointed to one listing. "I transposed two numbers. It's not three, four; it's four, three. Here, call right now. This is a good family friend, and someone I worked for. They won't lie, though; they won't say I was a good worker just because they were family friends. I promise."

Gram sighed and then dialed the number.

"Yes, hello, my name is Missouri Anna Winston and I'm calling from the Country Cooking School in Broken Rope, Missouri . . ."

Gram fell into a string of uh-huh's and I-see's as the

person on the other end of the line took over the conversation.

Finally Gram managed to fit in, "So, Freddie worked in your warehouse?" And, "Well, that's excellent. Sounds like he was something." And, "Oh, yes." And then she laughed. "I'll be sure to keep that in mind. Yes, thank you for your time. Have a great rest of the day." She hung up the phone and then looked at Freddie and me as we both watched her with matching expectant looks.

Gram sighed. "You are a mystery, Freddie, I must say."

"Why?" he asked.

"Your 'friend' gave you a glowing reference, but not too glowing. You were a good worker, but you have a tendency to sleep in sometimes."

Freddie blushed. "I hoped he wouldn't tell you that part."

"He did, but not without following up with the fact that you also stayed later than his other employees."

"I did."

"Look, Freddie, we should have leveled with you the first day, but we were concerned we'd hurt your feelings or perhaps show our own stupidity, but not only did we not have your references, we have absolutely no record that you applied to this school. Ever. You were a surprise. A big surprise."

"Oh. I'm sorry. I did apply, though. I was accepted. I'm sure of it," Freddie said.

I thought those were strange words to use. Why didn't he just insist, instead of sound like he was trying to convince us? But, I had to recognize that I'd talked myself into being suspicious of the young man with the bright green eyes more times than I should have. I'd painted a layer of doubt over every single thing he did. His explorations the night before might have been only a curious stroll. The clerk at the hotel might have been being only protective of her guests. Jake might not know a thing about people who live in Maine.

"What about the other references? We spoke with one of them and she was very complimentary, but we still haven't been able to reach the other names on your list," Gram said.

"Try again," Freddie said.

Gram picked a number to call but there was still no answer.

"I don't know what to say. Keep trying?" Freddie said. "Please?"

"We will," Gram said.

"So, may I stay? I don't want to leave. I'm not afraid. In fact, I really like Broken Rope and feel comfortable here and at the school."

Gram and I looked at each other.

"I suppose it's time to make a decision," Gram said as she sat back in her chair. She looked at me, but I didn't indicate that I wanted to talk to her in private. This needed to be her decision; I was too jaded. I'd told her about Freddie's activities the night before. She had all the information I had.

"Let me just say this, Freddie: you may stay," Gram said. "But I want you to stop being so goosey about spilling things. As a student of this cooking school, you will spill things, you will burn food, and you will probably even create something akin to a food disaster. It happens. You will not be asked to leave for such horrors. You have to understand, though, that we are still perplexed as to why you are here, and if the police find anything suspicious, out on your keister you will go."

"Oh. Okay, well, if you really don't have record of me, I can understand why you have doubts." Freddie scratched at the side of his head. "Maybe the proof will be in the pudding. More literally than figuratively. You'll see how passionately I will throw myself into learning all you have to teach. There's no ulterior motive to me being here, no reason for me to have lied."

I thought he might promise and then cross his heart. To me, his declaration of innocence was more suspicious than anything, but again, I was already stocked with a big supply of skepticism, and then there was all the coffee I'd drunk and Jerome's unsettling visit. I'd beg off from offering my opinion. For the time being.

"I hope so, son, because I don't kin well to people lying to me," Gram said as she moved forward again.

Freddie swallowed hard. "I understand."

"Good. Then we'll proceed from here." Gram sat back. "You need to find another place to live, though. The hotel will cost you a fortune. Find a room, or talk to the others and see if someone needs a roommate."

"I will. Thank you. I will."

"Good. See you tomorrow?" Gram said.

Freddie stood up awkwardly, knocking the backs of his knees into his chair and sending it sliding a distance across the floor.

"Yes, see you tomorrow. Thank you," Freddie said before he hurried out of the office.

"I hope we're not wrong about that boy," Gram said.

"Me, too."

She tapped her fingers on her desk a moment before saying, "Well, that was a day and a half, all lived in about half a day. It's just after noon. I suppose we will be able to get back to the real work tomorrow. You want to come over for lunch?" Gram asked.

"Let's go to Bunny's instead," I said. "I have a million things I'd like to talk to you about, and I'm thinking we need neutral territory."

"Uh-oh, that doesn't sound good. Are you all right?"

I nodded. "I'm fine. Really. But I've done some things, discovered some things. We just need to talk."

"Just as long as one of Bunny's cheeseburgers is part of the deal, I'm there."

"I'll drive."

Chapter 15

Bunny's was hopping. I had second thoughts about my choice of location; we might have had more privacy grabbing a sandwich at the saloon or pool hall, but Bunny, somehow using her Bunny superpower must have sensed that we needed a space to ourselves, got us a back corner booth. Three of our students were at the restaurant, too, but they would have to get used to seeing us outside of the school. It happened frequently.

Jules, Shelby, and Elian were across the restaurant and waved awkwardly when we first entered. They didn't know whether to come say hi or ignore us. We sent them a friendly wave but didn't go greet them or encourage them to come talk to us. It was just another step in the process. Soon, everyone would be comfortable with all the chance meetings. Broken Rope wasn't big enough to get away from everyone all the time.

Once we were seated, Bunny took our order and we got down to business.

"What's going on, Betts?"

"Gram, I went to the bakery last night. Gent asked me to. He also asked me not to take you."

Gram blinked. "Oh. I see."

"Gent asked me to come by myself because he knows how hard the past events are on you. He told me about what happened. I'm so sorry."

She tried not to, but Gram winced slightly. "Betts," she began, but she didn't go much further.

"I know. It's a waste of time to put energy into the ghosts when things could just end in frustration," I said. "You don't want that for me."

"Yes, that's true, but there's more to the story when it comes to Gent and his family. I know what Gent wants. He wants you to find his and his family's bodies. It's an impossible task. And, I told you that he broke my heart again and again. That's how, Betts. He broke my heart because I was never able to figure out what happened to them. The closer you look at the story, the more it will break your heart, too. They were good people."

"There's no record of their deaths or even much about them going missing. Why?" I asked.

Gram shrugged. "I tried, Lord knows I tried to tell everyone that something had happened to them. I was knocked silly the night of the fire and it took me a while to remember that I'd even gone to the bakery with them, and I still don't remember why I was there at all. Once I remembered I'd at least been there, no one would listen when I said they were there, too."

"That's horrible. All of it—that you got knocked unconscious, and that no one believed you."

"I recovered okay, but they found only the two bodies in the debris. The Cylases were poor people who had accumulated some debt. It was determined that they ran off to get out of paying that debt."

"That seems so . . . casual," I said as Bunny delivered our lunch.

"It was a different time, Betts. Maybe Broken Rope wasn't as Old West as it had once been, but people up and left places all the time, running from all kinds of things. It wasn't until later that social security numbers were required for employment. I'm sure that the people the Cylases owed money to searched for them, but of course they didn't find them. Neither did I. And when Gent and his family started coming back to visit, Gent and I tried everything. I'm sure he'll have you on the case, too."

"But I have more information, from the fire marshal, Evan, that might help. And, Gent remembered something, Gram, something that might make it easier."

Her cheeseburger was almost to her mouth, but she put it back on the plate and said, "And that is?"

"He remembered a name. Mary. The reason his family was called back to the bakery that night was because of someone named Mary."

"Mary?" Gram retrieved the burger, took a bite, and thought as she chewed. Once she swallowed, she said, "Well, that is something he's never mentioned before, but I don't know how it could possibly be helpful. I, we, knew a number of Marys back then. Maybe I can get this old konker of mine to remember some of their last names."

"You want to search with me?"

"No, dear, not a chance. I'm done with all that, but I know that won't stop you. I can help with at least that much, though." Gram took another bite. "Now, what's this about the fire marshal?"

I relayed the details of my meeting with Evan and his already established interest in the old fire. I told her about the smudges and the potential visual evidence of an accelerant.

"You mean, there really might be evidence that other bodies were there; the Cylases maybe?" Gram said and I thought she might be trying to blink back some tears.

"Maybe. It's all a maybe, Gram," I said.

"I'll be shot twice and hung to dry," Gram muttered. I thought she'd forgotten about the cheeseburger. "Not the best choice of words, I suppose."

"I'll try to find out more, Gram, I promise."

"Good. Okay. Good." Gram nodded herself back to the moment and once again reacquainted herself with the burger.

"There's more."

"Shoot. Give it to me. I can take it, whatever it is."

"Jerome's back," I said.

Gram put the burger down again and finished chewing the bite she'd taken. "I see. Well, he's never come back twice in the same year, so that is news."

"There's even more," I said.

Gram pushed her plate back slightly. "I'll just eat after you tell me the rest."

"He remembers lots, well, everything from his last trip for sure. His Swiss cheese memory has apparently become a little more like cheddar." I cleared my throat at the lame comparison. "He says he's not aware of being 'around' like we might have thought from the pictures, but he's always been aware of you, your safety and emotions. But, now, well, he says he's very aware of me—my safety and emotions."

"I see. And, what's he . . . sensing?"

"He said that the bakery building is dangerous for me. He asked me to stay away from it. I said I would."

"The building is dangerous. It should be torn down. Maybe he doesn't understand that it's a time . . . aw, shoot, I feel silly saying this, it's some sort of time-travel illusion or something."

I nodded. "I think he knows. He said that the bakery is dangerous because of what happened to the Cylas family."

"Their killer's still alive?" Gram said.

I shook my head. "Nothing that obvious or easy. It's blurrier than that, but he didn't, couldn't, go into detail."

Gram slapped her hand on the table. "See, these silly ghosts. Even if his memory is getting better, why in tarnation can't he tell you more? If he knows something from wherever he goes when he's not here, you think he'd be clearer."

I didn't know exactly what more to say at the moment so I took a bite of my own burger. Gram would have more to add, I was sure of it. And I was right.

"What about your feelings for him, Betts? Did seeing him . . . Don't let him ruin what you and Cliff have. Promise me."

"We had a chance to discuss that," I said. "He says he wants to just be friends."

The corner of Gram's mouth twitched suddenly. She tried to cover it with her fist but was wholly unsuccessful. She started to giggle. "I'm sorry, Isabelle."

I started to giggle, too. "It's so silly, isn't it?"

"No. But, yes, it's one of those things that the rest of the world doesn't have to deal with. And sometimes you just have to laugh."

"Yes, sometimes you just have to laugh," I agreed.

"Believe it or not, I understand. I've never really had . . . Saying that you have or had a crush on Jerome feels like I'm not giving your feelings due respect. I know it is or was more than a crush. Look, you were thrown for a loop. Our first ghost had to be Jerome, for goodness' sake. I was a kid so he never did the same thing for me, but, holy moly, he's all man, handsome, and a cowboy. You were thrown into this new existence where you could communicate with people who've been dead. When he and I were close in age, I had even less interest in the ghosts than I have now. I'd become used to them and had learned how to mostly ignore them. Sure, we'd chat, try to fill in some memory holes, but the ghosts used to spend most of their time here doing their things, looking around at the places that were important to their lives as they remembered them. All their people were dead, except for me. Their visits were brief and mostly unimportant. They can't haunt, not really. If they try to appear in front of people, they shorten their time here, mostly." Gram took a swig of her iced tea. I remained quiet while she formulated what she wanted to say next. "You know, I used to spend a lot of time wondering why they came here. I haven't spent many moments wondering why they come visit me, though. I just chalked it up to Jerome saving me and my mother from the fire. But I wonder if there's something we could do so they didn't visit anymore."

My heart sunk. "That might be for the best, Gram, but I think that would make me kind of sad."

"For a little while, maybe, but we'd get over it. It's not natural, you know."

"I know, but still . . . I'm not ready to ask them to leave. Yet."

"Okay, Betts, I'm not going to do anything to get rid of them, though I feel like I need a heart-to-heart with Jerome. You okay with that?"

I wasn't sure I was, but I remembered that I trusted Gram implicitly.

I nodded. "Sure."

"Good."

"And, Gram, what about our current murder victim? Roger?"

"I think the police will handle it just fine," Gram said. "You don't need to get in the middle of all that, Betts."

"I know that, but maybe we can help."

"I don't know how. I gave Jim copies of everyone's—not just Freddie's—paperwork. They'll look into it. We have to just continue to operate on that innocent-until-proven-guilty theory."

I looked across the restaurant at the three students who seemed to be having a good time. "But do you think one of them is a killer?"

Gram looked across the restaurant, too. "We just need to stay on our toes."

"I wonder if any of them knew Roger before coming here. No one acted like they knew each other, but remember a couple years ago when two of the students were, in fact, very good friends, but they didn't want to tell us that until we all got a good chunk of the year under our belts—what was their reason, something about not wanting their friendship to be a deterrent to them getting into the school?" I said.

"I do. Betts, no one is totally honest all the time and some of the time people lie about the silliest things."

I nodded as I peered at the small group again.

"I don't like Brenda," I whispered as I leaned over my plate. She wasn't with the trio at the other table, and I was being way too gossipy, but I was just rolling with the moment.

"I know, and I see what you mean about the notes and the snooty attitude, but she doesn't bother me as much as she bothers you."

"I know we made copies for Jim and Cliff, but could I take the students' files home today?"

"Certainly, but I'm going to repeat this—be careful. Be smart. Got it?"

"Promise."

"So, before I order some pie and risk not enjoying some cherries and whipped cream, is there anything else you need to tell me?" Gram said.

"I think you're caught up." I smiled.

"Good." She paused. "Now remember these: Loken, Gleave, and Silk."

"What are those?"

"Three Marys I remember. There might be more, but those are the first ones that came to my mind."

I wrote the names on a napkin and put it in my bag. I had some research to do, but for now I was going to enjoy the rest of my lunch with Gram and about fifty other Bunny's customers.

Chapter 16

My first stop was Jake's fake sheriff/archive room. I found him hovered over his keyboard, the "ghost" camera on the desk beside him.

"I can't find one thing that explains why this camera did what it did, Betts," he said. "Not one thing."

"It's broken?" I said.

"No, I don't think so. I've been able to record on it just fine today. But there is not one thing to explain the static and the lines. Yes, it's supposed to record ghosts, but in their ghostly form, or perhaps a shadow or light, but not static and lines."

I shook my head. "Even if it's not broken, maybe you just ran it wrong."

"That is possible, but not probable. It's a simple, simple camera. I 'get' cameras."

"I don't know, then."

"I'm going to run to Springfield. I ordered this online, but there's a camera shop there that's into paranormal and sells this model. Maybe they can help. You want to go with me?"

"Actually, I stopped by to see if you wanted to do some research with me—here or at the library. Jerome's back."

"Oh? I'm not so sure that's a good thing."

As I had done with Gram, I gave Jake a rundown of the conversations and events that had occurred since I'd last seen him. He reacted similarly to Gram regarding Jerome, but he was more excited than she was about the Mary lead.

"I do have to run to Springfield right now, but maybe later. I called the shop's owner and he says he knows these things"—Jake put his hand on the camera—"inside and out. He'll be taking the next few days off so I need to get there today. You are welcome to stay and use my computer and look through the archives if need be."

I looked around. I didn't think I would ever pull a file from one of Jake's shelves without him there to direct and scold if I did something improper. The same went for his computer.

"No, thanks, I'll just use the library."

"We've got to get Wi-Fi set up in your house, Betts, or at least at the school. Dial-up is a dead technology."

"Not dead. Just tired."

Jake laughed. "Well, I'm excited about having things to look into and hopefully getting to talk to Jerome—through you, of course, but right now, I've got to fly."

The Broken Rope library was housed in a building that was once a hospital for the mentally insane. It sat behind an old wrought iron fence and atop a high hill. The tall, brick building and the tree-filled grounds had been used in a couple of Hollywood movies, but none that had become particularly successful.

Of all the places in town, I thought the library would be the one place that would likely be haunted. But the head librarian, Sarabeth, had turned the inside of the building into a comfortable and peaceful setting where no ghosts bothered anyone; unless they were fictional specters found in some of the books on the well-stocked shelves.

"Betts, I was just going to lock up. It's closing time," Sarabeth said as we met at the front doors.

"It's only four." I looked at my watch.

"It's Thursday, dear, we close at four on Thursday. It's my date night with Boyd, and no one really likes to visit the library on Thursday nights. They're tired and can't seem to plan for the weekend until it hits them in the face."

"Shoot. I was really hoping to do some research. It's for Gram and for Jake. I'm helping Gram with some cooking stuff and Jake with some old historical stuff."

Both of those things were untrue, of course. Gram didn't need my help and Sarabeth knew both Jake and me well enough to know it would be a rare moment that he'd need me for research.

She pulled her chin down and looked up at me as her eyebrows drew together.

"You don't want to tell me the real story, do you?"

"I just need a little time. Not a lot." That wasn't true. I needed a lot, but I hoped my plan was working.

Sarabeth sighed, which was expected, but then she gave in.

"All right. But I'm not going to stay. I'll give you the keys. You lock up when you're done and bring them to me tomorrow morning. I get here at seven A.M. If you're late, I'll take away your library card."

I crossed my heart. "I won't be late. I promise. Thank you, Sarabeth."

"You're welcome."

Sarabeth's was the only car with a real spot in front of the building. Patrons and other employees parked in the side or back lots. I'd parked in the side lot this time and could see the Nova's nose if I stood right outside the front doors. I watched Sarabeth, in her floral-print dress and sensible shoes, make her way to her old Cadillac.

"Don't you forget to lock the doors, Isabelle Winston," she said before she got in the car and revved up its noisy engine.

"I won't," I said, but I doubted she could hear me.

I locked the door behind me and flipped the switch on the wall in the entry hallway. There was no sense at all that the building once housed mentally ill patients who had, by today's standards at least, endured cruel and inhumane treatments. Jake had told me about some of the horrific methods used back then.

The library's walls were painted with calming colors. The wall space outside each doorway was decorated with a sample of the types of books found inside that room. My favorite wall was the one outside the children's section. *Where the Wild Things Are* as well as *Goodnight Moon* and a number of other favorite covers had been perfectly reproduced. I walked past the children's room, though, and into the room with the computers and a desk adorned with the huge sign that said REFERENCE.

I pressed the power button of one of the computers and waited only a few moments for it to warm up. Sarabeth had long ago given me the sign-in and the password. She did this for almost all of Broken Rope's residents. It was easier on her that way. Though there were other librarians, Sarabeth knew more than they did combined, and her time in the library was rarely spent behind the reference desk or in her office. Instead, she was constantly moving around, helping patrons with anything they needed help with. Despite the fact that everyone in the world had a computer, the ones in the library were still well used, and Sarabeth gave out the usernames and passwords to those she trusted.

From the vantage point of the chair behind the computer at the end of the row of five, I could look out one of the building's side windows and onto the main road that was in the distance and down the sloping property. There wasn't much traffic out here, but every now and then a car drove down the road in one direction or the other.

Once the computer had warmed up and the search engine was ready to roll, I realized I had so many avenues to explore that I wasn't sure where to begin. I finally started with *Freddie O'Bannon.*

It wasn't an uncommon name. There were evidently a number of them throughout the world. On the first page of listings, I saw a teacher and a pianist, but even a few pages in, there was no Freddie O'Bannon in Maine. It was a long shot anyway. I knew that an "Isabelle Winston" search didn't lead easily to me. I wasn't into social networking at all, and there were many tech-savvy Isabelle Winstons to get through before you found me and the fact that I lived in Broken Rope.

The smell filled the library first, so I wasn't as surprised as I'd been the night before, but my heart rate did speed up, and I swallowed hard to try to moisten my suddenly drying mouth.

"You found me," I said as I turned to face Jerome. "Is one of your new tricks the ability to just pop to wherever someone is without knowing the exact location first?"

Jerome moved to sit in the chair next to me. "No. I followed you from downtown."

"I didn't know. I didn't smell you."

"I stayed downwind, I guess. I knew you were there because your automobile was there—I was outside the Jasper. I didn't want to disturb you with your friend Jake so I didn't come inside. I didn't think I'd bother you too much if I came in here."

"I see."

"I didn't ask last night, but I noticed my treasure is gone."

"It's now in a state-protected archive." I didn't mention that even at that moment I had a coin from his treasure still in my pocket. He didn't need that detail.

"May I ask what you're doing on that thing? I remember seeing them last time I was here, but I don't understand what they are."

"This, Jerome, is the world at my fingertips. It's a computer and it accesses pretty much any information that you'd want to find about any topic that you can think of."

Jerome whistled sincerely. "Gracious, that's something isn't it? Kind of like that Dina stuff you talked about last time."

"Dina? Oh, DNA. Yes, the world is much different than when you were alive."

"That's good, is it?"

"Mostly, I think. Sometimes, simpler is better. I'm not sure it's always a good thing to know everyone's business and have everyone know yours so easily."

"I wouldn't like someone in my business."

"I don't think you would. Anyway, it is convenient. I'm looking up our students to see what information's out there about them. Gram and I do this to a certain extent when we're first looking at their applications, but with Roger's murder, I thought I should look deeper."

"Huh. What have you found?"

"Not much of anything yet, but I've only started with Freddie O'Bannon."

I gave Jerome a quick summary of the students and what little I knew of them and the impressions they'd made on me and Gram. I told him about Freddie's surprise arrival and how wonky his references had seemed, though they looked like they could still pan out.

"I can venture out and watch them all a little. Maybe that would help," Jerome said. "It's not what I'm here for, but I'm happy to do so if it will help you."

I sighed. "So, if you're here to warn me to be careful and I promise to do as much—I don't want you to leave, don't get me wrong—but why are you *still* here?"

Jerome pushed his hat back on his head. "I don't know exactly, Isabelle. I'm worried about the Cylas problem, though. I feel like I need to be here as long as Gent and his family are here. Something's not right about their visit."

"You'll go away after they're gone?"

"Can't be sure."

"You'll come back again someday?"

"It seems likely."

I swiveled away from the computer and looked at Jerome. "What if I have a kid or kids? Will they be able to communicate with you?"

I thought Jerome blushed. "You and that Cliff fella going to have some kids?"

"I don't know! This is hypothetical. Just wondering."

"I see. I don't know, Isabelle. Seems it skipped a generation between you and Miz, though."

I wanted to understand the ghosts, their true raison d'être, so to speak, but at that moment, I thought I felt Gram's frustration more than I ever had. There might not be clear answers, or if there were, those answers might also change over time. Would I ever just be able to go with the flow?

"Mary," I said as I faced the screen again.

"Excuse me?"

"Loken, Gleave, and Silk. Those were three Marys that Gram remembered. I came to the library to use the computer, but I had another reason, too. Sarabeth's library has the one form of archives that Jake hasn't been able to collect yet: Broken Rope High School yearbooks. I thought I'd look there as well as try the Internet."

"Yearbooks. Now that's something I can understand," Jerome said.

"Let's go."

I led us back behind the reference desk, crossing a boundary I wouldn't dare cross if Sarabeth was in the building. I would have asked for her help if she was still there, but I liked that I could explore on my own. Sarabeth didn't like us commoners invading the reference desk space, and I didn't blame her. This is where she kept the good stuff, some of the more rare books the library held, some signed books, and, of course, a copy of each year of the high school yearbooks from when they first started printing them in the late eighteen hundreds. Gram had graduated in 1952 when she was eighteen. She'd once told me that many of her classmates were a couple years younger, but since she'd lived in the country for so long, she got a late start on an organized education. I couldn't believe I hadn't ever looked at her yearbooks, but I made a beeline to the back shelves behind the desk and easily found 1952 and the three previous years.

I carried them back out to a table next to the computers and turned to Gram's senior picture.

"I'll be, I remember Missouri perfectly," Jerome said with a smile. "Look at her, Isabelle. You and she could be twins."

Gram was lovely in her uplifted chin pose. Her smile was brilliant, and though I knew they touched up these pictures sometimes, her teeth had always been straight and white. Her thick hair was poofy and bobbed into a style she would never make the time for now. It wasn't possible to see the auburn color, but I'd been told that it matched mine. Of course, I never felt comfortable commenting on her beauty. I didn't think I looked that much like her but everyone else seemed to.

"Pretty," Jerome said.

I looked at him and his half smile.

"Hmhm." I blushed and then looked back at the book. "Gram remembered a Mary Loken." I turned the pages back to the Ls and found Mary Loken immediately.

Even in the bust-only picture, it was obvious that Mary Loken was petite. Her blond hair was styled like Gram's but the rest of her features added up to someone adorable, not someone beautiful.

"Any chance you know anything about her?" I said.

"Nothing at all. If she and Miz were friends, I don't remember anything about it."

"What about Mary Gleave?" I turned to the Gs but there were no Gleaves listed. I looked quickly through the smaller underclassmen photos, but there were no Gleaves there, either.

As I thumbed back to the senior pictures to search for Silk, I thought I might have seen the name flash by. I flipped back again.

On the page before the sophomore class pictures were small pictures of the sophomore teachers. The high school had never been big, but it was even smaller in 1952. There were only five sophomore class teachers, and the one who taught English was Mary Silk.

She was young, couldn't have been much older than high school age herself. I didn't know the requirements for being a teacher back then, but she must have had to attend some college.

"How about her, Jerome? Do you have any memory of her?" I pointed to the picture of the striking young woman with the short, short hair. Everything about her was severe; her sharp nose, her straight mouth, her small eyes, and her boyish haircut. She looked very teacher-like. "Jerome?"

"I might recognize her. I'm not sure, though. There's something familiar."

"I'll ask Gram."

I switched on the copier and carefully made copies from the books. I found a few activity pictures as well as some from other years. Before long, I had a thin file that I would show to Gram with the hope that something helpful would jog loose from her memory.

The last picture I searched for was Gent's. Apparently, he hadn't made it to school on picture days and he was dead by what would have been his senior year. I thought I might have found a picture of him and Gram sitting on the front lawn in a 1949 book, but I wasn't totally sure because the figures were small, the picture taken at a distance. I made a copy of it, too, and as I pulled the copy from the machine I thought I saw something else.

"There, right there, Jerome. Is that you?" I pointed to the shadow behind the seated woman I thought might be Gram—a shadow that looked like an outline of a cowboy hat.

"Shoot fire, Isabelle, I don't think so."

"It's in lots of pictures of Gram."

Jerome shrugged. "Maybe a part of me has always been with Miz. Maybe, but I don't know . . . Let me say that differently: I don't have a clear memory of watching her or watching over her, or being around her all the time. Nothing distinct."

I plugged in the Mary names for an Internet search and came up with only one interesting item. Mary Silk, the teacher, was still alive according to a listing at the Broken Rope retirement center, The Benedict House. There were no pictures, but I wondered if she still looked stern.

"How old do you suppose she is?" I asked Jerome.

"She didn't look old in her teacher picture. She might not be much older than Miz."

"I'll talk to Gram, but I think I'd like to talk to Mary Silk. The possible connection would have to be the long shot of all long shots, though."

"Stranger things have happened," Jerome said.

"Very true." I laughed as I looked at him.

And then looked away so he wouldn't see my eyes give way to the hollowness carving through my chest.

We can be fine friends. We can be friends just fine.

I returned everything to its correct spot, making sure all items were a little neater and a little less dusty as I went along. Sarabeth's sharp intuitive librarian instincts might make her notice that I'd looked at the yearbooks, but she'd also quickly determine that I hadn't caused any harm and I'd left things better than I found them.

I searched for interesting Internet tidbits on our other students, but nothing stood out. I did note that I was able to find at least a little something about all of them—addresses, social network pages—except for Freddie.

Finally, I switched off the computer, stood, and then pushed in my chair. As I left the reference room, I flipped off the light. I was so lost in my own meandering and overlapping thoughts, it wasn't until we were outside the building that I realized how late it had gotten. The sun had almost set all the way.

After I locked the doors and swung around to head to the Nova, I realized Jerome had transformed into his fully dimensional self. As I swung, my hand grazed his hand.

I gasped and then felt immediately foolish.

"Sorry," I said.

"It's all right. It'll take more than that to hurt this old man," Jerome joked, but he'd felt it, too, I knew he had. Not the touch, the spark that went with the touch.

He was suddenly so real, too real, too much like a living man to be a ghost. I stood and stared, the files fortunately filling my arms. If they'd been empty, I doubted I would have been able to resist touching him. On purpose. And with purpose. This sense that I had was beyond curiosity, beyond reason, beyond normal.

"Jerome," I whispered.

"Isabelle," he said as he put his hands on his hips and looked at the ground in between us. For a moment, all I could see was the top of his cowboy hat, and I wanted to touch even it.

"This is wrong, so wrong," I said.

He looked up and I saw the pain in the lines around his eyes, his tight-set mouth, and the mustache that took up way too much space to be fashionable but seemed so perfect to me.

"I don't know what this is," he finally said. "But it isn't wrong. Don't call it that. It's not natural maybe, but it isn't wrong."

"How do we . . . I mean, I don't even know what to do."

Jerome smiled slowly and sadly. "There's nothing to do except enjoy each other's company when we're able to."

"Platonically?" I said, not able to hide the disappointment in my voice.

He laughed then, a deep barrel of a laugh. "You are something, Isabelle Winston, but, yes, I'm afraid platonically is the only way to go here. Otherwise, this could step right on over to the world of wrong."

"I suppose you're right," I said, "but . . . well, I gotta say, if it weren't all so strange, I'd wish for more." I turned and walked toward the Nova.

Leading questions, leading statements. These sorts of things weren't the hardest part of law school, but they'd been my favorite. And I'd just used a statement to fish for something from Jerome. It was pretty elementary, and if Jake had been in the area, he would have pointed out my bold behavior and tsked at me.

"Isabelle," Jerome said when I was halfway to the Nova.

I turned, inwardly knowing that I'd gotten his attention just as I'd intended.

He was a vision to behold. Perfect with his slew of imperfections. The mustache, the somewhat uneven but bright blue eyes, the messy hair that could have used a brush and a pair of scissors, the rip in the right shoulder of his shirt—of course, in this form I could also see a patch of muscled skin through the tear so it wasn't so imperfect after all—his dusty pants and boots. He took my breath away.

"Yes, Jerome?" I said casually.

"I can see right through what you're doing and I'm not giving in that easily. I'm . . . well, I was a man of few words. I'm dead, I can't have feelings. I can't say the things you want me to say."

I laughed this time. "If you don't have feelings, then why are you looking at me like that?"

He rubbed his finger under his nose, but I suspected it was a stall tactic.

"I have to go, Isabelle. I'll check on your students and get back to you."

And then he was gone. I really hoped he couldn't see what I did next.

I dropped the files onto the Nova's passenger seat and myself onto the driver's seat. I started the engine but I kept the windows up and the doors locked as I blinked back tears of frustration and tried to catch my breath. No matter what, I couldn't let anyone see me this way. No matter what, Gram, Jake, and certainly Cliff could never know that I was this confused, this emotional, struggling so much with whatever these feelings truly were.

It was not natural, and though it might not have been wrong, it certainly wasn't right. And it made no sense at all. I barely knew him, had spent less time with him than I probably had with Cliff the first week we were dating. How did this happen? I wasn't shallow, or so I thought. Besides, though Jerome was attractive to me, so was Cliff, so were many other men, and I didn't fall in love with them just because they were nice to look at.

And no matter what he said about not having feelings, about "wanting to be friends," and whatever other noble comment he thought he had to add, I knew he felt the same way about me. I just knew it.

How had this happened?

And how was I going to get myself out of it?

"Damn," I said as I drove the car away from the library. "Damn."

Chapter 17

I soon decided that the quickest way to get over confusion regarding way too intimate feelings about a ghost is to get a call that some of my cooking students need to be bailed out of jail.

I hadn't been in the car five minutes when Cliff called. I wasn't going to answer at first because I thought he'd hear the disloyalty in my voice, but I was glad I did. It was better I handle this than Gram.

"Betts, I had to haul in some of your students. You want to come get them out?" he said. "I can call Miz, but I thought I'd try you first."

"I'm glad you did. What happened?"

"Disruptive behavior, but they're claiming it was all a misunderstanding. I'm not going to hold them for long, but

I thought we should make a bigger deal out of it so they get the message that they can't behave this way. If you come down and let them know that you know what they've been up to, they might shape up from here on out."

"Good plan. I'm on my way."

Main Street was open for parking, but there was a wedding reception being held in the saloon, and the attendees had taken all the prime spots. I squeezed the Nova into a space at the end of the street by the small stagecoach museum and then walked to the jail.

The party in the saloon was going strong and a bass beat shook the boardwalk. Even the jail's door knob rattled as I grabbed and pulled. Inside was one of the sorriest sights I'd ever seen.

Four of our students were there, seated in a line of chairs to the side of Cliff's desk.

The three I'd seen earlier at Bunny's were present: Jules, Shelby, and Elian. And the fourth criminal was Freddie, who looked much worse for the wear and much more subdued than the other three. In fact, Freddie's timid glance away from my eyes was only exaggerated by the other three's obvious anger and their ability to keep their glares firmly focused on me. Jules had her arms crossed in front of her chest and her toe was tapping so quickly I thought she might put a divot into the hard floor. Elian leaned forward, his elbows on his knees, and was purely disgusted, though I didn't think the disgust was meant for me. Shelby looked the least disturbed but she sighed heavily. She shook her head slightly as if to let me know that she could not believe she'd gotten herself into whatever it was that they'd gotten themselves into.

I sighed, too. It was rare that I or Gram had to pick up students from the jail but it had happened a time or two in the past. Usually, issues were resolved quickly, and they weren't unsolvable problems in the first place. According to Cliff, this wasn't serious, either, but Freddie's blackened eye and disheveled hair made me wonder.

Cliff stood as I approached the group. "Hey, Betts."

"Hello." I didn't mean to sound so teacherly when I spoke next, but I did. "Who wants to tell me what happened?"

Of course, everyone began to speak at once; everyone but Freddie, who continued to try to avoid my glance as he fidgeted in the chair.

Cliff stepped forward and put his hand up to halt the commotion. I was impressed by the immediate silence.

"Betts, the best I can understand is that Mr. O'Bannon crashed the wedding reception and was involved in a tussle with a bona fide invited guest."

"Freddie, you crashed a wedding and got a black eye?" I said.

Freddie looked at me and shook his head.

"Oh, no, that won't work," I said. "Truly, I don't have the time or the patience for the silent treatment or any effort you might want to make to protect someone else. I need to hear what happened—from everyone's point of view—so spill it. You first, Freddie. Cliff, you have any ice?"

Cliff nodded and disappeared toward the back of the building.

Everyone else in the room turned toward Freddie.

"I, uh, well, I thought I saw someone else in there so I went in to see what they were doing."

"Who did you see?"

"Brenda."

"Our student, Brenda?"

"Yes."

"Why isn't she here?" I asked him and the others.

"It wasn't Brenda."

"I was there," Elian said. "I'd crashed the party."

"You thought Elian was Brenda?" I said to Freddie.

"No, I didn't see Elian."

"But you saw Freddie?" I said to Elian.

Elian nodded. "Yes, and I saw him run into the guy he ran into. He spilled his drink."

"So, he, that guy, hit Freddie?" I said.

"No!" Freddie said.

"That's exactly what I saw," Elian said.

"I'm really confused. Freddie, how do you think you got the black eye?" I said.

Cliff handed Freddie a plastic bag full of ice.

"Thanks," Freddie said to Cliff. "No one hit me. I ran into something."

"A fist," Elian said.

"No!" Freddie said.

I looked at Cliff, who shook his head. "No one else except Elian saw Freddie get hit by anyone. Elian looked through the crowd for the man he saw accost Freddie, but he couldn't find him."

"I saw the man because I saw Freddie come into the party. I saw the whole thing. No one else was paying attention really. Everyone was just enjoying the party," Elian said.

"What did you think you ran into?" I asked Freddie.

"I don't know."

"Jules, Shelby, why are you here?" I said.

"Because we apparently picked the wrong person to be friends with," Jules said bitterly.

"Elian said he wanted to crash the party," Shelby explained. "We didn't want to go with him so we went to the pool hall to waste some time. We were there when Elian called us to come help gather Freddie. We went into the reception and found Elian and Freddie at the back of the room. Freddie didn't want to leave with Elian. Just as we had him convinced that we all needed to get out of there, the police officer"—she nodded toward Cliff—"came and got us."

"Someone reported uninvited guests. I went to clear them out, but they weren't as cooperative as I hoped they'd be."

"Sorry," Shelby said. "I shouldn't have been so vocal. I just thought it was ridiculous that the police were there."

"I would have left on my own, if they'd all just left me alone," Freddie said.

Elian and Jules remained silent on this point, making me think they must have been the most obnoxious about the police being involved and didn't want to relive the moment or share the details.

"No one else saw what happened to you?" I said to Freddie.

Cliff answered. "Not that I could determine. It would have been helpful if someone had. It was the bride who reported two men in the back of the room who seemed to be arguing, and who hadn't been invited. She noticed Freddie's eye but she claimed she didn't see a scuffle, either. She just wanted them out of there. If they'd gone quietly, we wouldn't be here now."

"We're all sorry for the ruckus we caused," Jules said, but I didn't think her words were chock-full of sincerity.

"It was bad," Elian offered. "We were way too noisy and should have just gone with Officer Sebastian."

Cliff and I looked at each other, and he said, "Apology accepted, though I'd really like to understand what happened to Freddie."

"Me, too," I said.

The four of them looked at each other, but it was impossible to read if they were relaying something, perhaps they'd formed some pact not to tell, but that didn't feel quite right. I didn't have a clue, but I wished I did.

"I think you may all go now," Cliff said. "I'd like for you to stay out of trouble but I think that goes without saying."

All eight of their eyes, including Freddie's black one, brightened.

"No bail?" Shelby asked. "No fine, whatsoever?"

"Not this time, but if there is a next time, it will be double," Cliff said.

"Thank you and we're truly sorry," Elian said.

Cliff and I stood back as each of them stood and then exited the jail.

I watched them leave and it seemed that they separated into two groups: Elian, Jules, and Shelby in one group and only Freddie in the other. More had gone on than any of them would fess up to, I was sure.

"What the heck happened?" I said to Cliff when the door was closed.

"I have no real idea. Clearly not what they said happened." Cliff moved one of the chairs around his desk and closer to his chair. "Come sit a minute if you have time."

"Were they really obnoxious when you tried to get them out of there?" I said as I moved to the chair.

"Yes. Lucky me."

"I apologize for them," I said. "I will have to let Gram know. She won't be happy, but she won't kill them or anything. This time."

Cliff smiled. "Good to know. And you don't need to apologize for them. They're adults. They're responsible for themselves." He lifted a cup from his desk. "Can I get you some coffee?"

"No, I should let you work. Jim wouldn't like officers' girlfriends hanging around."

"Just like old times when I worked at the museum. Remember when old Mr. Hafferty caught us making out in the back room."

"He was so mad." I smiled at the totally alive man who was smiling at me.

"I wanted to talk to you anyway. Evan stopped by."

"Fire Marshal Evan?"

"One and the same."

"He showed Jim and me some compelling evidence about the old bakery fire. He said you and he were discussing it the other day."

"Yes, we were."

There was no question to Cliff's voice. He didn't wonder why in the world I would be talking to Evan, to anyone, about an ancient fire. The surge of adrenaline I felt was the result of what had become my new normal of not telling him about the ghosts in Broken Rope. He didn't care or mind that I was curious about the fire, and I didn't need to explain anything to him, including those things I was purposefully leaving out. It wasn't easy having so many secrets.

"He's looking at it more closely as you know. He

wondered if we'd pay for an expert or two to take a look. I'm curious. I'm done here in a few minutes and thought I'd drive by the building tonight. I won't go in, too dangerous, but there's something I want to look at from the outside, make sure I have the locations in my head right. You want to go with me? Jake will be jealous we didn't invite him for the brief walk down history lane, but he'll get over it."

A wave of unease rocked me. I didn't want to go back to the bakery. I'd told people, both alive and dead, that I wouldn't. But we wouldn't consider going inside the building, and just looking at it couldn't possibly be dangerous. Besides, I'd be with Cliff.

"I'd love to," I said, squelching my earlier instinct.

"Great. Give me a few minutes to type up a note to Jim. Officer Jenkins will be here shortly.

Officer Jenkins was the newest officer in the Broken Rope police department. His arrival effectively bumped Cliff out of the rank of "newbie," which had been cause for celebration. Jenkins was big, young, and serious, and Cliff really liked him.

As Cliff typed on his keyboard, I glanced at the wall of handcuffs. Jim and previous police chiefs had collected handcuffs over the years and hung them on one of the front walls. The jail, the office of the official police, wasn't a tourist stop, but sometimes visitors stopped by anyway and asked to photograph the wall of cuffs they'd heard about. Most of the time Jim welcomed them in, but sometimes he didn't.

The wall was also what I considered my first contact with Jerome. I'd been in the jail when a pair of cuffs, without explanation, fell off the wall and to the ground. Shortly after

I left the building that night I thought I saw a cowboy down by the old Jasper Theater.

I glanced back at Cliff, again the man who was currently very alive, and pretty darn wonderful in his own right. He didn't have an odd and unfashionable mustache. His clothing had no tears and they weren't dusty. His hair was police officer short and he liked and kept it that way.

It had never occurred to me that I could have such strong feelings for two men at one time. For analysis purposes, I took out of the equation that Jerome was dead and thought about what I would do if I was truly faced with a choice.

And dammit, I had no idea.

"Ms. Winston," Officer Jenkins said after he came through the front door. "How are you this evening?"

"I'm good, Jenkins," I said. *Jenkins* was what he wanted to be called. "How are you?"

"I'm excellent, thank you."

Moments later, after Cliff finished the work on the computer and had changed out of his uniform into jeans and a casual collared shirt, we were out the door. The wedding reception had quieted substantially and the boardwalk was no longer vibrating.

"Should we take the Nova?" I said, the only other option being Cliff's police cruiser, which was his to drive even on personal errands.

"Sure. If the neighbors see my car, they might wonder."

I drove us out to the old building and pulled into the familiar slot.

"Good choice," Cliff said about my parking decision.

As we got out of the car, Cliff looked up at the building. "Look at this place. If I believed in ghosts, I'd say there must certainly be some inside there."

"Uh-huh," I said.

"Boy, would he be in for a big surprise," a voice from behind me said. The wood smoke smell gave him away.

I turned and acknowledged Jerome, but then I turned back to Cliff.

"It hasn't changed much since we were younger, except for some more broken glass and broken-out windows. I'm pretty sure the fire started down in the jutted wing part of the building. That's where I want to look, compare what I saw in the pictures. You want to come with me? If so, be careful of all the glass," Cliff said.

"Isabelle, you shouldn't be here. I told you that this is a dangerous place for you. Please be aware," Jerome said.

"Go ahead, Cliff," I said. "I might join you but I want to soak in the atmosphere a little first."

Cliff hesitated. I wasn't usually much for soaking in atmosphere. "Okay. Be careful."

"You, too."

I watched him walk down the outer edge of the property, right next to the street, where there wasn't much glass. When he turned in toward the building and into some tall weeds, I spoke while keeping my lips from moving too much.

"I'm not going inside, Jerome. I'll be fine."

"I don't know."

"What about Cliff. Is he in danger, too?"

"No, I really don't think so."

"Then why am I?"

"Because you can see ghosts."

"Oh, well, that explains everything. I'm not going inside. Cliff just wants to look at the outside of one of the walls."

Jerome made a grumbling noise, but I stepped away from him and took the same path Cliff had just walked.

"I think you'll be okay if you stay outside, but I'm just not sure," Jerome said as he appeared next to me. "Please, be careful."

"I will. I promise," I said. We moved in tandem, the only sounds being my footfalls. "Hey, I'm sorry for the library. I was probably way too forward. I was never good at shy and retiring. I'm sure I chased off a few guys in my time." I looked toward Cliff, who was standing at the bottom of the wing's wall and looking up at something close to the top of the building. I hadn't been as blunt when I was in high school, but I didn't think I would have chased Cliff away even if I had been.

"You didn't scare me away," Jerome said. "I just don't quite know how to respond to it all."

I started to speak.

"NO!" he said, but then he continued more gently. "No, don't ask me to tell you what I 'feel.' That's not a wise thing for anyone involved. I'm not supposed to feel anyway. Give me some time to figure out how in tarnation I'm supposed to behave and I'll talk to you more. But, Isabelle Winston, that's a good fella there. He's one that you shouldn't let go of no matter what."

I knew that. I'd already made that mistake once. I wasn't going to make it again. I truly wasn't using Cliff as a stopgap between visits from Jerome. I hadn't known I'd see Jerome so soon. I certainly hadn't expected the giant emotions that would overtake me when I did see him.

I looked at him and suddenly wondered if his visit, simply because it was such a surprise, not because he was a ghost I thought I was attracted to, had rattled those emotions so much that I'd become overwhelmed and might have misinterpreted them. Our good-bye last time had been dramatic, and I'd infused it with so many layers of "romance" that I very easily could have built it all into something it really wasn't. Maybe. I couldn't be completely sure, but it was as if a dim beam of light had suddenly been illuminated. The guilt I felt became bigger, but at the same time I wondered if the feelings I had for Jerome suddenly became smaller. Maybe I'd overreacted *to him*, but even though the guilt I felt was real and deep, I wanted to comfort myself with the fact that the overreaction might have been involuntary. Who can see this sort of thing—a crush on a ghost—coming? There aren't ways to prepare.

Still, I couldn't let myself off the hook that easily. I needed to shape up.

"Betts, come here," Cliff said. "It looks like Evan was right and I'm beginning to think we really should call in an expert before we tear it down."

I high-stepped my way through weeds and glass to join Cliff who had pulled out a flashlight I didn't know he had. He aimed the light up.

"Look there."

The darkness was similar to the other two times I'd recently visited the bakery building, almost complete except for some milky streetlamp spray. I looked up to where the flashlight was aimed.

"I just see the building," I said.

"Of course," Cliff said. "But according to some pictures

that Evan showed me of the original bakery, this is the spot they rebuilt."

"Okay."

"Our files show that this isn't where the ovens were located. I wanted to see if I had the correct spots in my head based on both sets of pictures."

I thought about my time inside the bakery of the mid-twentieth century. Cliff was correct. This wasn't where the ovens were.

"Huh. I guess they didn't know how to look at that kind of stuff back then," I said. "You know, studying how or exactly where a fire started."

"I don't know if they didn't know or if they didn't care," Cliff said. "There seems to be some controversy around the fire. Well, now at least."

"Really?"

"The police didn't investigate for very long or all that deeply. It became an accepted theory that the fire started as the result of a bad oven. Two people were killed, but Evan says even that needs to be explored further. I'm ready to agree with him."

"I don't understand." I thought I knew what he was getting at, but I wanted to learn as much information as I could.

"Evan thinks the pictures show evidence of more bodies. I might have found a note from an old police file that said the same thing, but I'm not sure how to present it to the world yet."

"A note?"

"It's still unclear, but it might be something."

"What does it say?"

"Nothing really, just . . . I don't know."

Evidently, he didn't want to tell anyone, me included, what the note said. As a civilian, it was none of my business anyway, but I was still curious. I continued down a different path. "Did anyone go missing at the time?"

Cliff looked at me. "That's a great question, Betts. Very investigative. It's something I'm looking into."

"You might ask Jake."

"He might have something on missing persons?"

"Sure." No. As a rule he wouldn't, but I thought I might somehow manipulate things so that Cliff eventually realized the Cylas family was the missing group. I could get Jake to come up with a "clue."

"Good thinking, Isabelle," Jerome said.

A sound that resembled the distant crack and rumble of a storm cut through the darkness.

"What was that?" I said.

"I . . ." Cliff began.

But he was interrupted by a train engine–like whoosh and then something falling from the sky. It was something big, and if I'd had my wits about me, I would have known that the object didn't come from the sky exactly. It came from the side of the building. A window, frame and all, was falling speedily toward us.

Cliff and I were standing amid weeds and uneven ground. The window came from about a hundred feet above, and even if we'd had smooth ground and no weeds, it would have been difficult to get out of the way.

A second later I heard, "Betts!" and "Isabelle!" Another second later, out of the corner of each of my eyes, I saw men leap toward me, Cliff from one side and Jerome from the other.

I instinctively crouched. And closed my eyes.

The noise was awful: too loud and ferocious. I felt the impact of the blow, but not as much as I would have if Cliff weren't on top of me. His lungs made some sort of air-release sound that I managed to hear through everything else, and I immediately wondered if he'd been killed.

"No!" I either thought or perhaps said aloud, I couldn't be sure.

When I opened my eyes and focused on not being panicked, I saw Jerome's grungy boot-clad feet right next to my knees. After the window finished its dive, the boots stepped back a bit and then I felt Cliff lift off my back.

"You're both okay, Isabelle," Jerome said.

Tears sprung to my eyes with his words, but I pulled myself up and offered him a quick nod of thanks before I turned to Cliff just to make sure. I knew what had happened; Jerome had saved us both. If it hadn't been so dark, he wouldn't have been so "solid" and somehow, some way, his state of being had saved not only me but Cliff, too.

"You okay?" I said as Cliff held his hand up to his head.

"You okay?" he said, too.

"I'm fine. What's wrong?" I reached for his arms.

"I'm glad you're okay. I'm really fine, too, just a little dizzy. I'm amazed we're not busted up into a million pieces. If you're sure you're okay, I'll be just fine." Cliff took his hand from his head and looked at me. I could see he was having trouble focusing and his speech bordered on slurring.

"You must have gotten hit in the head. We need to get you looked at right away."

"I'm fine, Betts, really. I barely felt the blow. I have no

idea what happened, but that should have either killed us both or at least hurt us pretty badly. I barely felt it."

"You need to get out of here, Isabelle," Jerome said as he peered up at the empty space where the window had once been. I didn't see anything but the hole, but I guessed he did. I'd have to ask him later.

"Cliff, I'm going to get the car. Stay here." I looked at Jerome.

He nodded. "I'll watch out for him, for you, too, but hurry your hide, sweetheart."

I high-stepped my way out of the weeds and ran to the car via the road. It was the long way around but it probably took less time. When I got Cliff in the car, he seemed much less dizzy, but I still wanted him to get looked at. I shut the passenger door and looked at Jerome as I made my way to the driver's side. He still stood in the weeds and surveyed the building as though he was looking for whatever item might fall next. He looked my direction.

"Thank you," I mouthed to him.

He tipped his hat and gave me a worried grimace.

Chapter 18

Cliff didn't have a concussion. He'd been knocked a little silly but it was nothing serious. The sleeve of his shirt had been torn and he had a small scratch on his hand and dust in his short hair. My hair was dusty, too, but that was my worst injury.

Broken Rope didn't have a hospital and our closest emergency room was in Springfield. But we did have Dr. Callahan, who had lived in Broken Rope for all of his almost eighty years. During the day, he practiced out of a small office just off the main boardwalk that happened to be about half a block from his house. In the evenings or in the middle of the night if someone needed medical attention, they would knock on Dr. Callahan's door and he'd tell them he'd meet them in his office. It didn't matter how early in the morning or how late at night it was, when he was home

Dr. Callahan wore a red plaid robe over bright blue pajamas. His robe was almost as big a legend as some of our old dead characters.

I'd knocked on his door and he met Cliff and me back at the office. He'd examined us both and proclaimed us healthy but too curious—and maybe a little low on common sense, but that usually righted itself. Or not. He was also adamant that the bakery building couldn't come down soon enough. Though our experience was the most disturbing he'd heard, he was tired of stitching up cuts from silly folks who didn't realize how dangerous broken glass and debris could be.

After the requisite lecture, he suggested a pain reliever, some relaxing tea, and a good night's sleep for both of us.

Now, as we sat at my small kitchen table and drank the tea and ate some shortbread cookies, Cliff was still struck by the positive outcome of the evening's events.

"I don't understand, Betts. It must have hit just right, but I feel no pain in my back at all. How is that possible?"

"We got lucky."

"I guess, but I will wonder about it forever. I felt the pressure of the hit, but it was as if something was in between me and the impact. It's unbelievable."

I came *this* close to telling Cliff about Jerome, about all the ghosts. When I'd told Jake, he had believed me fairly easily. Cliff wouldn't want to doubt anything I said, but the ghosts would be a bigger pill for him to swallow. Jake was more into the possibilities of the ethereal world than Cliff's straightforward, realistic, and logical outlook allowed.

I expected Jerome to show up and suggest I tell Cliff. It would be easier on all of us if Cliff knew, and if he believed me, of course. I didn't have the heart to rock his world so soon after the incident at the bakery. It had been rocked enough. Maybe someday, but not today.

As I put the cup of tea up to my mouth a glow appeared out the back kitchen window. It wasn't Jerome but Gent who'd found his way to my house. He stepped up on the small back porch, peered in the window, waved, and then popped into the kitchen.

"Betts, I'm so sorry. I tried to stop him, but he was stronger than I was. It was just like that night, the night we were killed. He was so much stronger. I couldn't stop him."

The cup was still at my mouth but I hadn't taken a drink yet. I looked at Cliff and then back at Gent. This was going to be interesting. I faked a cough and threw in the word *who* with it.

"What's that?" Cliff asked.

I shook my head at him, pretended to clear my throat again and looked as pointedly as I could at Gent. Cliff turned to see what I was looking at but gave up when I cleared my throat one more time.

"The killer, of course," Gent said.

I sighed and looked away from Gent. "Name. Names are good."

"Whose name?" Cliff asked.

"Oh. No, I said 'same.' All the *same*, we're okay and that's all that matters."

"Sure," Cliff said doubtfully. He was probably wondering which of us wasn't tracking the conversation, but since he was the one who was hit in the head, maybe he wouldn't push it.

"I don't know his name," Gent said. "A big man. I couldn't see him clearly. Yet."

Of course not.

"Come on, Cliff. Let's get you to bed. Dr. Callahan said we needed rest, you especially."

It wasn't easy. Cliff wasn't much for being taken care of and my attempt to "tuck" him in was met with furrowed eyebrows and grumbles of "I'm fine." Nevertheless, once he was safely under the covers and I told him I'd be back once I got the kitchen cleaned up—and, no, I didn't need his help, but thanks—he fell asleep quickly, cheek on his folded hands.

Gent had waited in the kitchen. He was in his country boy/farm boy clothes and I caught him peering at the toaster.

"Gent," I said quietly.

He jumped slightly as he straightened. "Are you and your fella all right?" he asked.

"We're fine, Gent, but tell me what happened."

"I could see you outside the window, you and those other two, you were all just looking up. I yelled that you should get back."

"We didn't hear you." I didn't think Jerome had heard him, either, which raised more how-does-this-ghost-stuff-work questions in my mind, but now wasn't the time for that math problem.

"I thought you must not have. The big man was angry that you were watching him, but I think he could only see you, not your fella or the other one."

More questions.

"I didn't see him," I said.

"I know. You'd'a moved back if you did. He was angry, so angry that he pushed the window down on you. The big man wondered why you didn't get hurt. He was so angry."

"You need to sit down, Gent?" I asked.

"No, no, I need to get back to my family, just in case." He looked at me with brightly panicked eyes. He was scared. "I don't know what's going on. Can we die again?"

"No, Gent, I'm pretty sure that only happens once."

"Then why is he here? Is it for you?"

"I don't know."

"Will you come see who he is? Maybe you and Miz can get rid of him."

"Let me talk to her and we'll see."

What was I supposed to do with a scared teenage ghost? I didn't know how to calm his fears, because I didn't know if they were valid or not. I was certain he couldn't die again, but I didn't understand why he could feel fear. Ghosts weren't supposed to have feelings.

But that, it seemed, might have already been disproven today.

Gent nodded. "Okay, okay, good. I'll come to talk to you and Miz tomorrow."

I wished there was more I could do for him, but I wasn't going back to the bakery. Maybe ever.

In fact, I *sensed* so much more than I would ever tell Gent. It wasn't difficult to connect the dots. Jerome had told me to be careful. I'd had a window hurled down at me. I was a threat to the "big man" ghost. I didn't know specifically why I was a threat, but it must have had something to do with the nature of my ability to communicate with the ghosts. Gram might not be as much of a threat. We'd already witnessed how the encounters with the dead had become something more, somehow elevated, and, frankly, something that we might need to be concerned about as my awareness of my ability grew. They just weren't as "formed" when Gram was the only one they could talk to. There was still a lot we didn't understand and there probably always would be. But, I had no doubt that I was at least being perceived as a threat. My advantage was pretty clear though. I just needed to stay away from the old building. I could do that.

"Gent, I found some Marys. Do you remember Mary Loken, Gleave, or Silk?" I asked.

"No. Yes. Well, I think I do!"

I literally crossed my fingers behind my back. "Which Marys?"

"Silk. Oh, I remember. She was there. Mary Silk was the reason we went to the bakery that night."

I almost cheered in joy, but I remained calm. "Why was she there?"

"I . . . I . . . Oh, Betts, I don't remember it all, but she was there. She was . . . Oh! She was a teacher. Yes, she was a teacher. Mary Silk." His fear had turned into excitement, and now it transformed to disappointment. "But she's surely dead by now."

"Actually, no, she isn't. She's old, but not dead."

And his excitement changed to pure joy. He whooped and slapped his leg. The slap was silent and reminded me of our last ghostly visitor, Sally Swarthmore. I smiled.

"Let's go talk to her right this second," he said. "I mean, you'll talk and I'll see if I can remember anything."

"It's late."

Gent looked around as if he needed proof that it was, indeed, late. He noticed it was dark outside.

"Tomorrow, then?" he said.

"I will talk to her, I promise, but I need to do it the right way. I might need to make an appointment. She's old and living in a care facility; we don't know much else."

Gent nodded. I could tell he wanted to argue but was too polite to do so.

"Thank you, Betts Winston. Will you come back to the bakery and see me?"

"After tonight, I think you'd better try to check in with me and Gram. I think I'm a little spooked." There wasn't enough money or chocolate in the world to convince me to go back to that place.

"I understand. I'll see you tomorrow. Good-bye, Betts Winston."

"Gent—wait, where are you shoes?" I said.

Gent shrugged. "I've wondered that, too. I just don't know."

I nodded. "Good-bye, Gent Cylas."

He waved and disappeared.

I relished the silence for a moment as I sat down in the chair and drank some more tea. I didn't want to think about what might have happened at the bakery, but frightening pictures flashed in my mind, nonetheless. It had all worked out okay, but that was because Jerome had been there. Both Cliff and I might have been killed otherwise.

"Damn," I muttered to myself. "I have a guardian ghost."

The thought wasn't as comforting as I would have liked. I shivered, took one more sip of tea, and then joined Cliff in bed.

Chapter 19

I did not tell Gram about the events at the bakery. Since I'd returned Sarabeth's keys promptly at 7:00, I got to the school a few minutes later than Gram expected me to. We still had some time without the students, but I didn't want to ruin her morning with all the previous evening's stories.

Freddie's black eye caused her to demand the details of *that* story. Once she heard said details, her mood soured and I decided I might not ever mention the window falling out of the building.

It turned out that the morning didn't start off great for anyone.

Except Brenda Plumb. She seemed to enjoy every second of the drama. She took notes, but surreptitiously enough that I thought I might be the only one to notice. Brenda's notes were the least of Gram's concerns.

Brenda claimed that she hadn't gone to the wedding reception, but had spent the evening watching television in the room she'd rented. Brenda had no idea why Freddie thought he'd seen her in the party.

Gram was dressed in a Missouri S & T T-shirt, the serious miner holding a pickax mascot only adding to Gram's stern attitude and lecture.

"Folks, we lost a student to a terrible tragedy: murder. I've already told you all that I'm a big believer in innocent until proven guilty, but the behavior exhibited last night doesn't give me the faith I need to have in all of you. I'm looking for higher standards here, particularly now and particularly *because* of the murder. You all need to make a decision right here and right now: shape up, show respect for each other, show respect for this school, this town, and show respect for the memory of one of your former peers, or take your leave. I know we might not have known him well, but these actions in the wake of what happened to Roger are even more appalling. Shape up or ship out, and I mean it. I can't have this. You need to understand that before you even arrive here, Betts and I feel like we know you pretty well. We also know there will be surprises, but wedding crashing and violent brawls aren't the types of surprises that we tolerate."

The students and I were accordingly quiet. The majority of the class hadn't been involved in the fracas, but Gram always made it perfectly clear that we were a team and our individual behavior affected everyone on that team. No one argued, no one protested.

And then, as only Gram could do, when she'd spoken her peace, she switched back into caring teacher mode.

Bread, we were going to continue with bread, but she was adding a twist today. She told me that everyone needed something fun, something to give the horrible week a touch of enjoyment, and even after the adamant speech, she stuck with the plan.

The project of the day would be bread pudding. Cliff had framed and given me his grandmother's handwritten bread pudding recipe, and when I showed it to Gram, she immediately decided that it needed to be shared with our students. Granny Sebastian had died a year earlier and Gram thought teaching the recipe would be a perfect way to keep her memory alive.

As supplies were gathered, though, we discovered that we were out of cinnamon, a key ingredient and one that we inventoried frequently. Its empty space on the shelf was a clear indicator of the turmoil that had distracted us over the last five days.

"I'll run to the store," I offered. We would order some from our suppliers, but they wouldn't be able to deliver until Monday.

"I'll go, too. I'll help," Freddie said.

It was cinnamon, so it wouldn't be a burden to carry from the shelf, to the register, and then to my car. I probably wouldn't even need a cart, but there was something in his voice that made me think he wanted some fresh air.

"Sure, Freddie, that'd be great," I said. Gram and I eyed each other. It was clear that she suspected the same thing but didn't try to stop us.

"I'm so sorry about all this," Freddie said as he sat in the Nova's passenger seat and pointed at his black eye. "I shouldn't have even gone into that party, but I was curious. I was sure I saw Brenda. It won't happen again."

"You said that no one hit you, Freddie, that you ran into something but aren't sure what. What did you run into? Come on, tell me," I said.

"I wish I could tell you." Freddie shook his head slowly. "But I don't know what it was. It was confusing, crowded, you know. I was in the middle of so many people, and then I just got hit."

"Then, it *could* have been by a fist," I said.

"I really don't think so. I think something happened to be flying through the air and it hit me in the eye."

I paused a moment before I said, "I'm having a hard time with that one, Freddie."

"I'm sorry." Freddie sighed.

"Me, too."

The store was unusually busy and it took us much longer than normal to get through the line. We chose the ten-items-or-fewer cashier and it quickly became clear that we would have been better off in another line.

"New cashier, I think," I said quietly to Freddie.

"I think so, too."

The cashier was a young woman who didn't look to be over twenty. We took our place in line just as the checkout perfect storm hit: the register's tape ran out, the store manager wanted to retrieve the large amount of cash out of the new cashier's drawer, and the cashier herself was so worried about making customers angry about the delays that she over-apologized.

I looked at the other now long lines with full carts and each three or four customers deep and decided it was just best to wait it out. As the cashier gushed, "I'm so sorry," her eyes flitted up and down the line, but on one such trip, her eyes stopped right on Freddie. Suddenly, she quieted as her eyebrows came together.

"Uh, do you know her?" I said to Freddie. The cashier's stare was unwavering.

"No, not at all," Freddie said. His face reddened, and he became uncomfortable, which is how I might have reacted, too.

The cashier helped the two people in front of us but continued to glance at Freddie. I began to wonder if she'd never seen a black eye before.

Fortunately, we didn't have to ask what was bothering her. As she took the two large containers of cinnamon from the belt and ran them over the scanner, she pointedly said, "Your picture was just in a magazine, wasn't it?"

"I don't think so." Freddie laughed.

"Really? You look so familiar. I saw a picture of someone who looks a lot like you, then. In that one, I think." She pointed to one of the magazines on the racks above the conveyer belt, one that was light on hard news but heavy on celebrity gossip. "No, wait, it was this magazine, but it was the one from last month. I can't remember the story, exactly, but I think it had something to do with restaurants or something."

I watched Freddie's reaction closely. He smiled sheepishly and looked away from the cashier.

"I really don't think so. You must be mistaking me for someone else."

"Wow, two people on the planet with those eyes," she flirted.

"Thanks." Freddie grabbed the bag of cinnamon that I had paid for during their discussion.

"That magazine?" I pointed.

"Yep," she said. "Last month's issue. His eyes are beautiful."

"Yes, they are. Thank you," I said before I followed the even more mysterious mystery student out to the Nova.

I thought about confronting him or taking him out to the library immediately and forcing him to sweat while I thumbed through the issue in question. I suspected that his picture was, indeed, inside the magazine, and finding it would explain just exactly who he was and what he was up to. Sarabeth kept copies of all the popular magazines for a few months. But I decided to say nothing at all. He wouldn't answer honestly, that much I now knew. I would research it first and then ask him some specific questions.

I got in the Nova and only said, "Phew, that place was busy. Thanks for the company."

"Sure. Anytime."

The temptation to tell Gram I had somewhere else to be and then hurry to the library was huge, but I resisted. Fortunately, everyone was quickly on task, and in no time we had some of the best Granny Sebastian bread puddings I'd ever tasted. I'd watched our students learn and create; I watched them improvise and make the recipe their own. It was as if today was the true first day of school.

Once the students were gone, I was still anxious to check the library's back issues, but it did occur to me that the cashier might just have been flirting with the cute young man with the pretty green eyes. I had to give her credit; it would never occur to me to flirt with someone by telling them I saw them in a magazine.

But my mission was further thwarted by two ghosts who thought it was necessary to be honest with Gram.

Gent and Jerome had both shown up; Gent because he wanted to talk to Gram and me, and Jerome because, apparently, Gent had begged him to come along. Though Jerome didn't say it out loud, I got the impression that he would rather not hang out with Gent Cylas. I didn't ask how they'd finally found each other, but given all the crazy circumstances I wasn't too surprised.

When they arrived, Gent immediately launched into what had happened the night before at the bakery.

"Betts! You and Cliff could have been killed!" Gram said.

"They might not have been killed; maybe hurt a piece," Jerome said as he leaned back against one of the center islands and crossed his arms in front of himself.

"No, no, sir, you saved them," Gent said to Jerome. He turned back to Gram. "This old boy saved them, I'm sure of it."

Jerome adjusted his hat.

"While it's good to see you again so soon, Jerome, I don't like any of this," Gram said. "As far as I know there has never been any threat to me or anyone alive from you ghosts. What's going on?"

For a long moment, we were all silent, but finally Jerome spoke. "Miz, things are different." He didn't want to blame me, but it was easy to figure out where the changes had come from. He avoided looking my direction.

"Different bad?" Gram said as she hoisted herself up to a stool.

"I don't think so," Jerome said as he looked directly at me this time.

I shrugged.

"I think they're just different," Jerome continued. "This

time we're faced with a little more danger but that won't happen all the time. And . . ."

"And what?" Gram said.

"Well, we have a pattern. I think I came back because I sensed danger, and it looks like I was able to do a little to prevent it, too. Maybe I'm balancing out the bad; maybe I'm not the only one who'll be able to do that."

Gram's mouth twisted as she thought. "Betts," she said a moment later, "you keep your hind end away from that bakery building, do you understand?"

"Yes. I'll stay far away."

Gent slumped. "I guess you won't be able to help," he said.

"I'm not going back into that bakery, Gent. Not a chance," I said, much more forthright than I'd been in my kitchen. "But I can still help. I'm going to try to talk to Mary Silk, and believe it or not, you've got a slew of town officials—law enforcement officers, the fire marshal—investigating the fire. They don't know all the details about you, but I'll try to find a way to inform them, to let them know they should be diligent about trying to find out what happened to you and your family."

"How are you going to talk to Mary Silk?" Gram said.

"She's alive," I said. "And Gent says she was the reason—the Mary—that his family went to the bakery for that night."

"Really? She was a teacher, a mean one if I remember correctly," Gram said. "She was strict to the point of not allowing us to fidget even a little in our seats."

"You want to come with me to talk to her?" I said.

Gram looked around the room, at me, at the ghosts, and then shook her head. "No, dear, I don't."

"I'm so sorry, Miz. I know this is all still painful," Gent said.

Gram seemed to pull her spine straighter. "I'm fine, Gent. I just don't think that it's possible to find you and your family's bodies. I've tried, too many times to count. I can't put my energy into that any longer, but it's not because it's as hurtful to me as it used to be. Been there, done that, that's all. It's fine if Betts wants to give it a shot, just as long as she stays the hell away from that building. Got it?" She turned to me as she said the last two words.

"Yes, ma'am."

"Good. Now, everyone needs to go away. I have some paperwork to do in the back and I don't want to have you all distracting me. Understand?"

"Want me to stay?" I said, hoping she'd say no.

"No, thanks, I'm good. Go. See you tomorrow."

Chapter 20

Gent disappeared quickly, though he told me that he'd find me later to ask what more I'd discovered about Mary Silk.

What I hadn't mentioned in front of him was that I'd already scheduled the appointment and had left a message for Jake to join me. The ghost of Sally Swarthmore had taught me that if I made plans that were somehow about the ghosts, it was best to keep them to myself. She had pestering down pat.

Jerome walked with me out of the school and to my Nova. The awkward discussion about feelings and my further doubts about their validity had been eclipsed by the fear we'd experienced from the falling window. Somehow this allowed the air between us to normalize and settle back to something comfortable, something similar to how it had been when we'd first become acquainted. There would be further awkward conversations ahead, but for the time being I enjoyed the ease.

"I don't know much about your students, yet, Isabelle. I'll keep looking. But you really will stay away from the bakery?" Jerome asked as we approached the Nova.

"Yes. I don't know why everyone keeps emphasizing that. The window falling was more than enough to keep even someone with—as Gram would say—'a few bolts loose' away from that place."

"We just want to make sure."

I nodded. "I'm going to visit Mary Silk this evening. I've asked Jake to come along. Want to come, too?" I didn't regret offering the invitation, but I was struck by the somewhat freakish nature of inviting a ghost to come along on our evening outing, like he was just another guy.

"Uh, sure." He seemed flustered by the invitation, probably sensing the same thing. "But I don't really know anything about Gent Cylas other than the little I've learned in the last few days, dead or when he was alive. He was after my time, and I don't remember meeting him when I visited Miz. I'm not sure I will be useful."

I shrugged, trying to be casual. "You don't need to be useful. Thought it might give you something to do."

"All right, then. I accept your invitation."

"Okay. Good. Be outside Jake's office in a couple hours."

"Isabelle . . ." he began.

"What?" I said as I put my hand on the car door handle.

For a moment Jerome struggled with what to say. The sunlight was so bright that he was almost transparent, but I could still see him searching for the words. The normal air between us started to waver again. I took my hand off the handle and stood straight. I didn't want the normal air to go away, but I would listen to what he had to say.

Finally, he just said, "Isabelle, be careful. I'll see you this evening."

And then he was gone, and I could finally make my way back to the library. But my phone buzzed, halting my progress again.

"Jake?"

"Got your message. Yes, I'd love to go with you this evening."

"Good. I hoped so. I'm running to the library right now to take a look at a past issue of a magazine. Can I call you back and we can make arrangements when I'm done?"

"Which magazine?" I heard his fingers start to work his keyboard.

I told him the pertinent information and he responded a couple seconds later. "I can pull it up here. No need to go to the library."

"Really? Great, I'm on my way."

Jake was in civilian clothes; this, more than even the students returning, always heralded the end of the summer. I didn't have time to dwell on it, but for a moment I missed his sheriff's getup.

"Come in, come in. I have refreshments. I ran down to the saloon after your call," he said as he pointed to two smoothies sitting on the center table.

"Yum. Thanks."

"You're welcome," he said as he handed me a smoothie while slipping an extra-long straw into the lid's slot. "So, magazine or what I've found out about Mary Silk first?"

I took a long sip. The news about Mary Silk sounded interesting, but I said, "Magazine."

I relayed the grocery store clerk's behavior and words, which made him as curious as I knew it would. He showed me he'd pulled up the issue of the magazine and then directed me to sit in his desk chair. He dragged a stool up to a spot where he could glance over my shoulder.

"This guy's been strange from the beginning, hasn't he? Maine, my foot. I just know he's from somewhere else," Jake said.

"Maybe. He's strange, but likeable, too. The clerk might have just been flirting with him. He's a cute guy, but I thought it warranted at least a quick look, especially if it's this easy." I clicked a right-pointing arrow on the screen, which turned the full-color page. "Is it legal to have this?"

"Sure, this is the magazine's site. They put up past issues right when their new issue hits the stands. We really have to get you much more Internet savvy. Everyone knows how to do this sort of thing. You're kind of getting a little embarrassing."

I ignored the comment, but then I literally gasped as I turned to page thirty-seven.

"Jake! That's him! That's Freddie." I pointed. "Or, I think it is."

Freddie, or allegedly Freddie, stood behind two people, each of which seemed to be blessed with the same wonderful dark hair and his bright green eyes.

Jake scooted closer and read the headline above the story.

" 'Successful Local Business Owner Killed After Catching Culprit Poisoning Bakery's Magic Ingredient.' "

"Yikes," I said, but then I continued to read the article.

Local family-owned and -operated bakery, Mario's Sourdough, has closed their doors, and the surviving family members say they will never open them again.

Even if their decades-old sourdough starter hadn't been contaminated, the murder of Gepetti patriarch, Mario Gepetti Jr., would have caused the family to discontinue their successful business.

On the morning of January 15, Mr. Gepetti Jr. arrived at his store at the normal time of 3:30 A.M. to begin baking the sourdough bread that has become famous throughout all of San Francisco as well as much of northern California. Investigators say that Mr. Gepetti must have come upon the culprit, who from all indications had already poisoned the starter, effectively 'killing' it. When a confrontation occurred, Mr. Gepetti was stabbed with a knife from the bakery's supply. Mr. Gepetti died instantly; his body was found by his son, Mario Gepetti III.

I turned to Jake. "Freddie is Mario III," I said.

"Looks that way. Keep reading."

The victim's father, Mr. Gepetti Sr., came to America from Italy in 1908. He was the classic definition of an American success. He arrived in this country with only three dollars and fifty-four cents in his pocket. He worked whatever menial jobs he could find until he managed to save enough money to open a bakery in New York City. Gepetti Jr. married a woman from San Francisco who convinced him to move back to the West Coast shortly after the nuptials. Gepetti Sr. had created the sourdough starter that Gepetti Jr. carefully transported across the country and had used as the spark for what is estimated to be hundreds of thousands of loaves of sourdough bread enjoyed by Mario's Sourdough customers, including several local restaurants.

The article continued to discuss the specifics about how a sourdough starter was made and how its future taste was a mystery, often a surprise, and could usually never be duplicated no matter what precise and similar steps were taken. It was close to a repeat of what Gram had said in class the day the students made their starters.

However, it was the end of the article that caused me to gasp and fumble for my cell phone.

It is believed that the poison used to contaminate the starter was from a plant that thrives in meadows across the western United States. Death camas is a bulb plant containing toxic alkaloids. Eating any part of the plant or bulb will cause drooling or frothing at the mouth, vomiting, extreme weakness, an irregular pulse, and confusion and dizziness. In cases of severe poisoning, the final symptoms include seizures, coma, and death.

It is unclear as to whether the killer intended to ruin the starter or poison it so that it might poison those ingesting the end result: loaves of bread. However, the Gepetti family states that poisoning the starter would have caused the starter to be unusable, therefore, if anyone would have attempted to make bread with it, they would have been unsuccessful.

"Holy . . ." I said as I dialed Morris, who surprisingly answered on the first ring.

"Dunsany."

"Morris, was it . . . death camas that killed Roger?" I said.

"Betts?"

"Yes."

"In fact, it was. I've heard of it killing lots of livestock in the West in the springtime. I'm researching it now. How did you know?"

"Come to Jake's archives right now if you can."

"All right. I'm on my way."

I called Cliff and told him to hurry over, too. And then I told Jake I needed the Tied and Branded's number. He scooted to the computer, typed for a second, and then pointed at the number on the screen. I punched it into my phone.

"Yes, could you connect me to Mario Gepetti," I said.

"One moment, please," the receptionist said before the phone rang.

I hung up before the first ring finished. I'd just wanted confirmation that he was there.

A few moments later, Cliff, Morris, Jake, and I were gathered in the archive room. I told them about the grocery store, showed them the magazine article, pointed out the method of poisoning, and reiterated every interaction I'd had with Freddie/Mario since the first moment he'd peeked his head through the school's front swinging door.

Cliff called Jim, who said he'd track down Mario and bring him in for questioning.

"So, do you really think Mario killed Roger?" Jake said.

"Do you think Roger killed Mario Jr., our Mario's father? There has to be some strange connection. Mario III came here as someone else. You"—he looked at me—"and Miz thought he faked his acceptance. He must have done exactly that. How in the world did he manage it?"

"We need to know more about Roger Riggins," I said. "He was from New Mexico, but that's all I remember from the file and my quick Internet search."

"He was married. We contacted his wife regarding his murder. She wanted to come out here, but we asked her not to until we knew more," Cliff said.

I said, "Hang on—when we were making the sourdough starter, I'm almost sure Roger was the one to bring up the story about the business being ruined because their starter was ruined." I thought back to the moment in the kitchen. "Freddie, I mean Mario, knocked over a bowl of flour right when Roger started the story. I sure can't imagine Roger was a killer, but I barely knew him. Maybe, Mario followed him here to kill him, but he knocked over the flour so no one would know the details of the story and connect the two of them together. I don't know. There's something missing."

"How did Roger behave toward Mario? If Roger had killed Mario's father, he would have probably been surprised—no, downright horrified—to see him in the class," Jake said.

"Roger was fine. Normal, from what I could tell, friendly. He was very math-teacher-like, but that's the only impression I got from the short time I knew him."

"We need to talk to all of the students, not just Mario. Look, I need to help Jim. Anything else you think I should know right now?" Cliff said.

"Go. I'll call you if I think of anything."

Cliff, undeterred by the audience, moved around the table, bent over, and kissed me. He lingered there for a little longer than was appropriate, and Jake cleared his throat. During the unprofessional and completely surprising maneuver, my whirring mind calmed to one thought only, and that thought was all about Cliff. No ghosts. Just Cliff.

"You stay out of trouble. Got it?" he said.

"Yes, sir."

"Jake?" Cliff said.

"I hear you. I'll be with her constantly. Lucky girl."

"Thank you, Jake," Cliff said on his way out the door.

Morris hadn't been bothered by the affectionate display, but he didn't see any reason to stick around any longer, either. He'd been researching death camas, trying to learn as much as possible about it when I'd called him, and he decided to go back to that research.

When he was gone, I said to Jake, "Gram will not be pleased with the new developments. She'll be really ticked that we fell for Mario's act."

"She'll be fine. Your grandmother has seen much worse than this."

"I suppose. I sure hope the year improves." I thought about calling her to give her an update but decided not to. She was keeping busy; that was probably the best thing for her. I switched gears. "What did you find out about Mary Silk?"

Jake reached to the folder on the middle of the table. "It's interesting. And you're going to be impressed by how I found it. It wasn't easy. In fact, it was damn hard and just by chance that I dug up anything at all."

The buildup was certainly impressive.

"Okay, okay, I know. Get to the point," Jake said.

I nodded.

"I would never have even thought about looking for someone named Mary Silk in the place that I found her but this research has taught me something very valuable. I need to keep a better record of those mentioned as surviving loved ones in obituaries."

"Like so-and-so was survived by so-and-so, and it usually mentions their relationship."

"Yes. Usually. Anyway, I'm connecting dots I only think are there, but it's the best guess I can offer." Jake handed me a copy of an obituary. I'd read a number of obituaries in the archive room and had become accustomed to the sometimes old-fashioned language or the smudged print. This one was clear, though, as if he'd retyped it on his computer and then printed it out. I looked at him with raised eyebrows.

"Believe it or not it's a genealogy program I recently purchased. You scan the obit and it creates that." He pointed. "Read aloud."

It is with a heavy, heavy heart that we print the remembrance of Mr. William Kennington today. Mr. Kennington along with his business partner, Howard Knapp, were killed in the tragic Kennington Bakery fire, killed horribly and surely painfully inside the walls of the business the two men created.

I paused and looked at Jake. "This is dramatic."

"Yes, things weren't so formulaic back then, at least they weren't for those at the *Noose*. Go on."

Though details are still scarce as to the official cause of the fire, we know for certain that the loss of Mr. Kennington and Mr. Knapp will leave a deep hole in the heart of our community. It must be added that Mr. Kennington's legacy is the distinct values of honor and integrity.

He will be remembered by all, but most especially his family and loved ones. His loving wife, Maude, and his daughter, Lila, will always hold him in their hearts. But his kindness extended beyond his family and beyond his employees. This reporter knows that Mr. Kennington also held a special place in the heart of local high school teacher Mary Silk, and it would be remiss not to mention her loss here.

Rest in peace, William Kennington, good man, good heart.

I put the piece of paper on the table and sighed heavily. "I have to say, Jake, that was bothersome to read, creepy."

"I know, but not so much back then, I guess. I find obituaries like that here and there."

"I still don't understand the connection to Mary Silk. If I were Maude Kennington, I would have thought that my husband was having an affair with Mary. I'd be pretty ticked."

"That's one interpretation." Jake nodded. "And that might be what was happening, but we can't be sure until we talk to Mary ourselves."

"Special place in her heart. What in the world does that mean? Wait, who wrote this?" Not that we could have conjured him or her up to help us out, but I'd recently met the ghost of a long-dead reporter. This didn't sound like his writing style, but I was curious.

"There was no attribution," Jake said. "It was an obituary so there might have been a reporter, or a cub reporter, or a secretary assigned specifically to obituaries. Or someone just might have answered the phone or taken the obituary order in person. Not possible to really know."

"I'd love more info."

"We'll ask Mary if she remembers. And?"

"And, great job, Jake." I smiled.

"Aw, shucks, 'twas nothing. Now, ask me about what I found out regarding the camera."

"Oh! What did you find out about the camera?"

"Just that my camera might be the biggest mystery of all. The owner of the shop had never seen anything like it. As I explained to you, it wasn't supposed to record any sort of activity with those lines."

"But it did."

"Yes, it did. The only conclusion we could come to is that it really worked."

"I don't get it."

"Well, there's an element of woo-woo and phony-bologna with ghost hunting, right?"

"Right."

"Maybe there really were ghosts in the area, and the camera behaved as it truly was supposed to behave—for the first time that this guy had ever heard of."

"That's spooky. Kind of."

Jake shrugged. "Dunno. I think it's kind of . . . awesome. Next time there's a ghost in the vicinity, I want to test it. Just let me know."

"You'll get to test it soon. Jerome wants to come with us to talk to Mary Silk."

"That just might be the best news I've heard in the last hour." Jake gathered his camera equipment off a shelf. "Summon him. Let's go find him. Whatever."

I didn't bother to tell Jake it didn't work that way. He knew better.

Instead, I led the way out to the Nova, and suspected that Jerome would show up momentarily.

Fortunately, he did.

Chapter 21

Only a few minutes later I was steering the Nova down the two-lane highway with Jake in the passenger seat next to me and Jerome in the back. I'd been right; Jerome had appeared downtown shortly after we left the archive room.

"I have to trust that you are here, Jerome, that you aren't some strange figment of Betts's imagination, and now I won't be able to record your presence. I didn't even think about charging the battery in this thing. It's as dead as you, Jerome," Jake said as he held up the camera. "This darn camera has proved to be more annoying than helpful."

"I don't understand," Jerome said.

"He can't be sure that you're really here, Jerome," I said to the backseat. "Jake, you saw Sally; you know the ghosts exist."

"He saw Sally?" Jerome said.

"He did. She appeared briefly for him."

"Hmmm."

"What? Isn't that okay?" I said.

"I don't know if it's 'okay' or not. I'm surprised. It's a tricky maneuver and it takes a lot out of us."

"It was brief, and Sally managed to stay around for a few more weeks afterward."

"I see. Tell Jake he'll have to take it on faith that I'm here. I won't appear for him. Sorry about that."

"Take it on faith, Jake," I said.

"I can do that. I hope Betts has been behaving herself. You do know she's missed you."

"Jake," I said. "Come on."

Jerome chuckled. I turned and looked at him briefly. He tipped his hat. "Would you please tell your friend that you behave just fine."

"Jerome says I behave fine."

"I was worried he'd think that." Jake sighed.

Benedict House, originally a school for the blind, spread wide in a low valley in the Missouri countryside. It was a three-story building with lots of big windows and a huge bell tower rising from the middle section where, at the bottom, big front doors opened into what used to be a cafeteria. Now those doors led to a recreation room, where a combination of noises greeted us and reminded me briefly more of a school than a place where old people now lived. A television blared from one corner. Four people, two men and two women, were involved in a lively game of Ping-Pong. Two other tables were being used for card games, the participants diverse except that every one of them had gray hair or no hair.

"May I help you?" A small walled reception area was tucked to our right. A round-faced redhead with a nurse's cap spoke through a window hole.

"We're here to see Ms. Mary Silk. Jake Swanson and Betts Winston," Jake said.

The redhead gave us the once-over before she looked at something on the podium in front of her.

"Sure, hang on a second. I'll come out and show you to her room," she said as though she didn't really want to.

A moment later she appeared from behind the reception area. The rest of her was as round as her face and she moved laboriously as if something was hurting.

"They're a noisy group today," she said as she nodded toward the activity room. "Sorry about that."

Jake looked at me and then back at the nurse. "No problem."

"This way."

We followed the nurse as she hobbled down a long hallway. I thought about telling her we didn't need an escort and directions would do, but I figured that might insult her so I remained quiet. I peered through open doorways as we passed. I saw some people in bed, but mostly I saw people sitting in chairs, perhaps watching television or reading a book or even knitting. There was a general sense of peace about Benedict House, and though Gram often joked about which room she wanted and though I'd move her in with me before I moved her some place where there was no family present, Benedict House wasn't a bad place to be.

It was clean and bright with sunshine, and it didn't smell funny; these were attributes that automatically made it somewhat appealing.

"I'm Dell," the nurse said as she put a chubby hand on a doorknob. She seemed to be in a better mood the farther we'd gone from the activity room. "If you need me, just push the red button next to Ms. Silk's bed. She'll be in her wheelchair and she'll be able to talk to you, but you'll need to speak up a bit. Sometimes, she's a little confused, but most of the time she isn't. She's an easy one."

I cringed at the "easy one" description. It made Mary somehow less human, but something told me that Dell didn't really mean it that way.

"Ms. Silk, yoo-hoo," Dell said as she opened the door and led the way inside.

Mary Silk was sitting in her wheelchair, but she turned eagerly toward us. Her hair was as gray as the other residents' and her wrinkled face unrecognizable now from the picture in the yearbook. She smiled and her bright eyes brightened a little more.

"Oh, Dell! You brought visitors," she said as she clapped. "Three of them!"

"No, Mary, I'm not visiting, but these two are." Dell looked at me. "Well, she might be a little confused."

"Oh, no, I mean the other three," Mary said.

I glanced toward Jerome, who shrugged.

"And another person who can see ghosts. Lucky people," Jake muttered quietly.

"Excuse me?" Dell said.

"We'll be fine," I said. "Thank you, Dell."

Once Dell left us alone and the door closed behind her, the first thing that Mary said was, "Come closer. I want to meet the handsome cowboy first."

We moved closer—and went with it. There wasn't time

to discuss why Mary could see Jerome, and it didn't much matter. She just could.

"Your name is Jerome Cowbender, just like the Broken Rope legend?" Mary said when Jerome introduced himself.

"Yes, ma'am."

"That's probably the most interesting and wonderful thing I have ever heard," she said with wide eyes.

Jerome smiled at Mary and she smiled at him. I didn't know if he was as transparent to her as he was to me. I didn't know if she knew he was a ghost or not. Again, at that point it just didn't matter.

"Ms. Silk," I said.

"Mary, dear, you must all call me Mary. I haven't liked being called Ms. Silk since my teaching days. Those are long gone now." Mary sighed but didn't lose her smile.

"Thank you. Mary, we have some questions for you from back when you were a teacher. Are you okay to answer them?" I said.

"Well, I'll try. Don't remember all that much anymore. It's been a long time."

"Sure. We understand, but we feel like you might remember these events. They were a pretty big deal."

"Oh." The smile faded slightly. "Well, go ahead, dear. Ask. I'll do my best."

"We were wondering about the Cylas family. Homer and Ellen, their son Gent and their daughter Jennie. Do you remember them?"

Mary's already pale face faded to a shade paler, and she put her fingers up to the hollow at the bottom of her neck. "I'm not sure I do," she lied.

I reached out and put my hand over hers as it came down and rested on the wheelchair's armrest.

"Mary, if it's not too much to ask, would you please think about it for a minute. Make sure. It's important."

Jerome moved to Mary's other side and sat on the edge of her bed.

"We'd sure appreciate it, Mary. We could really use your help," he added.

Mary looked at my hand over hers and then she looked up at Jerome. She inspected his face.

"Time passes so quickly, you know that, don't you?" she asked Jerome.

"Yes, ma'am, it surely does. It's not fair, but that's what happens. It's good to make the best of the time you have." Jerome looked at me. "Sometimes we need others to help us to do that."

I blinked but wasn't completely sure what he meant. Now wasn't the moment to ask.

"You're right, of course," Mary said. "I suppose they won't lock me up at this old age anyway. Maybe it's time to tell the truth."

Jake had been sitting on a chair next to a small table on the other side of Mary's bed and to the side of Jerome. He scooted his chair a little toward me and sat up. He sent me a small nod. He was encouraging me to keep going.

But, unfortunately, at one time in my life I wanted to be an attorney. That part of me had mostly withered with my exodus from law school, but it suddenly found a little life. If Mary had done something illegal, she should consult an attorney before she spoke to anyone, including us.

"Mary . . ." I began.

"Mary," Jake interrupted. "Betts is about to tell you that if you've done something illegal, you should talk to someone like an attorney before you talk to us, but I'm going to intervene here and make you a promise. We won't tell anyone what you tell us. I promise. I swear. Your secrets will be ours. You have no reason to believe us, of course, but as I think you've already figured out since meeting Jerome, we're an unusual bunch, from some unusual places. Look, we don't care even if you killed someone, by accident or on purpose, your secrets will be safe with us." Jake looked at me. "How could it matter to anyone other than people who are already dead anyway?"

I swallowed hard but kept my face steady as Mary looked at me and then at Jerome, who rubbed a finger under his nose but didn't look away from her glance. When she looked at me again, I nodded; one quick nod that would have gotten me disbarred, if I'd ever passed the bar in the first place.

"It probably doesn't matter much right now anyway, young man," Mary said to Jake. "Yes, I knew the Cylas family. Gent was one of my students; he was a wonderful boy. He, his sister, and his parents all worked at the Kennington Bakery, that wonderful . . . and that horrible place." Mary's eyes swam with tears, but none fell down her cheeks.

"What happened the night of the fire, Mary?" I asked.

"I taught William Kennington to read. He was my student, too."

"One of the owners of the bakery? He didn't know how to read?" I said.

"No, he didn't. And we would have all been better off if he'd never learned."

"It wasn't as uncommon as it should have been back

then. School, reading, none of it was mandatory as it is now," Jake said.

Mary sighed again. "That night, the Cylas family was there by accident. I'd been called to come in and help Howard read some contracts."

"Excuse me," I said. "So the Cylas family wasn't called into the bakery, too?"

Mary thought a long moment. "No. Gent had forgotten his shoes that day. He only had two pair—a work pair and a pair he wore outside the bakery. He forgot to change when he left the bakery and it was against the rules to wear your work shoes outside the bakery. He came back to switch his shoes. His family and a friend came with him, but I'm not sure why."

"I see," I said, understanding one more piece of the puzzle.

"I helped Mr. Kennington with the contracts, but it wasn't a good outcome. He was angry. I don't remember the exact details, but there were some inequalities when it came to the banking. Mr. Knapp was clearly making more money that Mr. Kennington, and they were supposed to be equal partners. Mr. Kennington called Mr. Knapp to the bakery. It was some time after both men were there that the Cylas family arrived, but no one knew they were there at first.

"When things became heated between the two gentlemen, Gent, with his friend—her name was Missouri, I remember that very well, were exploring the racket. Right as the two of them passed by the office, Mr. Knapp slapped me hard for 'talking foolishness' to Mr. Kennington."

"Oh no," I said.

"Gent and Missouri rushed into the office to help me.

Then events happened quickly after that. Mr. Knapp drew a gun, shot Mr. Kennington and then Gent. He missed Missouri with a bullet, but he charged and hit her over the head with the gun, knocking her to the ground. The rest of the Cylas family came running, but Mr. Knapp grabbed me and held a gun to my head and told them to sit down or he'd kill me and them." She paused as the events from so long ago must have come into focus in her mind. She turned to me. This time, the tears in Mary's eyes flowed freely down her cheeks. "Then he pulled the gun from my head and aimed it at them. He pushed me away, backwards. I was overcome with a need to try to save the girl named Missouri. I didn't know what to do. My instincts took over, and I swear it was like someone was guiding me. It was such a strange feeling. The building had big windows and they opened out. Missouri had fallen to the ground next to one, and she and I were now behind Mr. Knapp. As he continued to aim the gun at the rest of the Cylas family as they made their way to a bench, I grabbed the poor girl and heaved her out of the open window. I knew he would kill her. I thought it was her only chance. I don't even know how I lifted her up the little bit I needed to lift her, but I did. Of course I thought I might end up killing her too but it was worth the risk." She paused again and blinked a couple tears away. "Mr. Knapp told me that because of what I'd done to her, I was a killer, too. If I ever told anyone what he did, he'd tell them what I did. I thought he'd kill me, too, but he seemed to like to have that to use against me more than he wanted me dead."

"I guess you got lucky," Jake said.

"Probably, but the sadder and perhaps truer fact is that I

would have been missed. I was a teacher. The Cylas family was poor and not as well known. "

"I see," Jake said.

As the pieces came together, I realized that Gram had been thrown out the same window that had come down on me, Cliff, and Jerome. She shouldn't have survived. I wondered if Jerome wasn't remembering as much as he thought he was. I looked at him and he just shrugged and shook his head slowly. He didn't remember, but I had no doubt. He'd been there that day. He must have been. *Someone* must have been. Gram would have been hurt much worse or surely killed if someone hadn't been there to save her from the fall.

"Then he shot them all, the rest of the Cylas family. Oh, gracious, there was so much blood. Too much to clean up by the time he was done," Mary continued.

"Oh, Mary, I'm so sorry this is painful," Jerome said gently.

She sniffed and looked up at him.

"Who set the fire?" I asked her.

"That was his idea."

"But he died in the fire?" Jake said.

She shook her head. "No, that was Homer Cylas. We put Mr. Knapp's identification in Mr. Cylas's pocket and Mr. Knapp took his. Then Mr. Knapp set the first fire. And then . . . the strangest thing happened. We thought the fire would destroy everything. But it didn't. The fire burned the room, part of the building . . . the people, but then it stopped burning." Mary looked at Jerome. "I've often wondered if even in his death Mr. Kennington could have done something to douse the fire. Is that possible?"

"I don't know, Mary," Jerome said.

She nodded. "Anyway, when the fire didn't destroy everything . . . and everyone, we had to get three bodies out of there. Everyone would think that Mr. Kennington and Mr. Knapp were killed, but the others had to go. We took them . . . Oh, it was awful, but we took them and buried them."

"Mr. Knapp wasn't worried about Missouri's body?" Jake asked.

"No, he thought she was dead for sure, but she hadn't worked in the factory and he kept telling me that I'd killed her, that it was my fault. He probably thought that if they found her body it would be a distraction from the Cylas family missing, if anyone noticed them gone anyway. Missouri had no ties to the bakery, none at all. I don't think that evidence gathering then was what it is now, but I'm sure he thought that if they found any evidence on the poor girl, it would somehow point to me. He wasn't all the way in his right mind by then, I'm sure."

"I see," Jake said again.

"Do you remember where you took the bodies?" I asked.

"Yes, of course, I would never forget. There's a cemetery on the outskirts of town next to what used to be an old church."

"I'm familiar with it," I said.

"We buried them right outside the cemetery. In the woods. Later, I tried to use rocks for markers, and I've put flowers on their graves a number of times."

What Mary had done had been illegal. Technically, she'd broken a number of laws, there was no doubt. If she'd been caught in this day and age, she would definitely serve jail time. She probably would have back then, too. But, I wasn't telling her story to anyone who'd get the law involved. Jake and Jerome wouldn't, either. Beyond legalities, though, I couldn't fathom how she'd lived with what she'd done, but I had a small idea.

"Were you aware that Missouri survived?" I said.

"Oh yes! I was grateful to later hear that I hadn't killed her. It was a miracle really, a true miracle. And I was so happy. It was my only source of happiness for many years. I kept thinking she'd tell the authorities, but no one ever came for me. There were times I wanted them to. Sometimes I wanted to talk to her, too, but I just never could bring myself to do it. Mr. Knapp never knew she lived. I never told him."

Which might have explained why when he found out that she hadn't died he lashed out at me from his afterlife, or I assumed he was dead. He'd tried to kill me with the same window she'd been flung out of. Again, my connection to the ghosts was somehow bigger, clearer than Gram's. Mr. Knapp might not have been aware of Gram as he traveled through his death, but he must have somehow been clued in to me. I was going to have to deal with this extra sensory skill at some point, but not today.

"Where did Mr. Knapp go?" Jake asked.

"I don't know. He just left. He took cash from the safe and left. For years, I received letters from him with a San Francisco postmark, but the letters stopped about two decades ago. He must be long dead by now."

"What did the letters say?" I asked.

"Reminders that I was to remain quiet. Goodness, he even called a tribute article in to the *Noose*, mentioned me and everything. Made Maude Kennington suspect her husband and I had been up to no good. We hadn't been, but it was just Mr. Knapp's way of making sure I knew he could somehow hurt me whenever he wanted to. Even when I learned better, even when I understood things better, I didn't tell anyone. As time passed"—she looked at Jerome—"it all seemed to become unreal somehow and then, of course, I only felt guiltier about letting the years go by without saying anything. It's good to tell someone. I'm so sorry, so very sorry. Were the Cylases some of your kin?" she asked us all.

"No. Missouri is my grandmother," I said.

"How wonderful. I haven't lived in town for ten years. I do see some resemblance. You're just as pretty as she was."

"Thank you," I said. "Gram—Missouri—forgot what happened at the bakery that night. I think she spent a long time trying to remember, but it might have been too awful."

"Yes. Yes, it was truly awful."

"But you saved her life, Mary."

"In a terrible, cruel way, but I'm so grateful she lived."

"Mary, do you have any more details about where the bodies are buried? The woods next to the cemetery are pretty dense," Jake said.

She smiled at Jake and then looked at Jerome. "Go to the row with Jerome Cowbender's grave—the historical one, of course—and then walk toward the woods. Once you reach the border of the woods, walk fifty or so steps directly south. You'll see those rocks. Follow these directions, and I think you'll find them easily."

"Thank you, Mary," Jake said.

"Yes, thank you," Jerome and I said together.

"No. Thank you all." Mary sighed. "I'm more tuckered out than I have been in a long, long time, but telling the story has helped. It was a burden that isn't all the way gone, but it is some. Just some."

Mary was tired, so even though none of us wanted to leave, she made it clear that we needed to let her rest. We promised that Gram would come out and visit her. I'd twist her arm if I needed to.

As we left, though, Mary stopped us at the door.

"Jerome, I know exactly when I'll die. I don't have much time here, but I do have some. Tell me, is it . . . I don't know what I want to ask."

Jerome smiled and said, "You'll be fine, Mary. Just fine."

"Thank you," she said and blew him a kiss. He tipped his hat.

Once in the hallway, Jake turned to me and said, "What'd he say, Betts? What did Jerome say to her?"

"He just told her that she'd be okay, Jake. She'll have nothing to worry about," I said.

"That's good. That's very good."

Chapter 22

"He's gone-gone, like no sign of him anywhere?" I said into my cell phone.

"Nowhere to be found," Cliff said.

Gram, Jake, Jerome, and I were all at the cooking school. I'd called the meeting. After we told Gram Mary's story and the details of the magazine article, I called Cliff to ask him for an update.

"He must have gotten spooked by the grocery store clerk, knew that I'd try to track down the magazine," I said.

"Sounds likely. We'll keep trying, though," Cliff said.

"Do you think he's Roger's killer?"

"We're not sure, Betts. His disappearance is suspicious, but we just don't know. We'd like to find him to talk to him and because we're concerned for his safety."

I'd been plenty concerned myself, but a deeper sense of

disquiet now ran through me. My mind quickly replayed moments I'd spent with Mario III, but those moments didn't tell me anything new.

"Cliff, do you have addresses of where everyone is staying?" I said.

"Yes, but we've got all the students here at the jail. Jim's about done with them for now."

"That's good! Wait, no, can you ask some of them to stay?"

"Well . . . what's up, Betts?"

"Cliff, I have a hunch, but it only includes Brenda, Jules, Shelby, and Elian. You okay if I come down?" I asked.

"Seems a bit unorthodox."

"I know, I know. We can pretend you want to question me, but I'd like to . . . I don't know, look at those four, talk to them. I feel like there's something I've been missing. Maybe I can 'see' it."

Cliff hesitated, but then said, "I'll see what I can do. Jim or I will intervene if we think you're causing more harm than good."

"Makes sense to me."

"All right. See you shortly."

I hung up the phone and looked at Gram, Jerome, and Jake.

"Change of plans. I need to go to the jail. I have an idea about our present-day killer."

"What's the idea?" Gram said.

"It's not fully formed yet. I need to see some of them in person." It *was* fully formed, but my theory was weak and I didn't want to say it out loud just in case that caused it to lose steam. It was the only idea I had.

"So, Freddie—I mean Mario's gone?" Gram said.

"They can't find him yet."

"Shoot. I wish we'd picked up on things sooner."

"They'll find him," I said, but I wasn't so sure.

"We'll wait to hear from you before we trek out to the woods," Jake said.

"It's getting dark. Maybe we should wait until tomorrow anyway," I said.

Gram said, "Oh, I'm not waiting until tomorrow. I'll be checking for those rocks this evening. I've wanted to know what happened for a long time. You all have no idea how this has tormented me over the years. I'm relieved to hear the story, but until I see where those bodies are buried, I cannot rest."

"I'll go with you to the woods, Miz. Jerome, come with us, too?" Jake said.

Jerome nodded.

"He'll go with us," Miz said.

"Isabelle, you'll be careful?" Jerome said. "No going to the bakery, got it?"

"I'm not going anywhere near that bakery."

My idea was pure instinct and based upon where two of the students lived, where one said he lived, and the fact that one took way too many notes. I suspected that the killer, if he wasn't Mario Gepetti III, was Elian Sanchez, Shelby Knot, or Jules Broadshed. I really didn't think Brenda was a killer, but I threw her into the mix because of all the notes.

It was another instinct, the one I hadn't vocalized to

Gram, Jake, and Jerome. My weak idea was somewhat based upon something that could change or be changed easily. I thought that we might be able to figure out who the killer was, or at least who they might be, based upon the way they sounded, their accents or lack thereof. Jake had been so in tune with Mario's lie. I wondered if I could try to find an answer using the same sort of insight.

In the back of the jail I conferred with Cliff and Jim. "Do you know much about accents?"

"Betts, before we answer that, what's on your mind?" Jim said.

"Look, Fr—I mean Mario said he was from Maine. He's from San Francisco. Jake caught that during our first conversation. He knew Mario wasn't from Maine."

"Okay," Jim said slowly, but I could see that the pieces of my wimpy theory were coming together in his mind.

"I'm operating on the theory that Roger wasn't Mario's father's killer. I think that's the safe way to think right now; well, at least an avenue that should be explored."

"Right. So, someone else killed Mario's father. Mario followed them here, and they killed Roger," Jim said.

"Yeah."

"Why would they kill Roger?"

I shrugged. "I can think of a couple reasons. Roger was killed at the school. He might have been early on purpose but that's pretty rare this time of year. I think he was called there because he knew what happened with the Gepetti sourdough. He about told us the whole story but was interrupted by Mario spilling flour."

"So, therefore, the conclusion should be that Mario killed him," Jim said.

"Except, if Mario killed him, why didn't Mario leave earlier?"

"You mean—if he came here to kill his father's killer, why did he stick around after the deed was done?" Cliff said.

"Yes. It's that little nugget that makes me pretty sure that one of those people"—I nodded toward the four sitting in chairs at the front of the jail—"is a killer—of both Roger Riggins and the Mario in San Francisco, but hopefully our Mario, our Freddie hasn't been killed. Unless he's a killer, too."

Jim rubbed his hand over his bald head. "Betts Winston, you could be onto something. Or not."

"Right. Well, there's more. The poison used to kill Roger is from prairies in the western United States. Can we, with questions, and listening to their accents, determine if one of those people aren't from where they say they're from? I think I can eliminate two right now, but I'm just not sure."

"Who?" Cliff asked.

"Brenda Plumb. She's from Alabama and she sounds like it. And Shelby Knot. She's well known in Portland, and when Gram and I checked her out, we saw all kinds of pictures of her."

"But she's from Portland," Jim said. "The West. That's why you didn't think she should be dismissed?"

"Yes."

"Why is Brenda Plumb still here then?"

"She takes lots of notes. I don't trust her."

"But she doesn't fit with your theory," Cliff said.

"I know, but I thought it might be a good chance to figure out what all the notes are for."

Jim sighed. "Jules Broadshed?"

"Arizona. The west again."

"Elian Sanchez?" Jim continued.

"He says he's from Boston. He doesn't sound like it at all. We've had students from Boston, and not one of them spoke without at least a tinge of that Boston/Kennedy-type accent."

Jim shook his head slowly. "I don't know, Betts, this is more than a long shot."

I shrugged. "You've got people out there looking for Mario, so you're not wasting valuable time. It's worth a shot—even a long one. If it falls apart, it falls apart."

"I suppose so. However, let me ask the questions. Got it?" Jim said.

I nodded. "Don't forget about Brenda's notes."

The corner of Jim's mouth quirked. "I won't."

Jules Broadshed was the student who acted most as if she didn't want to be there. She fidgeted, looked uncomfortable, and tried to avoid eye contact with all of us. Shelby Knot and her tattoos seeped attitude. She wasn't pleased to be back in the police station, no matter what the reason might be this time.

Elian Sanchez looked like he would be fine if he just had something to do other than sit. He was clearly bored.

Brenda Plumb was not bored, not in the least. In fact, she sat up straight and alert. She didn't have her pen and notepad out, but I could tell she was itching to reach into her bag and grab them both.

"Ladies and gentleman," Jim began, "we have cause to believe that one or more of you isn't who they say they are."

I blinked at Jim. He got right down to business.

The only person who showed an exaggerated reaction was Brenda Plumb. She cringed. Jim caught it.

"Ms. Plumb? You have something you'd like to share with the rest of the group?"

"No," she said quickly.

Jim and Cliff shared a smile, but Jim moved on.

"I'm not sure how I couldn't be who I say I am," Shelby said. "If you need proof, I'm happy to pull up pictures for you. I'm pretty well known in Portland. I've had multiple stories written about me, many pictures posted on the Internet." She sounded both bored and annoyed.

Jim sidled up to Cliff's desk and half sat on the edge. "Actually, we know that, Shelby. I have a couple questions for you, though."

"I'm listening."

"Did you know Freddie before you came to the cooking school? Any of you know him?"

Again, Brenda Plumb was the only one to display an unexpected reaction, but again, Jim ignored her widening eyes and almost affirmative nod. I about jumped up and pointed at her, but I'd told Jim I'd just observe.

"I didn't know Freddie before I met him here," Shelby said, but her body language suddenly changed. Went from annoyed to curious. "Why? Is he okay?"

"We don't know. We can't find him."

That got their attention and they all seemed to straighten and become more interested in what Jim had to say.

"I don't understand," Shelby said. "Are we . . . Should we be worried about him?"

"We're worried," Jim said. "Anyone here know where he is?"

The four of them looked at each other as they shook their heads.

"Anyone want to tell us what really happened at the reception?" Cliff asked. "Clearly, we didn't get the whole story. Now might be a good time to get the truth."

"I wasn't there," Brenda said. "I wasn't anywhere in the vicinity. I don't know why Freddie said he might have seen me inside. In fact, I wasn't even downtown that day at all."

"Jules and I weren't there, either. We were at the pool hall." Shelby looked at Jules.

"It's true. We weren't ever out of each other's sight. I promise." Jules might not have been guilty about anything, but she was most definitely nervous, though that could be considered a normal reaction when talking to the police.

"Elian?" Jim said.

"I told you how I thought Freddie got the black eye. I found him afterward," Elian said.

"You like to crash parties, Elian?" Jim said. "Something you normally do?"

"What? No. I was just . . . It was just stupid."

"Where're you from originally?" Jim asked.

"Boston!"

Jim smiled. "Lived there all your life?"

"Yes."

"Ever traveled west, to California maybe?"

"What are you talking about?" Elian said.

"I just wonder two things. One, have you ever been to California? Two, why don't you sound like you're from Boston?"

Again, Elian said, "What?"

"I'm pretty sure you heard me."

"Well . . ." Elian flustered. "No, I've never been to California. And there are all kinds of accents in Boston. There's not just one."

"You sound so . . . plain," Jim said.

Elian shrugged.

"How'd the Sox do this year?"

"I have no idea. I'm not a baseball fan."

"Football, hockey?"

"No. I like to cook and bake with my free time. I don't watch sports."

I liked to cook and bake, too, but I had some idea how Missouri's college and professional sports team fared. Of course, not being a sports fan didn't make Elian a killer.

"Jules?" Jim turned slightly. "You ever been to California? Maybe recently even?"

Jules blanched. "Yes, I was there over Christmas."

"Oh, yeah? Tell me about it."

"I have an aunt who lives there. I stayed with her. We did some tourist stuff. We do every time I go."

"I see. Eat out much?"

"Yeah, almost every meal."

"Remember where?"

"Not really. I could call my aunt, though. She could look up the places."

"I just might have you do that. We'll see. Thanks for offering."

With Jim's friendlier tone, Jules relaxed a little. She attempted a smile at Jim, but it was weak.

Jim surveyed the students with suspicious, questioning

eyes. I would have found it intimidating; they did, too, but it was interesting to watch them hide it.

"Well, I suppose that's it for now. You may all go, but the regular instructions apply. Don't leave town. And, of course, if you see Freddie, tell him I need to talk to him and then you call me right away." Cliff handed out business cards to everyone.

As they all stood to leave, Jim said, "Ms. Plumb, you have an extra moment?"

"Uh, sure," she said.

Elian, Jules, and Shelby cleared out of the jail quickly. They probably hoped they weren't called back, too.

Brenda Plumb wasn't good at masking her emotions. I'd thought she was snotty and strange, but now she just looked scared. I wondered what Jim had seen that had caused him to call her back and let the others go. I remained quiet.

"Come on back and have a seat again," Jim said.

I was sitting in a chair that was closer to the two small holding cells in the back of the space than to the two desks in the middle. Brenda pushed through the short swinging gate and sat in the chair next to Jim's desk that she'd previously sat in.

"Coffee? Soda?" Cliff said.

"No, thank you."

Jim and Cliff both sat in their own chairs. It was as if they knew where to place themselves to form the best barrier. Cliff was more toward the front doors and Jim was more toward the back of the jail. There was no place for her to run, if that had even occurred to her.

"I think I forgot to ask you if you'd been to California recently," Jim said as he leaned back in his chair.

"Oh. Yes, well, in fact, I have."

"Care to share the details?"

"I merely traveled through. Back in March. I had a full day's layover in San Francisco before my flight to Hawaii—well, Los Angeles and then Hawaii."

"I see. And how much sourdough bread did you eat?"

Brenda cringed. "Shoot," she said, which struck me as gruesomely casual if she was saying it because she'd just been found out as a killer.

"Ms. Plumb?"

She bent over and reached into her bag. Both Jim and Cliff moved their hand to their guns, but they didn't pull them from the holsters.

"Oh, no, I don't have a weapon," Brenda said. "I'm pulling out my notebook."

Jim and Cliff relaxed when she produced said notebook.

"I was there in San Francisco the day that the news of what happened to 'Freddie's' father broke. I know who he is. I've known since the second I saw him at the school."

"Why didn't you tell us?" I piped up from the back of the room.

"I don't know. I thought maybe you knew. I thought it was supposed to be a secret you were keeping. I didn't think I was supposed to know."

"What about after Roger was killed?" Jim asked.

"Well. I've been working on that."

"I don't understand."

Brenda held up the notebook. "I've been taking notes since the first day. When I saw Mario Gepetti, I thought there must be something going on. I like to write and I thought I might write a story about it all. Or a blog. You know, there are lots of people who'd want to hear what a year at Missouri's Country Cooking School is like, and a Gepetti in the mix would only make it more interesting."

"A writer?" I said. "A plain old writer?"

"I'm not sure I'm a 'writer' but I like to write."

Brenda looked around at the three of us. We were all somewhat baffled by her admission, though there was no harm to what she was doing, I supposed.

"Look," she said, "I was going to go over these notes and see if I could find anything suspicious about anyone's behavior. You're more than welcome to look through them." She bit her lip as she looked at me. "Well, the police are more than welcome to look through them."

I wanted to laugh at the indication that she'd written something unfavorable about me in her little book. That was the least of everyone's worries.

"I didn't kill anyone, I promise," she said. "I wish I would have told Betts and Miz that Freddie was Mario Gepetti. If Mario killed Roger, I wouldn't know why. I think Mario's in danger. I hope he's hiding safely somewhere. But, there's something else going on here that's weird and, frankly, I think the other three that were just here are the most suspicious. Go ahead and look through my notes. You'll see why."

Jim reached for the notebook. "You may go now, Ms. Plumb, but the same holds true for you as it did for the other three. Don't leave town. And—be careful. Be alert."

"Oh, of course, I'll be careful. Thank you for your concern, but I'd just rather wait for my notebook."

"You may go," Jim said as he set the notebook on his desk in front of him. I didn't know if Brenda would ever see it again, but for the time being, at least, Jim was taking advantage of possession being nine-tenths of the law.

Brenda wasn't pleased, but she wasn't dumb, either. Without further ado, she hurried out of the jail.

Chapter 23

Brenda thought I could use more conditioner and give some attention to my flyaway-stricken hair, but other than that there were no entries about me in her notebook. It was a mellow criticism and one I'd given myself a time or two.

There were some interesting notes in Brenda's book that Jim thought might be helpful to his investigation, though.

I hadn't noticed how Shelby Knot had purposefully avoided sitting next to Mario the first day class was in session. In fact, Brenda had observed Shelby notice Mario beside her and made a quick move to another stool in the kitchen. She'd sat next to Roger Riggins, and Brenda wondered if Shelby might have been flirting with Roger.

I remembered Shelby saying that her boyfriend would be taking care of her vegetarian hot dog truck business back in Portland. Jim made a note on his own notepad to call Shelby's boyfriend to see if there were any issues.

Brenda had been very aware of Elian's quietness. She'd commented on how he frequently had an expectant look on his face as though he wanted to contribute to the conversation but then ultimately didn't say anything. She compared him to a turtle who kept peering out of his shell but then withdrawing again. She also wrote down that on the day we made the starters she'd seen him hanging out by the shelf where we'd stored them much more than what she deemed necessary. He could have just been curious, and hoped to see the process take place. Or he could have taken Mario's starter, waiting for a moment he could do so without being seen.

Brenda had also noticed Jules's oversized bag; but her observations had gone a little deeper. She'd seen at least one plastic zip bag inside Jules's bigger bag that contained greenery; perhaps foliage or maybe just some herbs she'd brought with her for cooking purposes. Or maybe it was death camus.

Of course, first on Jim's list was checking out Jules's bag and its contents. He'd be able to throw in a search of her rented room as well. As soon as we finished looking through the notebook, Jim hurried away to find a judge who'd grant him some search warrants that evening.

The jail became eerily quiet after he was gone. I, Cliff, and the cuckoo from the cuckoo clock were the only ones left as we waited for Officer Jenkins to show up for the night shift.

I sat in the chair next to Cliff's desk as he typed notes on his computer. We chatted briefly about the case, but mostly he typed while I watched. I'd thought my way around Roger's murder so many times that it seemed everyone we'd talked to might somehow be responsible. Jules, Shelby,

Elian, and Mario were all equally suspicious, but, then again, maybe not. Maybe we'd completely overlooked the killer. A chill zipped up my spine at the thought that a murderer who might never be caught was in our midst.

It must have happened more than I wanted to contemplate. If Mary Silk's story was true, Mr. Howard Knapp had gotten away with multiple murders. I still hadn't figured out how we would manipulate Jake's tie to the historical society to give the police clues about the bakery fire. The truth needed to be told, but it was most definitely going to cause a lot of ruckus before it did any good.

"You cold?" Cliff said as he stopped typing.

"No, just a little freaked."

"Understandable." He pulled his fingers off the keyboard and rolled his chair so his computer monitor wasn't in our way. "Jim will catch the killer, or killers, whatever we have going on here."

"I know, he's good. But they do get away sometimes, don't they?"

"Unfortunately."

"Cliff . . ."

"What's up, Betts? What else is bothering you?"

"We live in the strangest place, don't you think?" I said.

Cliff laughed. "Yes, Broken Rope is strange. I'm sure glad I came back, though."

"Me, too, but . . ."

"What? Just spit it out."

"You ever think we're . . . well, we're haunted?"

I thought he might laugh again, but he didn't. Instead, he rolled the chair even closer to me. "By what, ghosts? Past decisions? Literal or figurative?"

"Well, both probably, but I was thinking more the . . ." I was going to say, "ethereal kind," but my comment was interrupted by a loud metallic thud.

It had happened before, just prior to when I first saw the ghost of Jerome Cowbender outside the Jasper Theater. Jim had said that he'd never remembered the cuffs falling off the wall at any other time.

Jerome couldn't get inside the jail. The ghosts were met with some sort of barrier when they tried to enter certain places, though I still didn't completely understand the determining factor behind those places. Gram and I both thought that Jerome couldn't get into the jail because he'd spent so much of his life running from the law.

I'd concluded that the first time the cuffs had fallen had been because Jerome was trying to get inside, to Gram, who was being held for questioning at the time.

"That's strange," Cliff said as he stood. "I think you were here the last time these fell, too."

This time, I thought Jerome was trying to communicate again, and my gut told me he urgently wanted to talk to me.

I stood, too, and followed Cliff to the front of the jail. "I need to go."

Cliff had picked up the cuffs and was trying to find a place to put them on the crowded wall. His eyebrows came together as he looked at me. "Okay. So suddenly?"

"Yes, I just remembered that Gram wanted me to do something at the school."

"All right. So, we'll talk about the ghosts later?"

"Yep. I'm just being silly."

Cliff put his hands on his hips. "Really, B., you okay?"

"I'm fine."

I leaned in to give him a quick kiss good-bye, but his hand quickly came off his hip and he moved his arm around my waist. Cliff wasn't in the mood for a quick kiss.

And come to find out, neither was I.

Just like in Jake's archive room, it was a perfect moment. An instant that took away all the concern, the fear, and made me remember what I really knew was important. It was good to have it reconfirmed.

"It's too bad I'm such a rule follower, or I'd sneak out of here and leave the place unwatched."

I sighed heavily. "Yeah, too bad. There's always later."

"I'm planning on it."

"Me, too." And I truly was.

We disengaged and Cliff went back to his computer as I left the jail.

It was dark, Main Street was lit by only a few of our old-fashioned streetlights. During the tourist season, they were all illuminated, but as visitor count declined, so did the number of lit lampposts.

I saw activity in some of the shops, but almost everything was closed for the evening. There was no one outside, no person or ghost as far as I could tell. I looked around and back at the jail door before I whispered, "Jerome?"

There was no answer except for the sound of laughter that floated toward me from somewhere down the street.

I pulled out my cell phone and dialed Gram. She didn't pick up but that wasn't usually cause for alarm. Gram didn't pay close attention to her phone. But when I got the same non-response from Jake, I became concerned. He paid very close attention to his phone.

I hurried to the Nova and sped toward the school.

There were no cars in the lot. Gram's Volvo was gone. I'd brought Jake out earlier, so Gram might just be taking him home. From the dark lot, I tried both their cell phones again. No luck.

Still full speed ahead, I ran to the front doors. They weren't locked, which was alarming, but not so much that I didn't pull them open and go inside.

"Gram! Gram! Jake!" I said as I ventured through the front reception area, the kitchen, the classroom, and the offices. I was still spooked by finding Everett's body inside the supply room, but I opened that door, too. There was nothing out of place.

I stood in the hallway outside the supply room and pondered what to do next. A few seconds later I grabbed a flashlight out of a drawer in Gram's desk and retraced my steps back outside.

I flipped on the light and shone it toward the cemetery. "Jerome! Gram! Jake!"

Still no answer.

I knew that Gram had been set on finding the Cylas family's graves. I swallowed some nervous fear and said to myself, "There's nothing to be afraid of. No one is here. If they are, they are a ghost and can't hurt you."

There were many holes in my pep talk, but I was so set on finding Gram that I ignored them.

Down the stairs, over the rope without tripping this time, and through the cemetery I went. I shone the light on Jerome's gravestone and noticed that the coin was still there. I'd forgotten to ask Jake if he'd been the one to put it back.

I wasn't wearing my hiking boots or my flip-flops this time, and I was glad for sneakers and the sure footing they gave me on the uneven ground. There were intermittent bumps and sunken spots throughout the cemetery. The oldest graves had been dug when the cemetery wasn't as much a cemetery as it was just a spot of land where dead people were buried. There were a number of haphazardly placed and partially sunken grave markers in this oldest part, and I walked slowly and carefully through the maze to reach the edge of the woods.

The two-lane highway that ran in front of the school and the cemetery also ran in front of the woods, and there were some streetlights along the side of the road. But the trees were so thick that barely any light could make its way inside the woods. The flashlight would have to do.

"Okay, straight from the row with Jerome's grave about fifty steps or so this way."

I trudged forward over rough ground, though it seemed as though there might have been a narrow path at one time.

It was dark, but I was so focused on my footfalls and the ground in front of me that I didn't notice much else, except the slaps my face and arms suffered from the stray branches along the way.

"Forty-eight, forty-nine, fifty." I stopped and lifted the light.

I'd walked right into a small clearing. I didn't think that trees had once grown there. Instead, I thought the twenty-by-twenty plot hadn't for some reason been friendly for growing much of anything. Someone could easily come upon the clearing and think it would be a good place to set up camp, make a picnic, or perhaps bury bodies.

"Gram! Jake! Jerome!" I still didn't receive a response, but I was relieved I hadn't found them in an injured state.

My mind had conjured up pictures of them trekking out to the woods and then hurting themselves. Or them being hurt by someone.

I hadn't let it seep all the way into my consciousness, but the fact that Cliff and I had been accosted by a window presumably thrown from a building by a ghost meant that perhaps the ghosts were more dangerous than we'd ever realized. Jerome had warned me about staying away from the bakery, but if danger was at the bakery, surely it might also be at the place where the killer buried those he killed.

But there wasn't danger, not that I could sense at least. The clearing was dark and quiet, with no sign that Gram or Jake or Jerome had been there, but I suspected they had simply left the area as undisturbed as they'd found it.

The rocks used as grave markers were easy to spot. Three of them bordered the edge of the clearing. There was also a pile of smaller rocks in front of each of the larger ones.

As the light skimmed over the surfaces of the bigger markers, I thought I saw something on each of them. A closer inspection revealed that a name had been crudely carved into each big rock. Gent. Jennie. Ellen. Simple chicken scratches that brought tears to my eyes.

The graves hadn't been bothered. It had been a long time since they'd been dug, and from all indications, no one had searched for answers to the questions that the names on the rocks conjured.

Somehow, we'd find a way to have them dug up, inspected, whatever was called for by professionals. It would take some manipulation and some lies probably, but I was getting closer and closer to telling Cliff about the ghosts. Having a law enforcement officer "in the know" might help with all these mysteries from the past.

For now, though, I needed to find Gram, Jake, and Jerome.

It was easy to see the way back to the school, its front floodlight a welcome beacon ahead. I still stepped carefully and I still got swatted by branches, but I resumed my hurried pace.

It wasn't completely unusual that Gram or I forgot to lock the doors, but the oversight tonight suddenly sat funny with me. We'd had a murder on the property. Gram was diligent about safety. Now that I had time to think about it, the doors being unlocked was deeply bothersome.

I opened them again and searched the school one more time, but there was nothing out of place. I stood in the middle of the kitchen, plopped my hands on my hips and thought about where she could have gone. I tried her phone one more time.

And I heard it ringing—in both ears.

I pulled my cell phone away from my ear but didn't disconnect as I searched for Gram's phone. It was on the ground under the butcher block in the middle of the room. It might still be too soon to panic. Along with Gram not paying close attention to her phone, she'd frequently set it down and forget about it.

I couldn't help it, though; dread was beginning to build in my stomach. I disconnected the call and picked up the phone from the floor. I went to her call log and scrolled through. I'd called a few times, of course, but what got my attention was that she'd also received a text recently.

It said: *Meet me at the bakery. I'm scared. I know who the killer is.*

The sender attached to the text was only a phone number. The area code was 307. It took a quick Internet search on my phone to find that 307 was a Wyoming number. I wasn't aware that any of our students came from Wyoming.

"Oh, Gram," I said, but I still didn't know how upset or worried to be. I didn't know if she'd read the text or not, if she'd gone to the bakery or not, if . . .

I locked the school doors and then got into the Nova. I'd stay back from the building if I needed to, but if Gram was at the bakery, I didn't want her there without me.

Maybe that's why the handcuffs fell. Maybe Jerome was telling me to get to the bakery.

Or, perhaps, to remember to stay away from it.

Chapter 24

Gram's Volvo was there, in the same spot both she and I had parked in over the last few days. The bakery building was dark and even more foreboding than it had been.

"Gram," I muttered to myself, "where are you?"

I parked on the street, about a half block away from the building and got carefully out of the Nova.

"Betts!"

I looked down toward the end of the street, which was also the other end of the building and the place where the window had fallen. Jake was running along the edge of the property.

"Stay there!" he commanded.

I crossed my arms in front of myself and did as he said, but it wasn't easy. I wanted to know what was going on and he was taking way too long to get to me.

"Hey," he said, breathlessly. He held the camera under his arm. "You're not supposed to be here."

"I'm staying back. What is going on? Where's Gram? Jerome?"

"I don't know if Jerome is still here, but Miz talked to him before she went in."

"She went into the bakery! Isn't it supposed to be dangerous?"

"That's what I said, but she talked to Jerome and was convinced that it wasn't dangerous for her. Just for you."

"Why did she go in?"

"She wanted to tell Gent about the graves. We saw them. They were . . . sad and kind of sweet, too. Sad mostly, though. What happened to Gent and his family has been painful to her for a very long time. She wanted him to know right away just in case he needed to leave."

"What about the text?"

"What text?"

"This one." I handed Gram's phone to Jake.

"If she read this, she didn't give any indication. Hang on." He looked at the text again and then scratched the side of his head. "According to the time it was sent, I think we were already gone from the school. I think we'd left just shortly before."

"Have you seen Mario?"

"No, I haven't seen anyone but a guy I didn't recognize. He was just walking around. Didn't seem to be too interested in what I was doing. Miz ran me home first to get my spare battery and told me to try to film things. I haven't seen anything to film, but I've kept the camera rolling."

"Why didn't you answer your phone?"

Jake looked sheepish. "Oh, hell, Betts. I left it in the Volvo. I got such crazy results from the last time I filmed I thought there might be something messing with electrical stuff around here so I left it in the car. You tried to call, didn't you?"

I bit my lip but didn't want to make Jake feel worse than he did. "Tell me what the guy looked like, the one you saw."

"Oh. Short guy, short hair, bright orange shirt. I remember noticing how bright it was even in the dark."

"Elian, our student?"

Jake shrugged. "I haven't met the students yet, Betts. I only know what Mario looks like because of the magazine article and meeting him here the other night."

"Elian. It must have been Elian. Where did he go?"

"I have no idea."

"Jake, call Cliff, Jim, everyone. Tell them to get here and search for Elian. Show Cliff Gram's phone. Whatever, just get them here," I said before I started walking toward the bakery building.

"No! You can't go in there, Betts!" Jake grabbed my arm and dropped the camera.

"Jake, let go. I have to go in there. It's Gram," I said.

"But she's fine. It's you who is in danger."

"Handcuffs fell, Jake. Handcuffs fell."

Jake shook his head. "What?"

"Remember when I first met Jerome. I told you about the handcuffs falling in the jail?"

"Yes."

"I think it was Jerome trying to communicate with Gram since he couldn't get inside the jail. I think he tried again tonight. I think he wanted to talk to me. He's not around so

I'm assuming that he either left or is inside the bakery with Gram. If he's in there, they need help—or I just don't think the cuffs would have fallen. Let go of my arm, Jake."

"Betts," he said weakly, but he let go of my arm.

"Call Cliff!" I said as I ran to the building.

I hoisted myself up to the platform and pounded on a board over the old door.

"Gent, it's Betts, let me in!"

I stepped back and looked at the ground as I stepped forward again. There was no change.

"Come on," I muttered. "Gent!"

I was suddenly so worried for Gram that tears started to pool in my eyes and my throat started to hurt. I took a deep breath and tried again.

"Gent, please, let me in."

The world changed, from new and worn down, to just plain old-time new. The scene was similar to my two other visits. The door was intact and the plaque above it was shiny. But there was one big difference.

The smell of smoke was suddenly overwhelming. It went beyond Jerome's pleasant wood smoke scent to stifling.

The door opened and Gent signaled me inside. "Everyone's back here," he said. But he was scared, too; scared and maybe sad.

"Where's Gram?" I said.

"Back here," he said. This time his voice was full of despair.

I knew the smoke wasn't real; it couldn't be. But it was thick nonetheless. Before, I could see dim images in the background, but this time I could see only a gray haze everywhere.

"The building's on fire?" I said.

"How can it be?" Gent said. "I think it's a memory of the fire."

"I don't understand. Whose memory?"

"His." Gent pointed.

We'd made it to the middle of the large space, and as I looked around now, I could see the images I expected: bakery shelves, ovens against the wall, people, though everything and everyone was still surrounded by the hazy smoke.

"It's not real, the smoke's not real," I mumbled to myself, and I could actually breathe a little easier. Once we were fully in the area of activity that was defined by invisible borders, people and things were set in motion.

"Betts!" Jennie said. She was across from me and made a move toward me, but a big man put his hand on her shoulder.

"I don't think so," he said to her, his voice gravelly rough.

He was big, like Homer, but dressed in a suit that looked like it was from the 1950s. His short, curly dark hair was mussed and his face, though handsome, was set with a scowl that was pointed my direction.

"Who are you and why are you here?" he demanded.

"I'm Betts Winston and I'm looking for my grandmother," I said. "You're Howard Knapp?"

"I am, and I don't understand why you've brought me back here. I don't want to be here."

"I . . ."

"Isabelle."

I hadn't seen him—really *seen* him—until he spoke.

"Jerome," I said, relieved that he was there. "Where's Gram?"

He'd appeared beside me, but he stepped back now, giving me room to see that Gram was there, too.

"No!" I exclaimed as I ran around Jerome and to Gram, who was on the ground seemingly unconscious. I fell to my knees. "Gram, Gram!" I shook her arm.

"I hit her," Howard said. He was standing above me now. "Maybe this time she'll die."

I'd never once reached to someone's neck to feel their pulse, but this time I did. Thankfully, I felt Gram's. It was slow but steady and reassuringly strong.

"You bastard," I said. "You're dead, you idiot! Why did you need to cause more tragedy?"

I reached to lift Gram into my arms, but Howard put his hand on my shoulder just like he had done to Jennie.

"You're not going anywhere." He pushed hard. He was strong and forceful. His grip was as real as any man alive.

"Isabelle, listen to me," Jerome said. He'd crouched down, too. "He can't see me. He doesn't know I'm here. I can get Miz out of the building now that you're here. Remember what happens in the dark when you're around. I can lift her now."

I nodded hard, hoping to indicate that he needed to get to it right away.

"But, I won't leave until I know you're safe, too. Gent and his family don't realize it yet, but, they can fight now, too. Now that you're here. I don't know what good it'll do them in the long run, but it's better than going down without at least trying."

I shook my head as forcefully as I'd just nodded. "I'll get out. Just take care of her," I begged.

"Who are you talking to?" Howard said.

"I didn't do that to your grandmother," a voice from a distant wall said.

I turned to see Elian Sanchez leaning against the wall directly under a window—a window that no longer had glass panes; they'd been broken out. Elian held his hands over his thigh, but I could see blood seep through his fingers. He and the part of the building he was sitting in were still in the present time.

"He can only see you and Miz," Jerome said. "He's hurt from breaking into the building. He was going to do harm to Miz but he hurt himself first. Seems the building is full of idiots this evening."

"You're not taking her out of here," Howard Knapp said to me. "I've set the fire. It's only a matter of time and we'll all be gone for good, you and your grandmother included. These secrets will never be told."

"Elian, why? Why did you kill Mario's father and Roger Riggins?" I yelled. If all our secrets were in fact going down in flames, I wanted to know fully what they were.

"I just wanted to ruin their starter. They were so successful, the whole western United States wanted their bread and . . . my family couldn't compete. If the Gepetti starter was ruined, we might be able to have a successful business, too. I only killed Mario's father because he caught me. Roger . . . well, he'd left a note for Mario to meet him at the school in the middle of the night. Roger must have recognized Mario and wanted to see what was going on. When Roger talked about the Gepetti incident in class, I followed him. I intercepted the note. I thought he might turn out to be a loose end. I had to get rid of him." His voice was wavering. "Betts, I'm really hurt. Can you help me out of here?"

"You're last on my list," I said, though I didn't yell this time. He might not have heard me. I spoke up. "How did you poison him?"

"Easy, I put the poison in Mario's starter. I told Roger to drink it. He didn't know it was poisoned and I had a knife on him. I thought someone might figure out that it was Mario's starter that was missing. I thought that might throw suspicion his direction, at least briefly. Didn't work. Come on, Betts, I know I'll have to pay for my crimes, but I'm really hurt. Help me get out of here."

I looked away from Elian. I was okay with him suffering a little longer. Besides, I thought we had more important matters to attend to. "We're going to have to take him down," I said to Jerome as I nodded at Howard.

"He has a gun. I don't know if it's . . . real . . . if it can harm you and Miz. I can take care of him now that you're here, but I don't want you or Miz in the way of a bullet. I don't think I could handle . . ."

"On three, we'll knock him over together," I said ignoring Jerome's concern. "One . . ."

But before I could reach "two" something snapped and exploded in the jutted wing. I felt heat and the aftershock of a blast. It seemed we, ghosts and people, were all sent different directions.

I heard Elian scream and Howard curse, but I couldn't quite place where everyone was. It was getting hotter and smokier and more difficult to see and breathe.

"Jerome, get her out of here," I yelled again. "Gent, Homer, Ellen, and Jennie, we know where you're buried. We'll make sure everyone knows. While I'm here close to you, you can fight. You can fight the man who killed you, and you can't die again."

I'd hoped for a scuffle and it sounded like one ensued, though it made it more difficult to find where everyone was.

"Jerome!" I yelled as I found my footing and stood.

He appeared in front of me but not in the ghostly appear-disappear way, but as someone emerging from smoke. He held Gram in his arms. I reached to hold on to one of those arms and we tried to find a way out of the fire. I hoped Gram was still alive, but I also knew that if the smoke was real, she was inhaling toxins that could kill her just as easily as a bullet or burning flames could have. We needed to hurry.

We moved carefully but purposefully. After a couple wrong turns that took us to the ovens and then another wall, we found the door. I'd never been so relieved to see a door, but I didn't know if I'd be able to open it. I reached for the handle and turned. And it opened—not quite to the world of my time, but that dark murkiness that I was no longer afraid of, and relieved to see.

"Betts!"

I turned to see that Elian was in the building. He was still against a wall and under a modern broken-out window, and he was only about ten feet away; an impossible trip for an injured man but an easy one for me.

"Take her. I'll get him and be right behind you," I said.

"No! I'll get him. You take Miz."

"You won't be able to get him without me close by. You need to get Gram out of here. Go."

"Isabelle," he said.

"I'll be fine. Go!"

"Wait!"

"What?" Now wasn't the time to wait for anything.

"Isabelle," he said more quietly. The world was burning around us, but I suddenly needed to know what he was going to say.

"What?" I said again.

"I feel. I feel . . . and I feel for you. I'll be leaving again as soon as you are safe, but I'll be back. I don't know how often or when—not enough for you to wait for me. Live your life, Isabelle. Live happily. Love that fella."

"Jerome."

And then somehow, as he was holding Gram and the flames from the fire that I wasn't sure was real approached us, he leaned forward and kissed me. For the second time in one night, I was kissed, and kissed good.

When he pulled back, he smiled. "There, that was more appropriate than the last one."

I smiled, too. "I'm going to stand here for five seconds while you get her to the ground. We'll talk again. Someday. Go."

And, once again, Jerome Cowbender was gone from my life only seconds after making my toes curl.

"Betts!" Elian yelled.

For a brief instant, I thought about leaving him there, but I knew I'd never be able to do that.

I glanced back into the building, into the gloom, the murky, sort of fiery darkness. I couldn't see much of anything. If there was a threat, I thought I still had a few minutes.

I hugged the wall and made my way to Elian. When I was close to him, as close as a couple steps, the world changed again, and he and I were not only in the present time, we were about to become engulfed in flames, real ones this time. I now had no doubt that what we were experiencing was one hundred percent real, and deadly.

Here and now, the fire was hot and painfully smoky. I put one arm up to shield the heat as I grabbed for Elian with the other arm.

"Come on!" I said.

But whatever his injuries were, they were debilitating. He could barely stand. I had to lift him and he wasn't light. As I held him under his arms, I turned to go back the way I'd come, but that path was gone, now fully engulfed in real flames.

I was about to burn up in a fire with a killer, and I wasn't happy at all about it, but I didn't see any other way out.

"We're going to die!" Elian exclaimed.

It would have been nice to have my guardian ghost appear and save us, but it wasn't happening.

"Here, Betts, I'm right here," a voice said from the window.

Evan had made his way through the opening and was reaching for me. I couldn't find my voice, could barely find my breath, as I handed him Elian. But he continued to reach for me instead. In only a few seconds, he had me out the window in the arms of Cliff, who'd been behind him and maneuvered me down a ladder. Evan, with Elian, followed closely behind.

Other than those who'd originally died all those years ago, none of us perished in the fire; the fire that was real or the fire from the past. Yeah, weird and freaky.

The building was gone though, burned to ashes. It wouldn't need to be demolished, after all; just swept up and thrown away. Neither Gram nor I knew what would happen to Gent and his family now. Time would hopefully tell.

Evan and Cliff told me that they knew exactly under which window to place the ladder to find me because some guy in a cowboy getup directed them. They wondered who he was and how they could thank him.

I was hoping to thank him someday, too.

Chapter 25

"So, Cliff and Evan teamed up and acted like they believed my story about finding records about the Cylas family, but then subsequently losing them. They're so eager to find the truth that they ignored all the holes in my tale. They are taking care of the graves, and they vow to track down where Howard Knapp went after he left Broken Rope," Jake said.

"Good work," I said.

"I couldn't believe how the building went up in flames only seconds after you disappeared into it. It was good you told me to call them. I'm really grateful you and Miz got out."

Jake had asked for this meeting. It was Sunday, two days after the fires. We were in his archive room, and he'd once again supplied the smoothies.

"Me, too." I smiled.

"Betts, you really . . . well, you solved some mysteries."

I shrugged. "I'm just glad everyone's okay."

"Miz bounced right back, didn't she?"

"Yep, she's strong and no worse for the wear."

"Mario was found, and he's all right?"

"Yep. They found him on his way back to San Francisco. He's in trouble, but I don't know how much. He forged his acceptance letter—did I tell you how he did that?"

"No."

"His father had been accepted to the school three years ago. Mr. Gepetti planned on attending but changed his mind at the last minute. If we'd had the real name, we might have found him in our archived files."

"Brilliant, but why did Mario III come here?"

"Oh. He suspected that Elian was his father's killer all along. He knew Elian was from the Sanchez Sourdough family and has been trailing him, trying to find a way to prove he was a killer. When he heard that Elian got accepted to the school, he found his father's old letter. Elian told the police that he only coincidentally had the death camus with him, but I wonder. He'd killed once before and seemed to have gotten away with it. Maybe he was looking for another challenge, as awful as that sounds. Needless to say, Elian was pretty bothered to see Mario here, but he kept quiet about him not really being named Freddie for fear of his own crimes being found out, and at first he didn't think Mario knew who he was. Elian has been keeping busy away from his home in Wyoming. He never changed his name, but tried to be a little crafty, saying he was from Boston. Shoot, he even made up a wonderfully romantic and adventurous sourdough starter story. Seems Gram and I should have been more suspicious of his application and references than of Mario's."

"You didn't know."

"No. His family has a big bakery business up in Wyoming. They were pretty successful in the western United States, but last year they lost a big chunk of their bread business to the Gepetti's. It was rough, apparently."

"So sad," Jake said.

I continued, "Elian crashed the wedding reception, just for something to do, and Mario followed him inside. Mario and Elian had some sort of conflict or confrontation and Elian punched him. Oh—Elian had followed us that first night you and I were at the bakery and Mario followed him. I have no idea if Elian saw what you and I were up to. Apparently he became a little mesmerized by the whole story behind the bakery and the demise of the Puff Pockets. When he thought someone might be onto him, he texted Gram to come out to the building. He was going to . . . well, I think he was going to kill her, too—another loose end. Gram never even saw the text. She was there to talk to Gent, but Howard Knapp didn't want Gram alive, either."

"Oh my, I'm glad that building's gone. Bad juju," Jake said.

"Me, too. Anyway, Mario was going to try to find evidence or force Elian to confess, and then—he admitted this—he was going to kill Elian. That was his plan."

"Yikes. So, is Mario in trouble for wanting to kill Elian?"

"Probably some. Plotting to kill's not good, but he didn't, in fact, kill anyone, which would have been worse, of course. Cliff will let us in on any new scoop. Or, our resident reporter Brenda will. I saw her briefly yesterday and she was taking more notes."

"She, Shelby, and Jules all off the hook?"

"Yep. The greenery in Jules's bag was oregano. She wanted to use it this year. I don't know if Jim truly suspected Shelby of any wrongdoing, but she's clear, too."

"Good." Jake took a sip of his smoothie as he peered at me over its top. After he swallowed, he said, "And, how are you and Cliff?"

"Great," I said.

"You sure?"

"Yes, Jake, I'm sure. I have a little bit of a Jerome hangover, but I'll get through it."

Jake sighed. "I was afraid of that. Now . . . well, I don't know if I should . . ."

"Jake, what?"

He sighed again. "I hope I don't regret this." He scooted off the stool and went to his computer. "You know that camera of mine?"

"Sure."

"Well, it turns out that it works just fine, especially when I use a fully charged battery."

"How's that?" I moved behind him and looked at the monitor.

"When the fire started, I got scared, but there was nothing I could do. When Cliff and Evan and everyone else told me to get out of the way, I don't know, I just started recording everything. And, I caught this."

He clicked the mouse, which started a video.

In the center of the shot was the boarded-up door to the bakery building. Suddenly, it changed, as if it opened, but it really hadn't. It just became different; a space framed by red-hot flames.

And there we were. Jerome, looking real, holding Gram and looking at me. We talked and then, of course, we kissed. The kiss looked even better than it had felt, like something from a movie. I was surprised Jake hadn't added a soundtrack.

"He's a handsome guy, Betts. I get why you're attracted to him, but . . ."

I couldn't speak so I just blinked.

"But," he continued, "that's more than just a simple attraction. I'm sorry I've teased you about him. I think I get it now."

I found my voice. "He's gone, Jake. And, I'm crazy about Cliff. There's no question there, I promise."

"I know. And Cliff is here, right across the street actually. He'll never see this, by the way, but I made you your own copy." He handed me a thumb drive. "Look, Betts, I'm here if you need to talk, always. You know that, don't you?"

I nodded and my phone buzzed.

I cleared my throat. "Hi, Gram," I said as I answered.

"Betts Winston, I need you at the school."

"What's wrong?"

"Nothing, we just need to rethink this whole year again. I think we need to ditch bread for the time being and move on to something so fun it'll distract everyone from all the bad stuff. Probably desserts, but I could use your input. You busy?"

"I'll be there in a few minutes." I hung up the call.

"Miz?" Jake said.

"Yep, work is calling."

"Take the smoothie, too."

I smiled and put the thumb drive in my pocket before I reached for the smoothie.

"I'll see you later," I said.

"You will. And, unlike poor me, you'll probably see more ghosts, too."

I laughed.

"Love you, Betts Winston," Jake said.

"You, too, Jake Swanson."

I drove the Nova toward Gram and the cooking school. It would be wonderful to get back on track, back to a regular school year pace. Bread, desserts, it didn't matter to me. No matter what she wanted to teach, I'd be there, right beside her, and doing my best to keep up.

Epilogue

Fall transitioned easily into winter and the fourteen remaining cooking school students flourished. Particularly Brenda. In fact, she and I became good friends.

The memorial service took place on a cold but sunny day in January. The Cylas family was buried in our cemetery. Gent, Ellen, and Jennie were moved from the woods and Homer was moved from Mr. Knapp's plot. We—all the students, Cliff, Jim, Jake, Gram, and I—gathered around the new graves to celebrate their lives, and the memories that we would all now carry with us forever. Gent surprised Gram and me by showing up, too. He stood in between us, and as Jake spoke to the group perfect words about his family, Gent told us that he, his father, his mother, and his sister had, indeed, been able to fight back during the fire. And, they'd fought hard. He couldn't give us details, but he smiled happily as he told us that his family was finally able to move on. He thanked us, told Gram how much he'd always cherish their friendship, and disappeared. Probably for the last time, but we couldn't be sure.

"Did you see?" I whispered to Gram. "He had shoes on."

Her eyes were filled with tears but she nodded and said, "I did, my dear, I did."

Later that day we received word that Mary Silk had passed away that morning. She'd been so certain that her time to leave this earth was near, and somehow we thought she'd probably picked just the right day.

Recipes

GRAM'S INSTANT MIRACLE ROLLS

Gram calls these her instant rolls because the dough can be stored covered in the refrigerator for several days and used as needed. It seems she always has some of the dough in her fridge. You just never know when you'll need some homemade rolls.

3 ¼ ounce packages dry yeast
½ cup warm water
5 cups unsifted, self-rising flour
¼ cup sugar
1 teaspoon baking soda
1 cup vegetable shortening
2 cups lukewarm buttermilk

Dissolve the yeast in warm water and set aside. In a large bowl, mix the flour, sugar, and baking soda. Cut in the shortening. Add the buttermilk and yeast, mixing well. Cover the dough and chill for two hours. Place the dough on a floured cloth, roll out, and cut with a biscuit cutter. Set aside until the dough reaches room temperature. Bake in a preheated 325°F oven for 10–15 minutes. If desired, brush with melted butter before baking.

Yield: 36 rolls.

GRANNY SEBASTIAN'S BREAD PUDDING

Simply, seriously yummy.

2 cups whole milk
¼ cup butter
⅔ cup brown sugar (light or dark, you choose)
3 eggs
2 teaspoons cinnamon
¼ teaspoon ground nutmeg
1 teaspoon vanilla extract
3 cups bread, torn into small pieces (a harder bread works best—French, sourdough, even Brioche if you have that around; I use about 20 percent crust and about 80 percent bread innards, and tearing is important—do not cut into pieces.)
⅛ to ¼ (your taste preference) cup miniature semi-sweet chocolate chips (optional)
½ pint unwhipped whipping cream (this might be the most important ingredient of the recipe, according to Granny Sebastian)

In a medium saucepan over medium heat, heat the milk for 5–8 minutes, until a film forms over top. Combine the butter and milk, stirring until the butter is melted (5–7 minutes).

In a separate bowl, combine the sugar, eggs, cinnamon, nutmeg, and vanilla. Beat with an electric mixer at medium speed for 1 minute. Slowly add the milk mixture, stirring with a spoon.

Place bread in lightly greased 1 ½ quart casserole, sprinkle with chocolate chips if desired, and pour batter over bread.

Bake at 350°F for 45–50 minutes. Serve warm, either on top of a couple tablespoons of the whipping cream or with the whipping cream poured over the top of the pudding.

Yield: 9 small servings or 6 bigger servings.

BETTS'S BEST BANANA BREAD

Betts has been making this for years. Even Gram admits it's the best banana bread she's ever tasted.

1 cup sugar
⅓ cup margarine or butter, softened
2 eggs
1 ½ cups mashed ripe bananas (3–4 medium—Betts uses *really* ripe bananas)
⅓ cup water
1 ⅔ cups all-purpose flour
1 teaspoon baking soda
1 teaspoon salt
¼ teaspoon baking powder

Heat oven to 350°F, grease bottom only of loaf pan (8 or 9 inch).

Mix the sugar and margarine in a medium bowl. Stir in the eggs until blended. Add the bananas and water and beat with a mixer for 30 seconds.

Stir in the remaining ingredients just until moistened. Pour in pan.

Bake 55–60 minutes for a 9-inch loaf, or 1 ¼ hours for an 8-inch loaf, or until wooden pick inserted in the center comes out clean.

Cool 5 minutes in pan, then loosen the sides of the loaf from the pan and remove the loaf. Cool completely before slicing.

Yield: 1 loaf.

JAKE'S FAVORITE BLUEBERRY ORANGE MUFFINS

This is a really easy recipe, and fresh blueberries make it a perfect treat.

3 cups all-purpose flour
4 teaspoons baking powder
¼ teaspoon baking soda
¾ cup sugar
1 ½ teaspoons salt
2 cups blueberries
2 eggs
¾ cup milk
½ cup butter, melted
1 tablespoon grated orange peel
½ cup orange juice
1 ½ tablespoons lemon juice

Preheat oven to 425°F.

Sift together the flour, baking powder, baking soda, sugar, and salt. Add the blueberries and toss until coated.

In another bowl, mix the remaining ingredients. Pour the liquid mixture into the dry ingredients, and stir.

Fill greased muffin tins two thirds full. Bake for 20 minutes. Let cool in muffin tins for 5 minutes and then remove. Serve.

Yield: 18–24 muffins.

CLIFF'S PEAR BREAD

Cliff's favorite!

½ cup vegetable shortening
½ cup packed brown sugar
½ cup granulated sugar
1 egg
2 cups all-purpose flour, sifted
1 teaspoon baking soda
½ teaspoon allspice
¾ teaspoon cinnamon
½ teaspoon salt
2 cups chopped canned pears, drained

Preheat oven to 350°F. Cream the shortening, brown sugar, and granulated sugar. Add the egg and beat well.

Sift together the flour, baking soda, allspice, cinnamon, and salt. Blend into the shortening mixture.

Stir in the pears. This is a crumbly batter, but that's okay. Pour into a greased 9 × 5–inch loaf pan. Bake for 1 hour. Cool completely in pan before removing.

Yield: 1 loaf.

Becca Robbins is happy to help research a farmers' market and tourist trading post—until she has to switch her focus to finding a killer...

AN ALL-NEW ESPECIAL FROM NATIONAL BESTSELLING AUTHOR

PAIGE SHELTON

Red Hot Deadly Peppers

A Farmers' Market Mini Mystery

Becca is in Arizona, spending some time at Chief Buffalo's trading post and its neighboring farmers' market to check out how the two operate together. She's paired with Nera, a Native American woman who sells the most delicious pecans—right next to a booth with the hottest peppers money can buy.

When Nera asks her to deliver some beads to Graham, a talented jewelry maker inside Chief Buffalo's, Becca is grateful to get a break from the heat. Little does she realize that the heat's about to get cranked up even more—because Graham has been murdered, and she's the one who finds his body. She soon discovers that Graham was Nera's cousin, and that her uncle was recently killed, too, after receiving a threatening note. Becca begins to think the murders may have something to do with the family's hot pepper business. Now she must find the killer, before she's the one in the hot seat...

Includes a bonus recipe!

paigeshelton.com
facebook.com/TheCrimeSceneBooks
penguin.com

M1144T0712

Isabelle "Betts" Winston loves teaching the secrets of mouthwatering country food in her hometown, Broken Rope, Missouri—but when an all-too-current murder threatens the start of tourist season, Betts must find a way to solve it without getting burned . . .

FROM NATIONAL BESTSELLING AUTHOR

PAIGE SHELTON

If Fried Chicken Could Fly

A Country Cooking School Mystery

At Gram's Country Cooking School, Betts and Gram are helping students prepare the perfect dishes for the Southern Missouri Showdown, the cook-off that draws the first of the summer visitors. Everything is going smoothly until they discover the body of local theater owner Everett Morningside in the school's supply room, and Everett's widow points an accusatory finger at Gram. Now, Betts has to dig deep into Broken Rope's history to find the modern-day killer—before the last wing is served . . .

Includes delicious recipes!

"Each page leads to more intrigue and surprise."
—The Romance Readers Connection

"A breath of summer freshness that is an absolute delight to read and savor . . . A feast of a mystery."
—Fresh Fiction

facebook.com/TheCrimeSceneBooks
paigeshelton.com
penguin.com

M1106T0712